Starling Days

STARLING DAYS

Rowan Hisayo Buchanan

SCEPTRE

First published in Great Britain in 2019 by Sceptre
An Imprint of Hodder & Stoughton
An Hachette UK company

1

A CIP catalogue record for this title is available from the British Library

Hardback ISBN 9781473638372
Trade Paperback ISBN 9781473638389
eBook ISBN 9781473638365

Typeset in Sabon by Palimpsest Book Production Limited,
Falkirk, Stirlingshire

Printed and bound by Clays Ltd, Elcograf S.p.A.

Hodder & Stoughton policy is to use papers that are natural, renewable and
recyclable products and made from wood grown in sustainable forests. The logging
and manufacturing processes are expected to conform to the environmental
regulations of the country of origin.

Hodder & Stoughton Ltd
Carmelite House
50 Victoria Embankment
London EC4Y 0DZ

www.sceptrebooks.co.uk

The task of recording roosts in London is difficult owing to the number of small and ephemeral roosts.

The Winter Starling Roosts of Great Britain,
B. J. Marples

Augury n. *The practice of predicting the future, revealing hidden truths, or obtaining guidance on the basis of natural signs such as the flight of birds. From the Latin, augur: seer, prophet or official who observes and interprets the behaviour of birds.*

To everyone who struggles with black dogs or inner demons or any shape of sadness.

& To my family – always.

August

She wasn't expecting the bridge to shudder. It was too big for trembling. Cars hissed from New York to New Jersey over its wide back. That August had been hot, 96° Fahrenheit hot. Heat softened the dollar bills and clung to the quarters and dimes that passed from sticky hand to sticky hand.

It was night and the air had cooled but humidity still hung in a red fog in Mina's lungs. Wind galloped over the Hudson, pummelling the city with airy hooves. The bridge shifted, the pylons swayed, and Mina closed her eyes to better feel her bones judder. Even her teeth shook. The day's sweat shivered between her bare shoulder blades. The tank top felt too thin, and the down on her arms rose.

She took a step forward along the bridge. The tender spots between her big and index toes were sore from too many days in flip-flops. She took the sandals off. They swung from her fingers as she walked. Under her feet, the rough cement was warm. She wondered about the people driving their shadowy cars. Were they leaving over-air-conditioned offices, or bars cooled by the thwack of ceiling fans? Were they going home to empty condos, or daughters tucked under dinosaur quilts?

The bridge was decked out in blue lights, like a Christmas tree, like those monochrome ones shopping malls put up. Still, it was beautiful. Mina readied her phone to take a picture. She watched the granulated night appear onscreen. Perhaps her hands wobbled, because the photo was a blur. It was nothing she could send Oscar. But she wasn't sure it was a good idea to send him pictures. Not tonight.

She stopped in the middle of the bridge. Hello, Manhattan. Downriver, apartment blocks spiked upwards. She couldn't see Queens and the walk-up apartment building she'd grown up inside. Nor could she see the Park Slope apartment, in which Oscar was working late. He'd have a mug on his desk, the coffee gone cold hours ago. The photo of her would be propped up behind his computer. The sparkly stress ball she'd bought him years ago as a joke gift would rest at his wrist. Every hour or so he'd roll it between his palms. When he was working, he didn't notice time. She was sure he wouldn't yet be worried. She'd said she was meeting some friends after the tutoring gig. He didn't know she'd texted the group that she was feeling unwell and would miss movie night. He wouldn't expect her for at least two hours. No one was expecting her. She was unwitnessed. She lifted her face to the breeze.

The river was as dark as poured tarmac. They said that when a body fell onto water from this height, it was like hitting the sidewalk. Golden Gate had nets to stop jumpers. She imagined the feeling of a rope cutting into arms and legs. Your body would flop, like a fish. How long did they have to lie there before someone scooped them out? There was nothing like that here. People said that drowning was a good death, that the tiny alveoli of the lungs filled like a thousand water balloons.

She lifted one purple flip-flop and dropped it over the water. She didn't hear it hit. The shape simply vanished into the black shadow.

That was when the lights got brighter and the voice, male and certain, lobbed into her ears. 'Ma'am, step away from the rail.'

The police car's lights flashed blue and white and red. Once

2

she'd had an ice-pop those colours and the sugary water had pooled behind her teeth.

'Ma'am, step away from the rail.'

'Good evening, Officer. Have I done something wrong?' Mina asked.

'Please get into the car,' he said. There were two of them. The other was younger and he was speaking into a radio. It was hard to make out his words over the wind and traffic. Was he talking about her?

'This is a public walkway,' Mina said. 'It was open. I haven't done anything wrong.'

'Ma'am, get into the car.'

'I don't want to get into the car. Look, I was just getting some air. I was thinking. I'll go home now.'

'Ma'am, don't make me come over there.'

Mina had never been in a police car. She'd read once that the back doors only open from the outside. Who knew what would happen if she got into the car?

The window was rolled down and the cop stuck his head out. There was a lump on his upper lip, a pimple perhaps.

'Where are your shoes?'

'It's hot out,' she said.

'Where are your shoes?'

'I don't want to tell you about my shoes,' she said. 'I haven't done anything wrong. I'm an American citizen.'

'Ma'am, where are your shoes?'

She lifted up the single flip-flop she had left. 'The other one broke,' she said.

Behind him, other cars continued into the night. Did they even notice her standing in the dark, a small woman with bare legs and feet? She was aware of the bluing bruise she'd caught banging her knee on the subway door. In the shower that morning, she'd skipped shaving her legs. In the beam of his headlamps, could he see hairs standing up in splinters?

3

'Ma'am, I really need you to get into the car. I can't leave you here. What if something happened to you?' In his voice, she heard the insinuation that normal women, innocent women, didn't walk alone on bridges at night.

'I'm fine,' she said.

Mina knew her stubby ponytail was frizzy. Bleaching black to Marilyn Monroe-blonde had taken four rounds of peroxide. Now it stood up in breaking strands. If she'd conditioned it, would this cop think she was sane? If she'd blow-dried it, would he have let her go home? And, of course, there were the tattoos twining up her arms.

'We can talk about it in the car,' he said. His shadowed friend was bent over the radio, lips to the black box.

Mina was tired. It was the heat, or perhaps the wind. So she got into the car. The seat was smooth. Someone must've chosen the fabric specially. This must be wipeable and disinfectable. People probably spat on this seat. They probably pissed on purpose and by mistake. Between the front and back seats was a grille. She would not be able to reach out to touch the curve of the cop's ear or straighten his blue collar. The flip-flop lay across her knees.

The cops wanted to know her name, address, phone number and Social Security. She gave them.

'We're taking you to Mount Sinai,' said the cop.

'I was just going for a walk, clearing my head. I don't need to be in a hospital. I was just clearing my head.'

Damn. Repeating yourself was a habit of the guilty. Mina tried to slow her breath.

'See it from my point of view,' he said. 'You're walking alone on the bridge at night. I can't let you out. I don't know what would happen.'

Only then did she understand that they must do this every night, drive back and forth across the bridge looking for people like her.

4

'I have to go to work tomorrow,' she said. 'My husband will want to know where I am. Please, please, just let me go to the subway.'

'We can't do that, ma'am.'

The car left the bridge and fell back into Manhattan. She kept telling them she wasn't trying to cause trouble. She said it so many times that the word 'trouble' began to sound like 'burble' or 'bubble'. Heat rose in her eyes. She pushed the water off her face.

Finally, they agreed that she could call her husband, and they would go to the paramedics parked near the bridge. If the paramedics said she was okay, she could go home.

'Oscar,' she said. 'Oscar, I need you to come get me. They won't let me leave until you come get me.'

'Slow down,' he said. 'Where are you? What's going on?'

She tried to explain about the cops and how she'd been clearing her head and now they wanted to take her to the hospital. About how she needed him to be there.

The ambulance was parked under the highway. Was it, like the cops, always there? Always waiting for people like her? The cop got out of the car and opened her door. He didn't cuff her or even touch her. But her breath came double fast. The pearly pimple on his lip gleamed. He led her to the ambulance. The steps into the vehicle were constructed from a steel mesh. They hurt her feet. A hand reached out to help her. It was soft and firm and female. It was attached to a slim arm and a body in scrubs the colour of the swimming-pool where she'd made her first tentative laps as a pre-schooler. Mina smiled into the face and the face smiled back.

'Please take a seat,' the paramedic said, gesturing to the stretcher. A sheet was draped over the end, which made it look almost like a real bed. Mina sat on the edge.

'Can you wait here?' the paramedic asked. 'We're going to talk for a minute.'

Mina nodded, before she understood that *we* meant the cop. He stood on the sidewalk, his legs spread. For the first time, she saw his gun. It was no bigger than a bottle of Coca-Cola. Then the paramedic shut the door. That had to be a good sign. They trusted her to be alone. Her body was reflected as a peachy blur in the metal drawers. The sour light marked every pore, every scratch on her legs, the tiny specks of dirt under her toenails.

The paramedic returned with a clipboard. Mina noticed then how pretty she was and how neat her hair. The paramedic's lips were lipsticked a dark red. Mina had once owned a dress almost that colour—oxblood, the store called it.

'Nice lipstick,' Mina said.

'Thank you.' The paramedic smiled.

'I just want to go home.' Did that sound too desperate? Mina disliked the clipboard.

'We have to do a quick check-up,' the paramedic said. 'Can you give me your full name?'

'Mina,' she said, then paused. 'Umeda.' She'd only had her husband's name for six months and it still felt itchy. To most people, she suited the Japanese name. Mina was short, with a small, flat nose. People never guessed that her DNA came from heavy-bellied China, not Japan's skinny island chain. It was Oscar who puzzled people with his mixed-race face and English accent.

The clipboard was uninterested in the intricacies of naming. It wanted to know the same things as the police: name, phone number, Social Security and address. It was as if this one long number and these few lines could tell them all they needed to know. They would probably be the first things asked for when she was dead.

Mina gave detail after detail away to this stranger. She said, 'Can I ask your name?'

'Sunny,' said Sunny.

Sunny shone a light in Mina's left and right eyes. She asked Mina to stick her arm out and then wrapped a grey tube around it. Her touch was gentle as she sealed the Velcro. 'This is for blood pressure . . . Oh, that's a bit low.'

'Don't worry,' Mina said. 'It's always been low.'

'Mine too. It's common in women our age,' Sunny said, unwrapping the arm. Mina wanted to take Sunny's hand and feel the low pulse of the blood. She wanted to say thank you for not asking anything difficult.

'This won't hurt.' Sunny placed a plastic grip around her finger and took note of numbers on a machine without comment.

'So,' said Sunny, 'how have you been feeling? Emotionally?'

'I'm fine. I was just clearing my head.'

'Were you clearing it of anything in particular?'

Mina tried to see what the paramedic saw. What would Sunny make of Mina? This patient was an East Asian woman wearing a black tank top and black shorts. A woman with peonies tattooed up her arms to hide the fine trellis of scars from her teenage years. A woman who didn't bother blow-drying her hair. A woman who looked younger than she was. A woman in bare feet, who'd let her pedicure grow out so that only the tips of her toes were striped in gold. A woman with a single purple flip-flop. In Sunny's place, would Mina believe this woman?

A hard knock on the door.

'Oscar!' Mina said. There was her husband. He looked like a real adult. They would trust him. He had a linen shirt. 'That's my husband. They said my husband could pick me up.'

Sunny did not offer Oscar a hand into the ambulance. She asked him to wait outside. Once the door was shut, with Oscar on the other side, Sunny spoke: 'Mina, I need you to tell me how you've been feeling.'

'I've been feeling fine. I was just thinking.'

'What were you thinking about?'

'I can't remember now. Not with all of this.' Mina didn't know why she couldn't lie better. She wanted to lie. She wanted to say, I was thinking about my job or where we should go on vacation or the trash schedule. Her lips didn't know how to make anything about her life sound convincing. 'I just want to go home with my husband. They said I could go home with my husband.'

'And you're safe with him? He's never . . .' Sunny trailed off, and all the things Oscar had never done hung there.

'Oh, no, never. Not Oscar. I want to go home with him. My husband,' she said, 'he's here to pick me up.'

They'd been married for only six months, but they'd been together for a decade. The switch from boyfriend to husband felt strange. The word 'husband' sounded so stodgy, so like 'my attorney' or 'my Ford Focus hatchback'. Tonight, though, she loved it.

Oscar waited in the dark. There were portholes cut into the ambulance doors, but he couldn't see Mina. Earlier she'd been fine. She'd been reading aloud a review of some super-hero blockbuster. They'd made plans to have friends over that weekend. He'd felt like they were finally getting back into the swing of their lives. For six whole months she'd acted like nothing was wrong. Every time he'd asked, she'd said she was fine. 'Fine.' And now they were here.

Finally the door opened and the woman in scrubs stepped outside. She explained that they could not allow Mina to leave by herself. Her activity had been too concerning. But they could release her into his care. Did he think that she needed to be hospitalised? Had she been displaying signs of depression?

Oscar thought of their wedding night six months before.

He thought of how she'd swallowed two weeks' worth of wisdom-tooth painkillers. He thought of the first day of their married life and of her body in the hospital bed. The cot had been rimmed by white bars. They'd put her in a paper gown. Every time he visited her, she'd told him she wanted to go home. She'd told him it was a mistake. That she was fine. She hadn't meant to take all those pills. It was like when you bought a tub of ice cream and you only meant to have a scoop and somehow you found you'd reached the waxy bottom of the carton. She'd told him the only thing that made her want to die was the hospital and its stink of piss and disinfectant.

The paramedic was waiting, her head tilted accusatorially, seeming to say that he must have noticed something, must have seen something. Oscar said, 'I'll take her home. She's fine. Mina's distractible. She's an academic.' He tried to say *academic* as if wandering around bridges at night was part of the job description.

'You do understand you'd be taking full responsibility if anything happens?'

'Isn't that what I signed up for when I got married?'

The paramedic didn't laugh at the joke.

'So can I take her home?'

'After you sign the form.'

They caught a taxi mercifully quickly.

'Mina, what's going on?' Oscar asked.

She tapped the window. 'It's raining,' she said. And it was. As each drop hit, it brought with it a bubble of orange light.

'Mina, I'm serious.'

'Nothing. Nothing's going on.'

'I love you.' He said the words carefully and slowly, squeezing her hand.

'Love you too. But it was just a walk.'

'Mina, I'm your husband, not one of those people.' He waved a hand to indicate paramedics, police, psychologists—

all the people beginning with *p*. 'How long have I known you? Talk to me, Mina.'

'Stop saying my name.'

'Okay, but I know it's not nothing.'

'I was just going for a walk.' She slumped against the car door. Her face hit the glass.

'Mina,' he said, 'sorry. It's just . . .' He didn't want to shout at her, he didn't, but volume would feel good right now. 'You could've come home. We could've talked.' Oscar eyed the taxi driver. It was hard to see his face, though Oscar glimpsed a beard. It was impossible to tell if the man was listening. Surely he'd heard worse. This was New York, after all.

'You were working.' She closed her eyes, as if she knew how ridiculous the excuse was.

'How am I supposed to work when at any moment you could decide . . .' The things his wife might decide to do clamoured, too many to choose from. 'I love you, you can talk to me.'

She didn't reply and slumped further, rolling her shoulders. The rain ran ribbons of shadow on her face, and her eyes had a haze that implied she might be staring out of the window, or at the glass, or at a moving picture inside her head. He was reminded then that his wife was beautiful. Wild animals were beautiful in the same way. A sparrow or a fox carried an untranslatable energy in its eyes. She might've cracked that face against the Hudson River.

'Mina, look at me,' he said. Oscar moved his hand gradually, careful not to startle her. He clasped her chin. Gently, he swivelled her face towards him. He felt the hard bone of her jaw through her skin. 'Please, Mina, look at me.'

She frowned. Her eyes scrunched shut. The tank top had shifted, revealing the lace-lichen of her bra. Above that was a handbreadth of her smooth skin. It revealed nothing of her inner workings. Her eyes stayed closed against him. His phone buzzed but he ignored it. In the street a dog began to bark, and her eyes opened. It was impossible to see the pupils in the low light. His hand rested under her chin.

'Is this something to do with us?' he asked.

'Us?'

'Us, as in you and me, us.'

'Us,' she said slowly, like she was teaching herself English. 'No, not us. Nothing to do with you.' She gripped the hand that held her chin, forcing it away.

The cab stopped in traffic. Behind his wife's head, Oscar saw two pedestrians. They were kissing, their whole bodies pressing into each other. Both were so thin and shaggy-haired that their ages and gender were obscured. But the kiss was obvious. Oscar ran a thumb over the back of his wife's hand. 'Why, then?' he asked.

'I don't know.'

'You can't not know.'

'I was reading about that actor who jumped off and I just wanted to see it. The bridge, I mean.'

'You couldn't have used Google Earth?'

Mina shrugged. He let go of her hand.

Rain spat at the window. At some point, she began to drum out a beat, smacking the flip-flop against her lap.

Finally, she began to talk. She turned to the window and passing shadows stroked her flushed cheeks. 'I was at Alfie's this afternoon.'

'Which one is he again?' Oscar could never keep straight the kids Mina tutored to supplement the measly salary the university paid her as an adjunct lecturer.

'Sixteen, lives on the Upper West Side. Learning Latin because his mom thinks it'll help him stand out college-essay time. He's good at it too. Most of the kids don't want to be there. But Alfie just needs you to tell him he's doing it right. Chews his pencils until the wood shows through. Likes Roman

11

history—loves all that pontificating about tactics, even though he's so skinny he'd probably fall over if you tossed a baseball at him.'

'Okay, I think I remember.'

'Well, anyway, Alfie, he's no trouble. And I'd given him this passage to translate. It's about geese. Basically, the story goes that the Romans are under attack by the Gauls. After several defeats they're trapped on the Capitoline Hill. They plan to wait the siege out. The walls are steep and they feel safe. There are kids in the Capitoline, women and slaves. This isn't a battleground, it's home.' Mina made a circle with her hands in the shape of a protective wall.

'Okay,' Oscar said. He stroked his wife's palm. Whenever she spoke about those long-dead Romans, it was as if she were telling a family story. She'd pause at the good bits, savouring them. But the Romans and the Gauls would not pull his wife out of the river. They would not have to identify her body.

'One of the Gauls finds a way to scale the walls. And by moonlight they climb. The Romans are asleep, lying on their hard pillows. Some are probably snoring and some are probably drinking, and others slipping out of lovers' beds. None of them are expecting the Gauls. But the Gauls are climbing.' Mina's voice was going faster now, having found a rhythm. 'The Gauls have daggers and hunger and rage. They want gold and wine. They move quietly and quickly up the walls. But a goose hears the strangers. It shrieks, and soon all the geese of the Capitoline are shrieking and beating their wings. The Romans gather their swords and save the Capitoline. This is why geese are sacred. They saved the city.'

Mina paused, staring into the window as if trying to read something written on the glass.

'That's nice,' Oscar said.

'It happened thousands of years ago,' Mina said.

'I know.'

'And they all died anyway. The Romans and the Gauls and the geese.'

Oscar pulled her against him, feeling the weight of her familiar body. The heat of her skin pressed against his shoulder. He pushed back an image of his wife cold in the river and said, 'Okay, so you got Alfie to translate this story.'

'Yeah, he did a pretty good job. And I think he liked it.'

'But?'

'But I just started crying. I don't know why. I kept thinking about how straw in the mud then probably didn't look that different from straw in the mud now. And about how geese have these hard pointed tongues, and about how it feels to scream. And also about how tired I was. Suddenly I was just tired right down to the knuckles in my toes. And the room was so hot, too hot. And I was thinking about the subway home and all the tired bodies. And I just started crying. I couldn't stop. I told Alfie it was allergies, but I don't think he believed me. And he's just a kid and his nibbled pencil was just lying on the desk. He's just a kid and he's already so worried.' Mina pressed the heels of her hands into her face.

Oscar touched her neck softly, stroking it up and down, up and down.

'What am I supposed to do? I can't be this person. I can't keep crying. What will I do when the new semester starts?'

'Keep crying?' he asked. 'You said you were doing okay.'

She shrugged and looked out of the window.

'We'll figure it out,' he said. 'We'll get the right dosage.'

'We're just going to keep upping and upping and upping the number of fucking pills?' She pressed the hands harder into her face, so hard it seemed like she was trying to push her eyeballs back into her head.

'Maybe you should take some time off teaching,' Oscar

13

said. He kept his voice steady. They'd figure out the finances. He'd do the maths when they got home.

'I can't do that,' she said.

'You can.'

'What would I even do? Lie in the apartment and feel sorry for myself? I'd just get underfoot.'

'Figure out that monograph proposal. Apply to conferences.'

'I can't go to a conference. Oscar, I burst into these stupid tears explaining to a kid that *strepitus* can mean confused noise, crash, clatter or din. There's no single correct answer. He had to choose.' Mina began to pinch the skin on her arm, until he stopped her by lifting that hand and taking it in his own. 'And I can't just quit. It's so fucking hard to get these stupid little adjunct jobs, while you hope that something more permanent will show up. You pray for the magic words— *tenure track*. I can't piss the university admin off.'

'Didn't you say Crista took six months' leave to have a baby? And she's fine.'

'She had a baby to show for it at the end.'

'Just say you have some health issues.' Oscar kept his voice calm. Mentally, he scanned their accounts. If Mina took time off, they should be fine. It would eat into their savings. But, he supposed, you saved for rainy days.

'I guess I was also thinking about all the nights before the battle. The people had to sleep knowing that the Gauls were outside. All that waiting for the situation to improve.'

The cab stopped. Oscar pressed a limp twenty and a crisper ten into the driver's hand. 'Keep the change.' Anyone who'd listened to this miserable conversation deserved a tip.

Mina stared at the door and he reached over her to snap it open. She got out, moving stiffly. She tilted her head up at their building as if this was the first time she'd seen it. 'I can't do this.' She made a gesture with her hands to indicate a *this*

14

that encompassed their building, the street, the whole city. 'I just can't keep doing this.'

The flip-flop dangled from her hand. He snatched it. The foam sole was soft under his fingers, like flesh. The trash can was a few metres away and he overarmed it. The sandal landed neatly.

'We'll take a break. We'll get you out of the city. Just try to relax. Can you do that for me? Try to be happy?'

Oscar stood in front of his underwear drawer, realising there were no boxers. Socks, yes. Underwear, no. He pushed aside sock-balls. Nothing. Laundry was Mina's job. Cooking was his. Mina lay in bed, the sheets pulled up over her face.

'Are there any clean . . .' he began to ask, but stopped. Mina's hand dangled down the side of the bed, loose as a corpse's. He pulled on yesterday's underwear inside out. He'd drag the dirty clothes down to the laundry in the basement later. He walked over to Mina. Her hair had fallen over her eyes. 'Do you want some tea?' he asked, crouching to her level.

She mumbled and turned her face to the pillow.

They'd moved into the studio apartment when they were young and new to the city. Their two desks stood side by side against the window. On hers, a cactus grew in a cracked mug. The air-conditioner ruffled her papers. On his was his laptop, and last night's coffee. He wiggled the mouse and the unfinished July sales report appeared. Oscar worked for his father's import business—Umeda Trading. The two-man operation sold sake and Japanese beer to bars and restaurants in the States. Oscar managed the East Coast sales. The report was almost done. He'd planned to finish it last night. But then Mina . . . He started a new document.

How to Get Mina Out of New York
Vacation (Short. Expensive.)
Stay with friends/family. (Awkward to impose. No privacy.)
Work trip. (Possible.)

Work trip. A work trip would be the thing. It was time he got to know their suppliers. In the past, his father had always said Oscar's Japanese wasn't up to scratch. But Oscar knew many more words now.

He finished off the sales report, the numbers slightly lower than he'd anticipated. Not far off. It was the same fractional difference that existed between his friends' Tinder profiles and their actual faces. Thank God he'd never had to do Tinder.

The clock at the corner of his computer ticked to noon. So, nine Pacific Standard Time. He called his father. They ran through the sales report. Summers were tricky. Sometimes slow and sometimes not. It would have been nice to be in a stronger position to make his request.

'Dad, I need to leave New York for a few weeks. I have some meetings set up in the next week. But after that I don't think the clients will notice if I go remote.' He kept his voice low, not wanting to disturb Mina. Although at midday, could it be so bad if she woke up?

'And where is it you'll be?' His father's voice was cautious, neutral.

'I could go out to Japan, maybe Ibaraki, and get to know the supplier side of the business better.'

'I don't think that's a good idea. Your Japanese is a bit . . . You have to understand these relationships are delicate. If you're not fluent . . .'

'I've been practising my intonations.' The lilts of Japanese did not give meaning, as they did in Chinese. But mistakes conveyed inept foreignness.

'It's not the right time.' His father sounded irritated.

Why not? Oscar wanted to ask. The old suspicion flared. His father didn't want his contacts seeing Oscar's bastard face, the evidence of the affair drawn in the wavy hair and beaky nose.

'And what do you mean you need to get out of New York?'

17

If he had grown up with his father, it would have been possible to run to him like a child with a cut knee and cry, 'Daddy!' But, even after all these years working for Kenichi Umeda, the man was more like a boss than a dad.

Oscar paused. He had to ask the sort of favour you couldn't ask a boss. He should have rehearsed what to say, but his mind had felt disordered all morning, as if a burglar had come in the night and emptied all the drawers.

'The heat in the city is making Mina ill,' he said. He looked over to his wife's unmoving body. He would have expected her to at least look up at the sound of her name. Could she be sleeping that deeply?

'Then Tokyo wouldn't do you much good.' His father's deadpan California drawl was incredulous.

'I thought a change of air might help.' It was illogical, but better than saying, *My wife has gone mad*. 'Japan would be useful,' Oscar added. Maybe he shouldn't have asked his father. Oscar worked from New York and his father from LA. The man might never have noticed he was missing. Maybe he should have just sublet their apartment and booked tickets to Hokkaido. Up in the mountains, he would have time to smooth out his syllables and Mina could relax.

His father sighed. 'So it's anywhere but New York?'

Oscar did a shoulder roll, concentrating on each shift of muscle. It would do his back no good to tense up.

'If you really need to leave New York, there's something in London you could help me with.'

'England?' Oscar had lived in London until he was sent with tuck-box and rugby boots to boarding school. The city came to him in flashes—baked potato and beans, the tiger in the zoo that wouldn't stop pacing, the sharp angles of a 50p coin in your pocket, Bacardi Breezers drunk on park benches, the rum and fruit syrup coating the back of his teeth.

Oscar's father had flown over from LA for Oscar's birthdays.

18

There was always a neatly wrapped gift and a card signed by his father and Ami, his father's wife. Oscar, his mother and his father shared a cake in a restaurant. The waitresses sang 'Happy Birthday' and strangers smiled at them as if they were a real family, not a one-night stand and its result.

The man was nothing like the sturdy-bodied football-watching fathers of Oscar's friends. When Oscar tried to describe his father, he'd settle on details that never quite became a picture. The watch with a little calendar spinning out the day. Or the phone with the keyboard, on which he let Oscar play a game where you shot six-pixel aeroplanes out of the sky. The way he'd often begin his sentences, 'Well, in the States . . .' He'd ask about Oscar's grades, and reply, 'Well done, kid.' He only looked happy talking about the business. In those early years, it always seemed to be growing. Import, export, transport—Oscar had the sense of objects flying over-head, as his father gesticulated with fork and knife. It seemed as mysterious as selling moon rocks to Martians.

Back then, Oscar had thought, some day he'd be a busi-nessman. He'd thought this before he knew what business was. He liked the way men in suits walked as if they knew where they were going. It seemed like they were all wearing the uniform of the same team.

At the leafy campus in Rhode Island, Oscar enrolled in Economics. But in his final year the economy tanked and nobody wanted to take on an apprentice businessman. His father had sponsored his stay at the glorious institution so he was luckier than most. He had no debt. But all the news-papers were saying that a college diploma meant nothing any more. Along the halls, stories were muttered of graduates turned down from barista-ing, pool attending, dishwashing.

Oscar wrote CV after CV, changing the fonts from serif to sans and back again. He applied for internships, dogsbodying, shelf-stacking.

Finally, his father suggested that Oscar work for him until the world found its footing. Oscar was surprised. Although his father always paid the bills, he'd never exactly been there. Oscar didn't know if he could be all buddy-buddy with a man he barely knew. But there had been no other options.

Oscar became the East Coast sales director of the two-man operation. He followed Mina, that sliver of a girl he'd met senior year, to New York. Columbia University had offered her a funded doctoral fellowship.

He never became buddy-buddy with his father. When talking to his friends he described the man as Ken, or Kenichi. It seemed easier. The word *Dad* implied fishing trips, first-condom handing over, and being hoisted upon shoulders. Ken was simpler.

'You're thinking of expanding to the UK?'

'Not quite,' his father said. 'I have some apartments.'

Oscar had never heard of any flats.

'Bought them in the eighties. Dirt cheap. Ex-council. But a great location. Figured it would pay off. I think the market over there is peaking. They need sprucing up. You could go over there, handle that. The agencies that deal with this stuff always add on extra charges.'

Had his father really not thought to mention that he owned property in the country of Oscar's childhood? Another son might've raged that, even after all these years, his father had only just thought to mention it. Another son might've hung up with a prod of the touchscreen.

'I'll do my best,' Oscar said. Mina needed a break. And this would get her out of New York.

September

London. Oscar tracked the cab's progress on his phone. Neighbourhoods he remembered as grubby had acquired a spit-shine gleam. Mina napped against his shoulder. Her hair was sleep-mussed. The oversized hoodie gave her the messy, optimistic look of a child on a camping trip.

He squeezed her arm. 'Wake up. We're here.'

She yawned and smiled up at him.

The building's entrance was on a side street. As he got out of the cab, Oscar stepped over a Heineken's carcass, the bottle's mouth shattered. 'Watch out,' he told his wife.

He lugged their suitcases to the door of a brick building. The block of flats appeared to be only six storeys or so. He reached into his pocket for the unfamiliar keychain. His father had said to hold the black fob against the black box, screwed under the list of residents. Oscar did. A mechanism within clicked its assent and he pushed the door open with his shoulder. Mina trotted after him, tugging the smallest suitcase. She seemed happy.

The entrance hall was small and clean. The floor was tiled. A lift flanked a spiral staircase. Oscar pressed the up button. The door whined as it opened. The lift was about the size of a telephone booth. There was no way he, Mina and their three suitcases would fit inside.

'We'll take turns. You first,' he said. He wheeled in two cases and Mina slipped in between them. 'Dad told me the liveable one is on the fourth floor.' The doors closed over her face, and he felt a jab of worry. But what could happen to her on such a short journey?

The lift returned empty. He loaded in the final case. The wheels of the suitcase caught on the peeling linoleum. Once on the fourth floor, he was disoriented. The landing was small and there was only one door. Mina, her back to him, had it open. Beyond his wife's head was the sky.

'I think the apartments are off this balcony thing,' she said. He followed her onto the exposed walkway. A pigeon squatted on the iron rail. It scuttled back a few steps, the scaly claws moving with surprising speed. He looked down. They were high enough for a fall to break a woman's body. The four-storey drop ended in a courtyard. Industrial bins proffered up swollen black bags. But he didn't trust them to cushion a landing. Oscar frowned. He forced his head to turn away from the drop. He didn't want Mina getting ideas. The key wouldn't turn in 4B's lock. He jiggled it, pulled it out a fraction, gave it another twist. The door to the next flat opened. A white-haired head popped out.

The old woman grinned at them. 'Moving in?' Her accent was English, but hard to place. London metropolitan. A hint of something else? Northern?

'For a few weeks,' he replied. There was no need to give extraneous information.

'I'm Mina and this is my husband Oscar. It's so nice to meet you.'

The old woman took Mina's hand in both of hers. It was a strange sight. Mina and the old woman had the same haircut with the same frizzy texture, one white, the other peroxide.

'Have you lived here long?' Mina asked.

'Forty years.'

'That's amazing,' Mina said.

'Oh, I've seen some goings-on.' The old lady raised a sparse white eyebrow. 'You're from America?'

Mina put her palms up in mock surrender. 'What gave it away? Our terrible fashion sense?'

'You should've seen how the kids around here dressed back in the eighties. Hair out to here.' She waved a hand over the top of her head as if she were signalling for help.

Finally, the key gave way. He'd been turning it in the wrong direction.

Mina said, 'If you need anything, just let us know. We're right here.'

At least that hadn't changed. If you were over seventy, Mina would listen to your longest stories, carry your bag, and tolerate your blinking hearing aid without a fuss. She got some sort of energy from it.

4B was dark and the air tasted dusty. He slapped the wall for a switch. Click. But no light. The bulb must've died. He walked to where daylight edged the shutters and swung them open. The windows looked out on the looming concrete plinth of a Travelodge. The logo was emblazoned up the side in letters larger than a man's body. Not an ideal view.

The room was covered in a heavily-patterned wallpaper. Here and there it was scratched or peeling off. A cheap-looking pine table and chairs dominated the middle of the room. A tangerine sofa leaned against the wall. A paper lantern covered the useless ceiling light. The jumbled style of the room was uncharacteristic of his father, but Oscar assumed the furniture been left by renters. Student lets, his father had said.

On his phone, Oscar made a quick list.

Check supplies
Buy light-bulbs
Dust
Unpack

*

Mina stood before the supermarket's food-to-go compartment. Her head was loopy from travel and the world had a pleasantly unreal aura. She skimmed past the labels for Coronation Chicken and tuna fish, looking for the vegetarian options. The packaging was delightfully foreign. She recognised the unpronounceably British brand names from the layovers they'd spent in London on the way to Oscar's mother in Scotland. Just seeing them gave her a vacation-zing.

She reached into the cool cavity to grab a cheese sandwich and a bag of pre-chopped apples for the snack portion of the supermarket's meal deal.

Oscar had already gathered his food and was collecting cleaning fluids elsewhere. Her friends were jealous of Oscar's cleanliness. Mina refrained from telling them that she suspected he'd started wishing he could rinse her brain with lemon-fresh detergent.

She wasn't surprised when, back at the apartment, he brought up Dr Helene again.

'She's really okay with you quitting?' he asked.

Since the wedding 'attempt' had indicated her old medication wasn't working, Mina had tried two different pills. The first had swelled her body, and her lips had peeled pale strips of skin. The second was almost as bad. For a few months, she'd puttered from class, to library, to tutees, to drinks with friends and back again. Her brain had felt heavier and heavier with each subway journey as if she might sink down beneath the rails. So, while Oscar prepared for London, Mina had asked Dr Helene if they could try going medication free. Mina quit everything. The mental-health meds, the vitamins and the birth control. Everything. They'd brought over boxes and boxes of the brand of condom Oscar liked.

Oscar spread a spoonful of canned tuna across a rice cracker.

'Are you sure you don't want to eat something else?' she

24

asked. He was munching what looked like cat food and she was the crazy one?

'Tuna is very high in protein.'

Her simple cheese sandwich was soft and tangy and surrendered easily to eating.

'You didn't answer the question,' Oscar said.

'I told you, my treatment is under control. We're having Skype meetings once a month and I'm keeping a mood log.' For each good day she made an uptick, ∧, below the date on her calendar and for each day she felt bad she made a downtick, ∨. Too many ∨s must be reported, at which point they would review the plan of care.

Mina's crazy was not the madness of delusion or hallucination. It was what the articles on the matter referred to as *a mood disorder*. She felt too much or too little and was sad when she should have been happy. Hence the mood diary: a way to order those disordered moods. Her first doctor had said simple depression. But after the wedding, Dr Helene had mentioned the possibility of bipolarity. Impulsive decision-making was often a characteristic of mania. Dr Helene hadn't made up her mind. There wasn't enough evidence to be sure. The medical terms made Mina feel like a bacterium— something to be studied and labelled. She preferred crazy. You weren't supposed to use that word, but she liked the *z*, the way it slid across the mouth like a knife.

'She's not worried?' Oscar asked.

'I mean, it's not her first choice, but I promised I'd keep really good track of my moods and my sleeping. And I've been doing well with the monthly meetings.'

After the wedding, they'd had to meet weekly. To be moved to monthly was like having your training wheels taken off, a mark of success. Mina had not mentioned the night on the bridge to Dr Helene. If she had, Dr Helene would never have allowed her to go medication free.

25

'You're sure this is what you want to do? If you had the flu and cough syrup didn't work, you'd take antibiotics. You wouldn't just quit.' Oscar had had his hair cut just before they left the city. His ears stuck out, petite and vulnerable. Compared to the sharp jaw and aggressively earned biceps, those ears were strangely endearing.

'You could try another medication. What if Columbus had given up after his first failed voyage?'

It was a stupid comparison. Columbus just took it into his head to cross the ocean. Mina had needed her medication.

A different pill might've worked. She might've coped with whatever weight gain, weight loss, hair gain or hair loss it caused. But she no longer had it in her to perform the sacrament of putting capsule on tongue. She'd lost faith.

Mina forced herself to look at his ears as she spoke. If she looked at the ears, she had some hope of sounding calm. 'If Christopher Columbus had given up, the native peoples of America would have had a few more peaceful years. What if we find a new pill, and there's a flood or a storm and I get stuck without it? Or what if big pharma decides it's unprofitable? What then?'

Maybe in the hustle of invitations or budgeting the wedding, she'd forgotten a few doses. But brides weren't supposed to need anti-depressants. Maybe it was her fault. Maybe that was what had triggered it. Or maybe it wasn't. Dr Helene couldn't say for certain. She could only offer Mina more pills with names that read like Latin put through a meat grinder. Mina crumpled the sandwich box and threw it into the trash.

'Mina, what would you do without WiFi or hair dye or cheese sandwiches? You'd figure it out. But it doesn't make sense not to use something just because one day it might disappear.'

'This is different.'

'Mina, it's just helping your brain make the chemicals that other people's brains make naturally.'

'I just want to try to see if I can be happy for a bit. Without professional assistance,' she told him. 'I mean it has to be worth trying, right? Otherwise, my whole life I'm going to be taking pills and wondering when they're going to fail.'

She wanted to learn the floor plan of this sadness. In their New York apartment, she could walk in the dark. Her body was attuned to the obstacles and automatically found the clear pathway. If she could get to know this sadness, she might be able to find her way through it.

She could barely remember how she'd felt before being medicated. In the last year of Mina's high school, her grandma died. The death was not just an excuse for missing class or flunking a final. She'd lost the woman who'd potty-trained her on a yellow plastic turtle. The woman who'd brushed her hair when she was sad. The person who'd hugged her good-night almost as many nights as she'd been alive. For most of her childhood it had been just her and her grandmother. Her mother was long gone. Her father spent his days book-keeping and his evenings at night-school, training to become an accountant. By the time her grandma died, he'd got his accounting certificate. The school counsellor called him to say Mina's mourning period had become 'inappropriate'. Little red cuts had danced up her arms. So she'd accepted the offered pills.

Oscar sighed, swiped a flake of tuna from his chin and said, 'I just want you to be safe.'

'We're only going to be in London for a few months. If I'm not feeling better in a few months, I'll let Dr Helene pop something down my throat. But let me get my head straight.' Maybe in a few months her throat would feel supple and she'd be ready to swallow capsule after capsule.

'You promise?' he asked.

'Cross my heart and hope to die,' she said. And made the gesture flicking a big X across her chest.

'Mina!'

'I'm joking, I'm joking. I promise.'

They unpacked their things. Oscar eased each of Mina's jeans over hangers, smoothing down the narrow denim calves. Later they fucked and his hands ran down her sides and over the tops of her hips, and his fingers pressed down until pelvic bone pressed back.

'Mine,' he said into her ear. 'Mine.' In the moment, it felt true. The little naked body was his. The knees that turned slightly inward were his. The way her face twisted was his. Each shift and bend of his wife was his.

'What are you?' he asked, knowing she would reply in a way she never would dressed and calm, her face smooth.

'Yours,' Mina said.

Her back arched and Oscar saw how it would have arched the same way in the cold black river, her lungs rising surface-wards as her limbs flopped towards the bottom. And then he pushed the thought away.

'Mine,' he said.

Afterwards he held her, the condom still clinging awkwardly to his dick, the contents ready to slosh out. But his arms strapped around her shoulders. His nose against her neck, he took in the warm, sweet, salty smell of his wife.

Outside the florist, wooden crates were crowned with succulents and cacti. Back in New York, Mina had a cactus in a mug. It'd been *her* mug, when she and Oscar first moved in together. Then it had cracked and she hadn't wanted to throw it away so she'd planted a green pincushion inside.

She reached out to pet a succulent rosette. It had a slight fuzz, like the hair that grows on a girl's back. This wasn't what she'd come to buy. Perhaps the neighbour would like one. Mina decided she'd leave it on the doorstep with a note. She hadn't seen the woman since they moved in the week before, but she wanted to be neighbourly.

Mina's grandma had filled their apartment with ferns. So many ferns that they stained the light green. She'd said the plants cleaned the air. At the end, she'd been too weak to lift the red watering can. Mina had taken over. Each night before SAT prep, she prodded the spout between the leaves.

Mina chose a pink-tipped succulent and carried it inside.

As she opened the shop door, the brass bell clanked hello. Colours burned from plastic pots. The florist kneeled over a basket of calla lilies. She pushed the sleeve of her denim dress up her arm and plunged a hand into the bucket, rearranging the stems.

'Hi,' Mina said.

'Can I help? Are you looking for something in particular?' the florist asked. Her hair was pulled into a black bud at the top of her head.

Are you looking for something in particular? was the sort of question Dr Helene asked Mina. She never had a clear answer.

'A dinner party,' Mina said. 'I'm looking for flowers for a dinner party.' The guests were Oscar's friends. They knew nothing of her breakdown and she wanted to greet them with flowers. For a few hours, she could be the wife Oscar deserved.

'Any preferences? Colour? Type?' the florist asked.

Reflexively, Mina gripped her arms where the inked flowers climbed. It was odd how tattooed and naked skin felt exactly alike. The inked peonies were perennially opening, the buds always on the verge of blooming.

'Peonies?' Mina peered through the greenery looking for those soft fists of pink and white.

'Sadly, they're out of season. We get some real beauties in the spring.' Gold-rimmed glasses hung from a chain at the florist's neck. Light fell through the glass, scattering daisies of sunlight. One spun across Mina's shirt and she stood very still, letting it rest there. The florist described the late-summer options. They decided on chrysanthemums.

Arranged in three buckets, the chrysanthemums came in pink, yellow and chicken-heart red.

'When does chrysanthemum season end?' Mina asked.

'If you're looking for locally grown, November,' the florist said.

How good it would be to think of time in terms of the opening and closing of flowers—to wake up and think, Today is the day of the snowdrops.

'I'll take the red ones,' she said. The florist beribboned the flowers. The translucent plastic wrapping crinkled and the tissue shushed as Mina adjusted the bouquet under her arm and stepped out into the city.

A girl walked past, a backpack turtling her slim shoulders, chattering happily up at her father. Her dress was blue

30

gingham and swirled around her knees. A breeze tickled Mina's neck. A week in, London still felt new.

She'd wanted to leave New York, this body, this life. This dragging out of limbs. But maybe the answer was a change of place, a change of currency, a change of light. The sun, that summer tyrant, felt tolerable here. In this sabbatical, Mina might find a way back into happiness.

She'd begin with tonight's dinner party. It was the first time they'd have guests since landing in England. Oscar's oldest friend Theo. Theo she'd met before, a large English man with a face as bland as rice pudding whose only topic of conversation seemed to be their school days and the cricket score. But in Oscar's childhood stories, Theo had always been the hero and Oscar the lieutenant. Perhaps he was one of those men who lost the zest of their boyhood.

Theo was bringing his sister. About her, Mina knew nothing.

Oscar lined up the knife with a tomato's belly button. The knife was as sharp and fresh as the tomatoes themselves. The red skin slit easily. He tilted the chopping board and they skidded into the salad bowl. The mumble of voices wafted up from the street.

It would be good to see Theo again. He always acted as if the order of the world was natural. Being with him, you briefly believed that everything was in its rightful place.

For five years of boarding school, Theo and Oscar had shared everything. They'd been shoved together in science class. They'd lived on the same corridor. They'd lain on the school lawns eating slices of chocolate biscuit cake Theo's mum had covered in tinfoil and sent in the post. Together they'd figured out how to bypass the school firewalls. Theo had guarded the IT-room door, ready to distract any incoming teacher, while Oscar watched some unclad blonde appear pixel by pixel through the stingy connection. He would copy and paste her into Microsoft Word, click Print, and flick the copy number to 2. The result: two black-and-white prints. Oh, the days of youth!

Mina walked in clutching flowers. 'Success,' she said. They were strange flowers, dark and heavy-headed, but no stranger than the mismatched plates they'd picked up from the Oxfam shop. Theo wouldn't care about flowers.

'Try one of these.' Oscar held up a quarter-tomato between thumb and forefinger. Mina bent her head, like a bird, to eat from his hand. Her mouth slid around his fingers and the red wedge.

'Need any help?' she asked.

'Almost done.'

Mina preferred guests who arrived in the winter. In the frigid months, they'd have to stand by the door, unzipping and unbuttoning. She'd get a good look at them. As it was, Theo and his sister simply stepped into the apartment.

'The lovely bride.' A big male body hugged her and clapped her shoulders, like he was trying to dislodge something from her throat. She tried to smile. A bony female hand thrust into hers. Each finger had a thread-thin silver ring. The sister. Mina looked into her face and stopped.

She hadn't seen a face like that in a long time. Years, maybe. She never knew what to do when she did. A certain type of woman glowed. A type that Mina knew she should not stare at, but her eyes swivelled towards anyway. This sort of woman could not be defined precisely. Phoebe had smooth white cheeks. Red curls feathered her skull. But other features could summon the same feeling. Mina remembered a woman with eyes the hazel of a boa constrictor and another with lashes like bear-traps.

'Fee-bee,' Mina said, enjoying the way the rhyme tasted. Phoebe, Phoebus Apollo, sun god. How could her parents

32

have detected the glow when she was only a round-bellied baby? Or perhaps the name had blessed the baby. Phoebe's pink shift dress matched the shade of the kneecaps that emerged below the hem. Mina remembered something about redheads not being allowed to wear pink. She couldn't see why.

'Let me get a good look at you.' Phoebe leaned towards Mina. 'You're just like the photos.'

'What photos?' Mina asked.

'The wedding photos. I saw them on Facebook. You two were adorable.'

Mina thought the girl in the photographs looked Photoshopped, her teeth glinting like broken glass. 'They were very flattering,' Mina said.

'No, really, you look just like them.' Phoebe's face was still so close. Something about her filled Mina's mouth with the taste of fruit. Specifically, a fruit so ripe that its juice runs down the hand and has to be licked from the palms and wrists. It was probably the hair. The blood-orange waves swayed as Phoebe moved.

'Oscar's lucky to have you.' Phoebe's top lip slowly thinned into a smile.

Mina's mouth followed suit. The expression came almost easily. She'd spent most of the past hour using a mirror to practise smiling like a normal person. 'Thank you,' she said.

'And, Oscar, you're a married man now! How does it feel?' Phoebe punched his shoulder.

'I figured it was time. We've been together . . . what? How long now?'

Mina knew that Oscar knew. She heard the pride in his voice. They'd made it so far. They'd got married on their ten-year anniversary. That was seven months ago. Seven months that somehow felt longer than the preceding decade. Was he still glad that he'd asked? As if sensing her worry, he ran a gentle hand down the side of her arm.

'Since it's hot out, we threw together some salad.' Oscar changed the subject. 'Sit wherever.' He was already pouring Theo a glass of wine. Mina was struck by the kindness of that *we*. She had chopped nothing. But there he was including her. Heat rose to her face. Who was she to be looking at a woman like Phoebe when she had a husband so ready to enfold her in pronouns: we, us, our life together? As if they had not two lives but one.

The men took the table's wide shanks, leaving the women the head and tail. Mina had a clear view of Phoebe. It was impossible not to look. She'd never seen a redhead with such blank skin. Not a freckle, a mole, a vein, barely a blush. It was so clean you could bite into it.

There was a sloshing of water and a chugging of more wine into more glasses. Hands grabbed tussocks of bread. Salad was passed. The sunset tie-dyed the sky outside and splashed the room. Forks, floors, walls and skin were spattered with gold. We are so lucky, Mina thought.

Theo proposed a toast. 'To the happy couple! I'm only sorry I couldn't make it to the wedding. Thank you for being so understanding.'

He'd called to say he couldn't come to the wedding only a few days before it began. Some case that just couldn't be delayed.

The glasses sang their clinking song.

Theo addressed Mina. 'How's teaching?'

Mina had given up the contracts at the three universities where she taught Introductory Latin. They'd accepted her excuse of health problems but had sounded as sceptical as she felt when a student explained his absence as being due to a bad case of Domino's pizza indigestion.

'I'm focusing on my research,' she said.

'How's that going?'

34

'It's going. You know how it is.'

Salad leaves were stabbed. The olive oil was passed.

'Nice wallpaper,' said Phoebe, raising an eyebrow. 'You must be Morris fans.'

The flat was papered in a dark blue and green print. Mina supposed you would call it floral. Between the flowers squatted indigo-eyed birds. A mischievous renter had scribbled eye-patches, monocles and moustaches on a few of the avians.

'Morris?' Mina asked, looking again at the walls and the pop-eyed birds.

'That's a William Morris wallpaper, you know, the designer. I suppose he's British, maybe not as big a deal in the States.'

'Or you're a nerd,' said her brother, reaching over and ruffling that hair. She batted him off, baring her teeth.

Oscar laughed and said, 'We didn't choose it. Must've been my father's wife.'

'It's cute,' Phoebe said. Wine glossed her lower lip.

'So tell me about it,' Mina said, to keep Phoebe talking. One of Phoebe's canines tilted jauntily to the side. Mina wanted to see it again. Her own teeth were depressingly orthodontia-ed.

'William Morris. William Morris.' Phoebe paused to dip her bread into the olive oil. 'To be honest, I don't remember much other than that he was a bit of a socialist and really into medieval stuff. Oh, and his wife fucked around behind his back. Janey was this gangly girl who was an artists' model for Morris's best friend. Anyway . . .' Phoebe took a breath and another swallow of wine. Mina felt the *Anyway* like an arm around her shoulders, as if she and Phoebe were walking down a well-worn path together. 'Morris asks her to marry him. And she says yes. She doesn't come from money and here's this rich guy. They set up house. They embroider the curtains together and everything. Then Morris's best friend, the one Janey was modelling for, starts sleeping with her. All

35

their friends know it too. What does Morris do? He potters off to Iceland and waits for it to pass. Can you imagine? Inside he must've felt like . . .' Phoebe's bony hands made a strangling gesture.

'Pheeb,' Theo said.

'All right, all right, I'll behave. Anyway, as a good feminist I should probably be on Janey's side. She didn't want to marry some rich lump. But I have a soft spot for cuckolds, being one myself.'

'Pheeb,' Theo said again.

She poured herself another glass of wine. 'If your husband left you for some slut, you'd have feelings,' she said. 'Sorry, I shouldn't call her a slut. Maybe I should say the brave, independent woman who is sleeping with my soon-to-be ex-husband. Would that be the correct take on it?'

'Phoebe,' said Theo. 'Can you not have a tantrum at table?'

Phoebe took another long drink and rubbed her mouth with the back of her hand. The knuckles came back smudged pink. Mina had the strangest urge to soap the little palm under the tap. It didn't make sense that someone would leave this person. Even just watching Phoebe drizzle a swirl of balsamic dressing over her salad and lifting a red sphere to her lips made Mina feel like the world might be a bearable place.

Oscar thought that Phoebe's face had hardened. He supposed she was twenty-eight now. Twenty-nine? The skin had tightened on her cheeks. And that thin mouth. It was odd to think he'd kissed it less than half a life ago. It had been a summer party at Theo's house. Her tongue had tasted of sugary Pimm's, and her soft body had been close to his. His own body had been fresh then too, not that he'd realised at the time. Hormones and lust ran like sap up his veins. He'd been scared to tell Theo about the kiss, so hadn't. Summer ended.

They'd gone back to school. For a while, the taste of Pimm's made him think of that kiss, not with longing or desire but like a man looking at a tree in his garden and thinking, Ah, yes, that is my tree. Finally, he'd moved to America where they didn't drink Pimm's, and without the fruity cordial, he didn't often think of her.

Did she remember the kiss? He looked again at the thin lip, dusted with flour from the ciabatta. She was divorcing a man Oscar had never even met.

'I thought we brought champagne.' Phoebe put on a squeaky childish voice, 'Didn't we, biggest brother?'

'Yes, littlest sister, we did. But I think you've had enough of the grape already.'

Siblings were weird creatures, not quite friends, not quite anything else. There was a savage, cultic whiff about their relations that Oscar didn't understand. He was thankful that Mina was another only child.

Phoebe found the champagne and walked across the room with it raised above her head, as if it were a prize. They drank it out of the wine glasses. Oscar and Mina wouldn't be in England long enough to need champagne flutes. The empty plates lay, tomato seeds congealing on the china.

'Happy to be back?' Theo asked.

'Of course, why wouldn't I be?' Oscar said. Was Theo worried about him? It was hard to tell. They were old friends, but not the kind who gushed about feelings.

Phoebe's hand reached around him to take his plate. He grabbed the edge. 'Don't do that,' he said. 'You're the guest.'

'Exactly. You fed me,' she said. 'Now let go.' She rapped his fingers, which still gripped the plate. It stung and he wondered if she'd intended to be so loud, if this was the person that shy girl had grown up to be. She was bending towards him. The thin dress hammocked downwards. No bra then, only shadow and skin. He let go of the plate.

'I win!' Phoebe said. 'I win.' She curtsied to the audience. His fork tinked as she dropped it onto the china. Mina asked if anyone wanted coffee or chamomile tea.

What did they think of his wife? It was hard to tell. Theo had met her a couple of times, when Oscar had come back to visit his mother, but the two were essentially strangers. It was hard for Oscar to see Mina as someone distinct from his memories of her. When Theo looked at Mina he saw no bridges, no pills, no body sleeping into the afternoon. He'd never been sleepless, trying to figure out what the hell had gone wrong. He'd never felt her neck droop as she fell asleep on his shoulder. He'd never sat in a parking lot holding her and watching the Perseid meteors melt across the sky. Or witnessed a smile break from tears. Mina was a person like any other to Theo.

Somehow, the conversation wiggled back to the wedding.

Theo leaned back. The top two buttons of his shirt were undone and the hair tufted out. 'So your dad gave the best-man speech?'

Oscar nodded. The speech had been short. Something about pride. Something about happiness. Something about luck. After Theo's last-minute cancellation, Oscar could've asked a friend from college, but that would have rubbed in that they were second choice, so he'd gone with the man who knew his bastard son in a largely professional capacity. As a boy, Oscar had never really missed his father. Once he was at school, he didn't miss his mother either. He loved her, worried about her alone in that cottage, but didn't miss her. He'd always had a sense of himself as being on a solo journey. A ball lobbed against a clear sky does not miss the hand that threw it.

Mina was the first person he could imagine missing so he'd married her. He hadn't understood then that you could marry someone, live with her and miss her anyway.

Theo said, 'I'd started writing my speech, and now it'll never be heard. Well, not unless this lovely lady tires of you and you have to find wife number two.'

'Oscar's rarely boring,' Mina said. She smiled in that way where her eyes arched in happiness.

'Or you could give it a go now,' Phoebe said.

Theo rubbed his chin theatrically. 'Let me see. The speech opened with the first time I saw Oscar kiss a girl.'

'No one wants to hear that,' Oscar said.

'I do!' Mina waved a hand in the air.

'I'm sure I've told you already,' Oscar said.

Theo coughed. 'It was one of those school socials. They filled the gym with disco lights and S Club 7 hits. We were thirteen and the only thing to drink was Tesco cola in plastic cups. Though someone snuck in a couple of those aeroplane bottles of vodka stolen from his dad. The school was all boys. The girls got bussed in. There were these strips of paper. You wrote your email on them and tried to give them to as many girls as possible. This was before any of us had mobiles.'

Phoebe banged a palm on the table. 'The kiss, get to the kiss!'

'Okay, so the real challenge was to see if you could pull a girl.'

'Pull?' Mina asked.

'Snog. French kiss. Make out. It was what we were calling it that year. The trick was to get a girl to slow-dance, move your face close to hers and go for it. Oscar was doing so well with this girl in a green tube top. She had the beginnings of boobs, which, believe me, was a precious quality at the time.'

Oscar interrupted. 'You remember this too well. It's disturbing.'

'Hey, I was thirteen. My best mate was about to pull. All of you stop interrupting. So Oscar, he gets right up close. All her friends are barely dancing, they're watching and flicking

39

their hair. Our lot were wondering if any of her mates would be up for it and tallying how much time was left before the girls were packed back into their bus. And my mate here. He freezes. Just stops.'

Oscar remembered the way the lights flashed on the faces in the onlooking circle. Inside his stomach, the school dinner had pulsed along with the music. His lips found the girl's mouth. It was unexpectedly sticky. Gloss? Cola? He'd pressed his tongue onwards until it hit a wall of teeth. The tongue stopped there, pressed against the enamel ridges. The week before, he'd smoked his first cigarette and he'd almost put it in the wrong way round, filter tip out. Theo had mocked him for that. The girl was worse. The cigarette had had no idea what was happening. The girl had her hard teeth and her closed eyes. Green powder was pasted over the lids. He hadn't known where to go. Should he fight his way past the incisors? Paint them with his tongue? He'd stopped. Beyond the round slope of the girl's cheek, he'd seen Theo's face watching him fail. He'd fled, hiding in the gym toilet until the night was over.

To Theo he said, 'On second thought, I think I should have written that client a thank-you note for keeping you away from the wedding.' Oscar tried to make his laugh sound as genuine as Mina's. She jangled with amusement.

'Oh, that's adorable,' Phoebe said.

'Don't worry, he more than made up for the errors of his youth, once we got to sixth form.' Theo laughed and glanced at his watch. 'Oscar had youthful indiscretions aplenty but, sadly, I must love you and leave you as I have an early start tomorrow.' He drained his coffee cup.

Mina was surprised it was time for their guests to go. She glanced out of the window. All the lights in the Travelodge had blinked themselves to sleep. Oscar let out a thick yawn.

Theo kissed her on both cheeks. The slight stubble was

40

rough. This was Europe, Mina thought. They kissed here.

Phoebe squeezed Mina in a hug. Without letting go, she said, 'We'll see each other again soon. Yeah?' The breath was warm against Mina's cheek, more kiss-like than whatever Theo had dabbed against her face. Mina smelled champagne and the last breath of perfume.

Mina couldn't think where they'd see each other again. Then she realised it was an invitation. She nodded. 'Yes. Yes. I'd like that.'

Mina's eyelids opened slowly. The lashes stuck together. She rubbed her face, pushing away flecks of sleep dust. The crescents under her eyes were wet. Her nose felt blocked. Her head hurt. She'd been crying in her sleep again. What was there to cry about? The nightmare hovered beyond reach.

From another room came Oscar's grunts. 'Twenty, twenty-one, twenty-two . . .'

He must already be back from his run. Oscar ran almost every morning. When he was worried about over-straining his knees, he'd take his skipping rope into the park. Sometimes, she used to go with him to watch. He did repetition after repetition as the rope spun over his head. Sitting on a bench, she'd sing him old playground songs.

'Fortune teller please tell me
what my husband's name will be:
A?
B?
C?
D?'

He'd ignore her, the rope whipping overhead, but always he'd let it drop on O. And she'd laugh. Then he'd start up again.

But lately, she was too tired to get up with him. She didn't want to start the day earlier than she had to. And he'd stopped offering to take her, letting her hide inside sleep.

Sunlight spread-eagled across Oscar's empty side of the bed. She touched the imprint of his head. A black hair curled

42

there. She picked up this vestige of her husband. The Victorians kept the hair of the dead. Should she have lopped off a chunk of her bleached mess for Oscar? A considerate suicide might argan-oil it first. He wouldn't find that funny, would he? Who would? Anyway, dust was partly human skin and they'd lived together since the summer after college. He'd inhaled years of Mina. Tiny particles of her swirled in his lungs.

'Three, four, five . . .'

Oscar must've started a new exercise. How long had she been lying there? In the bathroom, Mina splashed water on her face. She shoved the toothbrush over her teeth, put in her contacts, and paused. Her pillbox wasn't there. Of course not. No more pills. The habit of more than a decade ghosted her limbs.

Mina swirled peppermint mouthwash and spat. Walking to the kitchen, she found her husband dangling in the doorway. Oscar hung from a pull-up bar. His body compressed into a ball, then stretched into a line. Dot, dash, dot, dash, dot, dash, dot. What did that say in Morse code? Sweat glossed the back of his neck.

'Have you eaten?' she asked.

He dropped to the floor. 'Mmm . . . Not yet.'

The sink was full of last night's dishes.

Mina heated the electric kettle and sliced a yellow moon of lemon. 'You never told me his sister was so pretty,' she said, dropping the lemon into the bottom of the mug. She sprinkled on a constellation of sugar and poured over the steaming water.

Oscar's expression was odd. 'Phoebe's fine,' he said. 'She's not my type. Bit desperate.'

She's more than fine, Mina thought. More than pretty too. The lemon had risen to the top of the mug. Mina sipped, and the wedge bobbed against her teeth. There was no reason for Oscar to understate Phoebe's beauty. He knew that Mina found women as attractive as he did. Sometimes when they sat on the subway, they'd catch each other eyeing the same girl and laugh. Looking was not touching, they both knew that. Oscar had never been jealous and neither had Mina. But then again, since the wedding she hadn't been in a girl-watching mood.

'I guess I remember her when she was a kid.' He took a tub of yogurt from the fridge to mix with his protein powder.

'Do you think Phoebe meant it?' she asked. It had been so long since she'd made a new friend. These days, the girls from her PhD years were busy with assistant professorships or books or babies.

'Meant what?' Oscar asked.

'The see-you-soon?'

'I don't see why not.'

Oscar pushed aside the breakfast things and opened his laptop to his to-do list program. It was already past nine o'clock. He couldn't allow the new flat and time zone to trick him into thinking it was a holiday. Exercise was set to a daily repeat. He clicked the task to indicate completion and the font flicked from red to green. Quickly he typed:

Estate agents—value flats
Japanese
Fill orders
Email Dad update
Mina
Mum

The first should be easy. In this city, estate agents seemed to be as common as Starbucks.

'Mina? Are you ready?' he called, to the next room. He

didn't want to leave her alone with the four storey-drop more than he had to. A wife was not a dog. You couldn't lock her inside, even if that would make you feel like she was safer.

'Almost.'

'Can you wear a long-sleeved top?' Tattoos were common, these days, but why give more information about their lives than was necessary?

Oscar flipped his phone to the Japanese-language app. Big-eyed animals pranced across the screen carrying kanji. If you read the word correctly, carrots dropped from the sky to feed the animals. If you got it wrong, they cried. He got a score of ninety-five per cent. He'd confused 嘘, a lie, with 盗む, to steal. The animated rabbit didn't care that he'd been almost right. It wept baby blue tears. Ninety-five per cent wasn't bad but wasn't good enough. He would practise. Practise every day – that was the trick.

After a white chef in Williamsburg started reeling off Nihongo, like it was a test of Oscar's pale eyes, Oscar had signed up to take the JLPT—the Japanese Language Placement Test. It was in December. He aimed to pass level N3. The ability to understand Japanese in everyday situations. He liked the idea of having a certificate.

Mina appeared wearing a green shirt buttoned at the cuffs. Her unmarked hands flowered innocently out. He smiled at his wife, grateful that she'd understood what he needed.

He said, 'I want a sense of what we might get for the flats and how much work is worth doing.'

'You really want me tagging along?' she asked.

'I can't want to spend time with my wife?' he asked. 'Come on, it's not like you have anything better to do.'

Something unhappy moved across Mina's face.

'I didn't mean it like that,' he said.

'You're right. It's not like I've been so productive lately.'

'I love you. Come with me, please. It'd make me happy.'

Mina was silent in the lift down. She pushed a hand through that frizzy hair. He hadn't wanted her to dye it but he hadn't wanted to be the sort of man who tells his wife what to do with her hair. They both stared at the aperture in the door and watched the floors slowly passing by.

When they reached the door of the estate agency, he said, 'Wait a sec.'

In the window there were glossy photographs of flats with street names in big letters, then details written much smaller. 'Lh' for leasehold. 'Fh' for freehold. For just under a decade, he had worked for his father. He'd made calls. He'd negotiated deals. But he didn't think this much had moved between his fingers.

In the property photographs, the floors were polished wood or carpeted in cream. Gilt-framed mirrors hung above the mantelpieces. There were no creepy birds on the walls.

'That's nice,' Mina said, pointing to a garden shot.

'There must be something wrong with the house, if all they're showing is the roses.'

Inside, a glass-doored fridge was lined with Perrier bottles. A woman approached in a suit the pale grey of a MacBook Pro. Her shoes made sharp clicks on the marble floor. This place must have huge overheads. Then again, cash-rich buyers wouldn't go to a shabby agency.

The woman introduced herself. She was smiling widely. They must look like easy targets—a well-dressed young couple about to buy a first home. She shook his hand too tightly, making rigid eye contact. It seemed a trick learnt in a YouTube video about likeability. Oscar had watched those too. He smiled right back into the tiny voids of her eyes.

In the second estate agency Mina watched her husband. Already, he seemed fast and fluent. He used phrases like 'no onward chain' and 'looking for a cash buyer' and 'competitive

46

commission'. When had he had time to gather up those words? He was handsome in the freshly pressed suit.

Oscar clearly had no need of her help. Mina folded her hands in her lap. The lights of the office glowered down. At every desk, agents were emailing, calling, making deals. She stared into a vase of oval peace lilies. The soil was covered with white pebbles, like those after-dinner mints they give away in Chinese restaurants.

'I'm here on behalf of an individual who is looking into selling some property in this area.' Oscar stood straight-backed. An individual? Mina smiled. It made Oscar's father sound like a Mafia boss. The first time she'd met the man, he'd been wearing salmon-pink golf shorts and playing with the latest iPhone. He'd reminded her of an older version of the Asian-American guys she'd known in college, who'd gone into Big Data, banks, or start-ups. The guys with the coolest watches, who knew the best bars but who, despite it all, carried a slight air of nervousness, as if their parents might be listening in to their bullshit.

As they left, Mina said, 'I think I need a coffee. You do this next one by yourself. I mean, it's not like you need me.'

'Will you be okay?'

'It's coffee, not intergalactic flight.' Her husband seemed fine leaving her alone, as long as she had some task: buy flowers, pick up the dry-cleaning, go to the supermarket. He seemed to think she'd hurt herself simply because she didn't have enough to do.

A mess of kids scrambled past her knees. They were arguing about something that had once belonged to the larger boy and had been stolen by the shortest girl. 'We're blocking the way,' Mina added.

'Fine. Maybe you can work on the list.'

'Yeah,' she said. 'The list.' She knew he was worried, but she'd tried to die, not become a child in need of worksheets.

The coffee shop glinted with white hexagonal tiles and varnished wood. She ordered and found a table near the door. It was the last free space. Laptops gaped from every table. In front of her, two young men with beards the size of small dogs bowed over the same screen. They kept jabbing at the display. This was less a coffee place than a fancy open-plan office. A waitress appeared with the coffee in a blue enamel cup. Mina blew across the foam. Enamel cups could go on the list.

The list was supposed to be all the things that made her happy, as if happiness were a matter of filling a checklist. But she would write it for Oscar. She wanted to promise him that she would be happy again and be a person capable of making him happy.

HAPPY, she wrote in the notebook. The capital letters looked hysterical, like the work of a mad woman. In smaller script below she wrote, *enamel cups*. She glanced around the café. Hexagonal tiles, she thought. Did hexagonal tiles make her happy? Would they make her happy in all scales, or only when they were as big as her palm?

Did coffee make her happy? It did and it didn't. This coffee was nice enough. But it brought with it all the other cups she'd ever drunk and all the Minas she'd been when she was drinking them. Blanked-out, head-fogged, Mina drank dough-nut-cart coffee on her way to Alfie's and it felt like nothing would ever have enough caffeine.

She tried to think of happier coffees. She'd sipped from a thermos sitting on the library steps after a great day's research. She'd had her own carrel. She'd enjoyed teaching Introductory Latin. It was sad to watch the students tire of the subjunctive and slip away into Econ or Poly-Sci. But a few would stay, their brains adapting to the lap and flow of the language. Though they never wrote to her after the class was over, she was content to have added them to the scholarly stream. She was a ripple in a river that stretched back more than two thousand years. She was so sure she'd found her place in the world. The May that she sat for her thesis defence, cherry blossoms were bursting out all over the campus. She'd written her dissertation about shadows in Ovid and Virgil. The topic was obscure, but she'd enjoyed the obscurity. And the word itself: *umbra*. Long and low, like a hum.

She'd had a side project too, one her adviser had encouraged her to turn into a monograph or at least a series of articles: *The Women Who Survived*. Few women survived the Greco-Roman myths and legends. The stories were thick with death. Leucothoë was buried alive by her father as punishment for fucking the sun. Eurydice was killed twice, first by a snake and second by her husband's hungry look. Clytemnestra was murdered by her own children. If not killed, a woman might be transformed. Daphne's long and lovely arms split into the leaves of the laurel tree when she fled Apollo. Poor Clytie shrank to a violet for love of the same god. Scylla slipped into poisoned water and found her legs, hips and tenderest parts turned into writhing, rabid dogs.

The women who made it out, alive and intact, seemed worth noting—Penelope, Iphigenia in Aulis, Psyche, Leda. The project had started as a list she kept in a Word doc for her own amusement. Then she thought it might be a book, though feminist theory was out of vogue. But if she could swing a book with a good academic press, it might get her a tenure-track job. But who was she to write about survival? And, in any case, she hadn't yet found the pattern. What kept these women going?

Her hands picked up her phone. There were Facebook messages from New York friends, asking if she was having fun in London. It was clear they expected the answer to be yes. She thought of Phoebe holding the champagne in the air.

The weight had etched a line of muscle into her arm. In the red of her hair, threads of gold matched the top of the champagne foil. Over the course of the meal, Mina had forgotten to feel tired or nervous: it was as if her selfhood had slipped away and she was only an audience to watch Phoebe's smile. Would Phoebe survive if this were a myth? Mina considered it. No, probably not. Some god would see her, snatch her up and wreck her with his desire. Or a jealous goddess would curse her for the hair bright as the sun's rays.

It came to her that she'd been wrong about Phoebe's name. The name Phoebe didn't come from the sun god at all. Phoebus Apollo was the grandson of the female Titan Phoebe. For once it was the woman's not the man's name that had come first. Phoebe was a moon goddess. Mina thought of the freckled moon and of Phoebe's smooth cheeks.

Mina typed *Phoebe* into the Search bar before realising she had no idea what Phoebe's last name was. Then again, she should be in Oscar's Friends. Yes. In the profile picture Phoebe hugged a huge dog. Her arms were swallowed by the fur. It was hard to tell from the perspective, but Mina thought the dog must be the size of a fairground prize, those big stuffed animals that hung from the ceiling and were essentially unwinnable. Its fur was the colour of the cardamom rolls displayed on the café counter. Mina reconsidered the bearded men bent over their laptop. Phoebe's dog had enough fur to clad a whole start-up's worth of chins.

A dog seemed important. Phoebe had never mentioned it. Mina realised that she couldn't exactly reconstruct Phoebe's face. There in the picture were the hair and the big eyes. But the dog covered her chin. What was the chin like? Pointed, Mina thought. It couldn't have been pointed like a bird's beak. There must've been some softness. How soft? At what angle? It was like Mina had been staring at a light-bulb and now its shadow hovered in the centre of her vision. It wasn't just that

50

she was beautiful, Mina decided. It was her energy. Phoebe thrummed, while everything about Mina felt slow and water-logged.

Mina sipped coffee while looking into the dog's round eyes. When the cup was finished, Mina clicked *Add Friend*. It might've been the caffeine but she felt like there was too much blood in her head.

Oscar visited five agencies, all of which promised to get him the best possible price for the flats. By the time they returned to the apartment, it was his father's morning. Oscar rang. 'Dad, it's me,' he said.

He described each agency, their 1.5 per cent fees, and their similar showrooms. He wondered if the only real difference was the font of the signs. 'A few suggested we stagger the sales, given we're selling two properties in the same building. And I think it makes sense, especially because of the state 5B's in. You were right. It's much worse than 4B. Tenants wrecked the place. One of the kitchen cupboard's come off its hinges. There's a weird stain on the bathroom wall. And I think they took the mattress.'

'To be expected, I suppose.' His father sighed.

'I thought I'd start pricing the work.'

'Go ahead,' his father said.

Then father and son flopped into a gully of silence. After business was concluded, there was never much left. Oscar didn't know what father-son chats sounded like. Briefly, he considered telling his father about Mina. What should I do about my wife? How do you keep a person safe from them-selves? But he tried to sound like a professional when talking to his father. And so far Mina seemed to be doing okay. At dinner, she had acted like her real self. The slump had lifted from her shoulders. Anyway, his father wasn't exactly an expert in the art of marriage. Only a few years after marrying

Ami in a Los Angeles courthouse, he'd knocked up a passing English girl—hence Oscar's existence.

'And how's Ami?' Oscar asked.

'Ami's well. She likes the new house.'

Oh, yes, they'd moved. It was hard to remember when he barely saw the man in person.

'How is Mina?' his father asked.

'Mina is fine.'

Oscar had always known she was ill. She'd told him when they met—at a party on the art school's campus. The art-school kids with their dip-dyed hair and too-loud voices were playing a song he didn't recognise. Muzzy charcoal sketches of breasts, asses and dicks were stuck to the wall. There was this girl leaning against the fridge with her eyes shut, and the smallest smile on her lips. He must've been wearing the wrong thing because the first thing she asked when he tapped her on the shoulder was, 'You don't go here, do you?' Oscar didn't learn until much later that neither did she. She was not learning to weld or carve but was kept awake by conjugations of irregular verbs.

On their first date, she told him that she was bisexual, vegetarian and on meds. The facts spat out in quick succession were almost a challenge to be met. In the years that followed, she had low days, when she cancelled their plans and they stayed in to watch old movies, and nights when she woke him up and wanted to be held. But that had been manageable. He'd never guessed she might try to kill herself. It was like finding out the dog you thought was a husky had remembered it was a wolf.

Mina lay on the couch watching pigeons land and take off from the windowsill. Her whole life she'd been busy. She'd been busy with SAT prep, with AP prep, with college, with the PhD dissertation, with the job hunt, with tutoring spoilt high-schoolers, with networking, with writing articles, with her first adjunct teaching position, with getting married, with trying not to let her Greek slip, with putting together a pitch for the book, with trying always to think of the next thing. Even lying in bed, when her brain sank into viscous darkness, she'd known all the things she wasn't doing. But at least she'd known how to begin those things. How do you begin being better?

She balanced the notebook on her stomach, watching it rise up and down with her breath. Her pencil was blunt. She needed to sharpen it. Oscar was sitting at the table with his back to her. The silky tag of his shirt stuck up. Mina put the notebook down and walked to her husband. As she approached he held up a hand, like an air-traffic controller stopping a plane. She didn't take offence. Oscar was bad at being interrupted mid-thought.

Mina took a knife from the kitchen. She edged the steel into the pencil. Pressing into the resistance and feeling it give way was pleasurable. When the knife reached graphite, it danced forward. This was always how she sharpened her pencils. She liked the uneven look it gave them. She did this before editing her work. She always edited off-screen. It felt good to put a physical action to all those abstractions. When asking what Virgil meant to symbolise by *umbra*, it was nice to see the shadow of her pencil angle across the page.

She opened the notebook. The list she'd written had only two items, enamel coffee cups and hexagonal tiles. A list had to have more than two items. Underneath she added: *sharpening pencils*. What else made her happy? She looked down at her feet. Those she felt indifferent about. The socks were fine. Could black jeans go on the list? Denim curved into scallops at her knees. She had five pairs. Black jeans were easy, but they'd fade from black to old-newspaper grey. No garment could offer what she wanted. She didn't want a dress:

she wanted a battleship's hull. She didn't want a shirt: she wanted the UV insulated tiles of a space shuttle. She wanted something that protected. Black jeans were merely second best.

The bigger problem was that she had a second list: the reasons that her presence on the planet wasn't doing any good. It was posted on her neural pathways, like a highway billboard that every thought had to drive past. She wasn't sure when the sign had been erected. Maybe it had always been there but the pills had stopped her looking up. Until they hadn't.

Can't cope with jeans belonged on that list. *Has an interesting job, nice husband, good life, but can't seem to enjoy them* belonged on that list. *Fucking ungrateful* belonged on that list. It was a trap: being unhappy because you were unhappy. Hating yourself because you're the sort of weak idiot who hates themselves. Mina looked over again at her husband, who was diligently making his own list on the white screen. She pinched her arm, digging her nails into the skin. Snap out of it, she thought.

She put down the list and reached into her satchel for the diary. She lined it up on the table next to the notebook. The diary had a green leather cover. Attractive stationery was weak ammunition against the world, but it was what she had. The day she'd bought the diary, she'd pencilled a tentative uptick. A little stab at hope. There was another for the dinner party and another for moving in. Such hopeful mountain peaks. It seemed a shame to ruin them. A shame to add the bite of ∨. So she didn't. She made a little ∧, not because she felt okay but because she thought it was too depressing not to.

In her back pocket, the phone hummed. Facebook announced that Phoebe had accepted her request and was officially her Friend.

Cute dog, Mina typed. A nice neutral start. Everyone she

knew in New York who had a pet or a child loved to talk about it.

His name's Benson.

Cute name. Surely she had a better word than 'cute'. Would an emoji worsen this idiocy?

It's after Benson & Hedges.

Mina had no idea what that was. A law firm? A comedy duo? She googled. At the top of the screen appeared a golden cigarette box plastered with the usual warning about how cigarettes will kill you. It always seemed like such an expensive way to die.

The cigarettes? she typed.

He was my gift to myself after I gave them up.

What is he? That sounded rude. Mina added, *What breed I mean?*

His mother was a Pomeranian. His father was a mystery.

But he's huge.

Note the mystery.

I'd love to meet him sometime. The *Delivered* sign appeared, and then there was silence.

Mina tiptoed towards her husband. She tucked in the label. The heat of his neck warmed her knuckles.

He turned and kissed her hand. 'Got your phone on you?' Oscar asked.

'Why?'

'I need to download an app.'

'Can't you do it on yours?' There were no secrets on her phone. But the device was hers and it felt oddly private.

'It needs to be on both our phones.'

He turned his computer around to show her the website of a family tracking app. Apparently it would notify him when she arrived home, when she went out, where she was in the world. There were pictures of happy men, women and children delighting in their constant surveillance.

'That's creepy,' she said. 'I'm not doing that.'

'Mina.'

'What? I'm not a wayward teenager.'

'I'm trying to take care of you. I need to know where you are.'

'You don't need to know. It's not going to kill you. You won't evaporate if you don't know that I'm buying groceries or whatever.'

'Mina,' he said, too calmly, and she regretted using the word 'kill', because she could see all the retorts bobbing in his throat. 'I need to know you're safe.'

She knew she should be grateful. Many men would have left. Many women, too. Most sane people wouldn't want anything to do with someone like her.

'Fine,' she said.

'Thank you.'

Oscar watched as Mina turned off the lights and crawled into bed next to him. He pulled his arm around his wife. Her head tucked just right under his collar bone. Her body warmed his.

'I'm sorry,' she whispered.

'For what?' Oscar asked. He could feel his muscles go taut. 'What's wrong?'

'For all this.' She banged on her skull with a loose fist.

Nothing new. Okay, then. They could sleep. He felt like he hadn't had a full night's sleep all month. 'Don't worry about it,' he said. 'Go to sleep.'

But she didn't. He could feel it through the dark. Eventually she said, 'Tell me about when we were perfect.' Her face pressed against Oscar's breastbone, as if she were trying to nuzzle inside. His hand rested on the small of her back, which was warm from the shower.

'We're not perfect now?' It seemed like the response he should give.

'You know what I mean. Before all this.'

'We were perfect when,' he began. And he told her of the afternoon after the results of a big Greek test. She was always better at Latin than Greek. He'd wanted to celebrate her A grade. But she'd had a shift at the ice-cream parlour. The one where the servers had to sing to you if you gave them a tip. So instead he met her after work. She made him a waffle cone of mint choc chip, and he hadn't said anything about refined sugars, although by then he was already on a high-protein regime. As she passed it to him, she sang in her flat, husky voice. He'd forgotten the lyrics but he still remembered that she closed her eyes as she sang. The ice cream tasted of the winter just gone. When they kissed, so did her lips. And he'd hoped they'd be kissing next winter.

'Mmm . . . Tell me another.' Mina ran her fingers along his jawline, her breath soft and even. One thigh was tucked around his.

'Do you remember the first of my birthdays we had together?' he asked. She nodded, her lashes beating against his chest. They'd been dating a few months. He hadn't even mentioned his birthday. But she'd found out somehow. 'And the cupcake?'

'It was just a cupcake,' Mina said.

'With twenty-one candles.' It was more flame than flour. She'd knocked on his dorm-room door, and when he'd opened it, there she was lit from below by the blaze.

'Did I ever tell you there were supposed to be twenty-one cupcakes?' she asked.

Oscar blinked. 'No?'

'Yeah, I baked twenty-one cupcakes and there was supposed to be a candle in each. But I must have timed it wrong because they all burnt. Our kitchen smelt charred for days. I borrowed, stole, an egg, and I had just enough flour and sugar for one last cupcake.'

'You never told me that.'

'I guess I was embarrassed,' she said. 'Another.'

'Mina, we need to sleep. All the articles say it's not good to mess with your sleep cycle.'

'Please, Oscar.'

'Okay, one more.' He described the parties they'd thrown after moving into their first New York apartment. Mina had just begun her PhD and he'd just started work. He'd ordered crates of Japanese craft beer and taken notes in the name of research. Everyone told them they looked perfect together. His accent was just so cute.

He'd watch Mina talking on the other side of the room, surrounded by yet more friends. There was always the hum of music in the background and too many people talking for him to catch her words. But he'd see everyone around her fall into laughter. There were tea-lights on every surface. They'd felt immune to fire in those first years. By the end of the night, he'd have Mina back, folded in his arms.

'Another,' she said.

'Mina, I can't.' His shoulders and head hurt. His lids were falling. He willed himself to summon up the past. His brain flicked to the narrow dorm-room bed they'd shared, so narrow that her hair had got into his mouth and her tailbone nuzzled his dick as she slept. But sleep tipped him forward into darkness and dream, and he didn't tell another story.

The bathroom was only an arm-span wide and dominated by the large tub. Mina pulled back the plastic curtain and turned on the shower. She slipped the razor along her legs. Fish day, she thought. That was what they called them in their secret couple-script. Fish days and bear days. On fish days, she shaved legs, armpits, and plucked her eyebrows. On fish days, she was slippery, soft, almost but not quite liquid. Bear days were the days in which black fur rose from her skin. Those were the days when the scraping away of follicles was too much. They made a joke of it, Mina curling her hands into paws, flicking the nails like claws. Oscar said he loved her either way. He said he wanted her either way too. But she knew he preferred fish days. If she couldn't give him a clean and tidy brain then at least she could offer him this: a body and skin that provided no resistance.

She got out of the shower and towelled down. Oscar was out of the house, running. In the bedroom, she pulled up the app. There he was, his little body going around and around the city. She had the odd notion that if she found the right button she might be able to drag him across the tiny buildings. His dot was almost back at the flat.

This was a good city. It was good of Oscar to have brought her here. They said that to be loved you had to love yourself. Bullshit. How were you supposed to love yourself if no one else could see anything of value beneath your skin? No, she thought, it was the other way around. To love yourself you had to be loved. She was lucky to have Oscar. She was lucky to have a man who looked at her like she was a precious creature.

She decided to fill him a bath. The bathroom was still steamy from her shower. She turned on the taps. There was a pause, a *hurk*, and a gurgle. Mina fumbled in the bag of toiletries she'd brought from New York, until she found the sachet of bubble bath. The sample was the size of a condom packet. In New York, they only had a shower with an earnestly bent neck. But the package's elegant *cardamom* and *rose* had been too seductive to toss. Finally, it would have its use. She squeezed and slime glooped out, turning the water milky. As a last thought, she turned off the hot water leaving the cold to run. Oscar's skin was delicate and sensitive to heat. The tall, serious man was endearingly wimpy about hot coffee and showers. She dipped her fingers into the water, a breath too cold for her and perfect for him.

He arrived, red-faced and panting.

'I ran you a bath,' she said.

He put a hand on the wall to steady himself and held up a finger, smiling through the gasping.

'I thought it would be nice for your muscles,' she added.

He thumbed her chin with his hot hand. 'Thank you.' She watched him ease into the water, one foot and then the other.

'Hey, keep me company?' He beckoned.

'There's no room,' she said. But she dropped her towel.

She manoeuvred so that he had one end and she took the other. She propped her ankles against his shoulders. The curls of his hair stuck close to his head. Looking at the long-muscled frame of her husband on the bath's white plinth, she thought of a Roman statue. Or would Greek be more accurate? The Greeks had carved their statues all the way around. The

Romans carved only the visible parts. If the back of a statue faced the wall, they left it rough. She knew she was supposed to admire the pragmatism. But it disturbed her. The larger empire was built by people who cared only about how things looked, not how they were.

'What's wrong?' Oscar asked.

'I'm fine,' she said, and batted his cheek with the side of her foot.

'Hey!' he said, and grabbed her heel, laughing. 'Fish day, huh?' He ran a hand along the inside of her leg.

'Yup,' she replied, and the pleasure of his noticing bubbled in her chest.

For a while they lay, softening and wrinkling. Heat misted the mirror. She had the premonition that she would remember this tableau, these two recently married people sharing a bath, and the thought scared her. It seemed ominous. She didn't want this to be a scene she looked at in retrospect as she stood alone in front of some future sink, wondering where the years had gone and why she'd let everything drift away in a cloud of steam and self-pity. Her eyes felt hot. She didn't want to cry. This was supposed to be a happy time.

'Mina, what's wrong?'

'Nothing,' she said, hating herself for snapping. She jumped out, kneeing him in the chest in her hurry.

'Ouch,' he said.

'Sorry. I'm going to be late for my appointment.' As she made the excuse she realised it was true. She grabbed the first clothes that came to hand, black jeans, blue t-shirt, and a hoodie. The bra was old, the cups awkwardly warped but the gynaecologist had probably seen worse.

Since coming off the pill, her period had vanished. She had no nostalgia for the eight-day ordeal. But Oscar had asked her to get checked out to make sure it was nothing serious.

Their insurance would cover it. It had seemed easier to make the appointment than to object.

The gynaecologist looked like Anna Wintour. It was the perfectly bobbed hair and the long tendons that supported her thin neck. What would the editor-in-chief of *Vogue* make of having a gynaecologist doppelgänger? Diplomas hung on the wall. Their golden seals beamed like tiny suns. Mina had once been to an astrologer and that woman had had framed diplomas too. The gynaecologist wanted to know if Mina was trying to have a child. No. No. Her hand went to the small swell of her stomach. Her ovaries were squished in there. She didn't know exactly where. The cotton of her shirt was soft, and she left the hand there—holding herself.

'So why did you decide to come off the pill?' The gynaecologist looked at her the way Mina suspected Anna Wintour looked at a model who'd put on a few pounds. This woman was not a therapist, psychologist, psychoanalyst, psychiatrist, spiritual-healer or mindfulness coach. This woman's job was ovaries, wombs and fallopian tubes.

'I just thought it would be good to take a break from medication,' Mina said.

The gynaecologist's plucked eyebrows pulled together.

Mina added, 'Not for religious reasons or anything. But I've been on the pill since I was fifteen. Heavy irregular periods.' Her gift from puberty was a rope of pain that knotted itself above her pubic bone, mood fluctuations and the sort of PMS that misogynists think all women get.

'And you're not a virgin?'

'I'm thirty-two. I'm married.'

The gynaecologist made a note. 'I have to ask these questions. How many times a week would you say you have sex?'

'It depends. I mean, there isn't a pattern.' Some weeks, Oscar looked at her more like a doctor than a lover. He looked at her as if he was trying to find what was wrong, and then Mina curled up inside, like a weevil. Other nights, their bodies collided in sorrow-hunger that was all teeth and tongue.

'I see. And do you use protection?'

'Yes. Condoms, after I went off the pill.'

'Very good, and since you quit have you noticed any changes to your body?'

The gynaecologist asked about body hair, unexpected weight gain, and surprising pains.

I wish I was dead, Mina thought. Blue sky tipped in through the big window. She was in a tasteful office. She'd eaten enough for breakfast. But there her brain went again, I wish I was dead. Mina felt like the background music should change. The lighting should change. The blue sky stayed blue. The gynaecologist still looked like the editor-in-chief of *Vogue*. Mina felt queasy. The world was full of good and funny things and her brain did this. She smiled at the gynaecologist, a big smile with lots of teeth. The woman looked alarmed.

Mina stood on the medical scales with the rubber ribs of the mat digging into her feet. The machine's metal tongue pressed the top of her head. I want to die, thought the brain. Which was silly because she was dying all the time. In a few years her brain's myelin would begin to decay. What was the hurry? Why upset Oscar? Why make everyone angry and tired? Take the fact that she'd ruined her wedding. She couldn't even remember why.

Her friend Alex, who'd majored in film, had videoed the ceremony. They'd got married upstate in the woods. The video began with the pine needles shimmying in the breeze. Her wedding dress sprouted like a button-mushroom among the moss. A tinkling piano soundtrack overlaid the scene. Unfilmed was the girl who'd go back to their cabin and swallow all the pills left over from her wisdom-tooth extraction, garden-variety painkillers, and sleeping pills. She must've gone to her washbag and rooted past lip balm and toothpaste, until she found the orange tube with the long name, a box of Tylenol, and a packet of those green sleeping pills. Had she taken them one by one? Tipped them all into her palm? She couldn't remember what had made her swallow. Was it her brain saying again and again, I want to die? Or was it more specific? Mina had no idea. The number of pills and the feel of them on her tongue had vanished.

Part of her had died or got lost in the attempt. Some cluster of cells. Brain damage, she supposed, of the most minor sort. There were different types of memory loss. Her grandma began to forget words because her nerve cells were decaying. When the words failed, she'd put her hand on her mouth as if reaching to catch them. On the other hand, a black-out from drinking usually meant your brain had never made memories at all. Had the electric score of Mina's wedding night ever been written inside her skull?

Big deal. She'd forgotten the events of so many days. She'd forget all this eventually. She might as well smile through it now. She smiled and realised that, yet again, it was inappropriate. The gynaecologist's rubber-gloved hands were examining Mina's interior.

'Sorry, I was away with the fairies,' Mina said. Where had those words come from? She would never put it like that. The gynaecologist nodded. Mina's phone hummed in her bag. She flushed with further embarrassment, as if it were a movie she'd interrupted, not the careful prodding of her own body. The gynaecologist said she'd need more tests. Mina nodded, okay, okay.

Could there be something actually wrong with her? She hadn't wanted to come to this appointment. She didn't miss the Rorschach prints of blood on her underwear. She didn't miss the way her head ached and her body swelled. Tests. What were they testing for?

Anna Wintour was standing up and leading Mina to the door. She was telling Mina that the woman at the desk downstairs would help her make the appointment.

Above the elevator, a panel displayed a lazy scroll of floors. A nurse was waiting. Her scrubs were printed with itty-bitty shapes. Were they supposed to be confetti? Who thought of celebrating in a hospital? Mina checked her phone.

Tea with me and Benson tomorrow? Phoebe's message hung above the home screen. Phoebe. She couldn't say the word without smiling.

Oscar had agreed to meet Theo during his lunch break. Oscar was early. He opened *Nudge*. It was the only book he'd brought with him to England. The battered yellow paperback had enough dog-eared corners that it was easier to find those that had been left pristine. The book's premise was beautifully simple: what if you made it easier for people to do good things than bad? What if, rather than opting into organ donation, everyone was automatically made an organ donor? It would be easier to share your heart and liver and brain than not. People usually did the easiest thing. Those passionately against it could opt out.

How could he nudge his wife into happiness?

He thought of the list she'd made—sharpening pencils, hexagonal tiles, black jeans. He pictured Mina sharpening pencils, wearing black jeans, against a backdrop of hexagonal tiles. Even thought-experiment Mina didn't look happy. Couldn't she have said sunset walks on the beach? Or puppies? This shouldn't be so hard. He knew his wife. What did she like? What made her mouth slope upwards?

Flowers, maybe flowers. He'd been shocked when she first came home inked with peonies. But she'd said she wanted to see something beautiful when she looked at herself. And who was he to disagree? Sometimes when they fucked, she gripped

65

the bedhead and the blossoms seemed to swell. Oscar didn't notice Theo until his old friend was looking down at him. They exchanged the usual greetings.

'I'll have to be fast. I'm needed back in chambers,' Theo said. 'I was thinking we could get a sandwich and eat it outside.'

Theo's rugby-player bulk was there under the suit, but softer now. Oscar thought if it came to a tackle he could force his friend over. Oscar had got in shape.

'How's work?' Oscar asked.

'Trial prep is dragging out. The usual.' Theo rolled his eyes.

The sandwich place was nearby. Theo ordered without looking at the board. Oscar said, 'I'll have the same.'

'We can sit on the lawns in Lincoln's Inn,' Theo said.

They cut into a narrow street. The alley opened onto an ornate brick building. Theo sat on his document case and Oscar dropped to the ground. The grass was rough under his palms.

'Did you see the match?' Oscar asked. Above Theo's head a piece of brickwork broke from the wall and cast itself into the air. It morphed into crooked wings and a hooked beak. Oscar watched it aim for the sky.

'Hawks to catch the pigeons,' Theo explained.

Theo hadn't had a chance to watch the game. So Oscar caught him up on the disputed last minute penalty. 'How's Pheeb?' Oscar asked.

'Driving me crazy. She needs to get her own place. It's been six months since she and Brendan split. When I offered her the sofa, I assumed it'd be temporary. Figured they'd patch things up.'

'Couldn't she go to your parents'?'

'They had to downsize a few years back so it's really their sofa versus mine and mine's in London.'

Oscar had a vague memory that something unfortunate had happened to Theo's family in the financial crisis. By then they'd gone off to their separate universities and Theo wasn't the kind to talk about that stuff. It was so many years ago. They'd both had spots and iPod Minis.

'If you need another sofa to offload her onto, the orange monstrosity in our flat is free,' Oscar offered. 5B was a wreck, but if Phoebe stayed in 4B . . . It would be nice to have someone else around. Someone who could keep an eye on Mina.

'Ah, it's fine. I mean, family is family. You take care of your own.'

'I suppose,' Oscar said.

'How's the missus?' Theo asked.

'Good. Good. We're going to Mum's this weekend.'

As they stood, they crumpled their sandwich wrappers. Theo tossed his towards a bin. He missed, ball tumbling to the side. Oscar underarmed his. As soon as it left his hand, he knew the angle was off, but a gust saved him, and the ball slid in.

'Let's do this again soon.' Theo clapped him on the shoulder.

As Oscar passed Waitrose, a flash of petals caught his eye. He stopped. Right at the entrance, flowers gazed up at him. He scooped up pink roses. Interspersed between them were those flowers that look like bits of popcorn. 'Roses and baby's breath,' said the sticker. That must be some unhealthy baby. He stopped, uncertain. Tonight they'd be taking the train to his mother's. These flowers would sit alone. Flowers today were an impractical choice. The bunch was heavy. But that morning Mina had seemed sad, her attention scattered. It would be good to surprise her with a treat. He decided he would bring his wife flowers.

Oscar could see Mina as he opened the door of the flat.

She was stretched out on the sofa. Her shirt rode up and her pale belly was exposed. Her eyes were shut. A window was open, and the sounds of traffic and shoppers spooled into the flat. He placed the roses by the door, giving the faintest rustle. He walked quietly towards her. His socked feet were silent on the varnished wood.

As he got closer, he saw that her trousers were unzipped. Her hand was slipped underneath her underwear. Pink stripes contoured her fingers as they moved carefully under the cotton. Oscar smiled. 'Honey, I'm home,' he said, in his best American drawl.

Her eyelids flicked open. Her pupils shrank against the light. Her hand darted into the air.

'Don't stop on my account,' he said.

Her hair was flung out into a blonde jellyfish. The roots were growing out seabed-dark. He ran a finger from smooth to rough. She squirmed, laughing. He did it again. Her feet kicked against the soft arm of the sofa. Oscar leaned down and kissed the roots. When they'd met, all her hair had been black, and if he tried to catch a strand it slipped away like water. This dyed fluff tickled his nose.

They fucked like teenagers on study leave or new parents on date night or like any people speaking in the language of tooth-graze and finger-grip.

Afterwards, Mina laid her head on his bare thigh. He stroked the edge of her ear.

'Sex in the middle of the day. I feel so decadent,' she said, dragging out the last word, stretching her legs and arms.

'I'm glad,' he said. 'How was the doctor's visit?'

Mina wrinkled her nose. 'They said I need more tests.'

'I bought you flowers. They're by the door.'

Mina rolled her head to look at the distant pink blob. 'Thanks,' she said. 'That's really sweet.'

'They're roses,' he added, when she didn't move.

Mina sighed. Clearly, roses were an ineffective nudge. Oscar wanted to sigh too. But you didn't get to sigh when you were the healthy one.

'Mina.'

'What?'

'What's wrong?'

'I don't know. Just feeling kind of bleurgh.'

'Why?'

'Look, I don't know.' She stared at the ceiling.

'What can I do?'

'I'm okay. It's not a big deal. I'll get over it.'

'You're really okay?'

'I am! I'm going for tea with Theo's sister tomorrow,' she said.

'Tomorrow's Saturday.'

'So?'

'So, we're going to visit Mum, remember? We're booked onto the sleeper train out of Euston tonight.'

Mina looked at the flowers, her face turned away from him. There was a smudge of dirt on her cheek. He licked his thumb and wiped it away.

She said, 'Wouldn't your mother rather see you alone? One-on-one time, that sort of thing?'

'I told her we were both coming. The tickets have been bought.'

Mina sat up, her face tight, and carried the bouquet to the kitchen. She laid out the breadboard and began to hack at the flowers with the knife. The knife was cheap. The stems only dented under her blade. She slammed down harder and two stems snapped to reveal white insides.

'What are you doing?' He tried to sound reasonable.

'Cutting off the ends. Flowers last longer if you do that.'

'Let me do it.' She was doing it wrong. She should use scissors. Why was she trying to do so many at once?

'I'm fine,' Mina said, smacking the cutting board so hard that it shook. 'Just let me do this, okay? I don't need to be supervised all the time.'

He went for the knife. She stepped back, and somehow his hand clenched around the triangle of the blade. The steel pressed into his palm. The edge was too thin to be cold or hot. It was only sharp. He'd caught the blade at a bad angle, but everything would be fine if she just gave him the knife.

'Let go,' Mina said. 'I'm almost done.' The roses lay crooked-stemmed on the board.

He looked down at his fist on the blade, and her hand around the black handle. Mina was bloodless at the knuckles. The point of the knife was directed straight at his stomach.

'No, you let go,' he said. 'You'll hurt yourself if you do it like that.'

'I'm just trying to cut the pretty flowers my husband gave me.' Each word was flat and too calm, like a subway announcer's voice.

'Mina, what's going on?'

'Nothing. Nothing's going on. This'll only take a minute.' Her hand jerked, pulling the knife towards her.

The moment was short and bright with pain. Blood opened in his palm. It looked like he was holding the gleaming drops. His nostrils felt hot.

There was a clatter as the knife hit tiles.

'Sorry,' she said. 'Sorry, sorry, sorry, sorrysorrysorrysorry.' The words flowed into a river of noise. Mina's eyes were wide and panicked. Her hands were shaking. She stepped towards him. He let her wrap his hand in kitchen towel. They hadn't bought plasters. The flowers lay half amputated on the kitchen counter. She kissed the back and side of his hand, again and again, as if she thought enough kisses might close the wound. Blood expanded on the paper towel. 'Sorry,' she repeated. His

70

hand felt heavy as if the pain were an object with a weight of its own. His neck hurt, and he rubbed it with the hand not swaddled in kitchen towel.

'You cut me,' he said. Not knowing what else to say.

And, absurdly, Mina began to cry. His wife cried wet and messy. Her mouth made a wide-open curve, like those tragedy theatre masks.

He needed to punch something. His other hand was hot. His face was hot. He forced himself to breathe from his diaphragm to stay calm.

'You didn't tear any vital tendons,' he said.

'I'm so sorry.' She slid down until she was sitting on the floor in the kitchen. 'I didn't mean to. I was just, I don't know, just upset. And I don't know. I needed to do something useful. I just wanted to cut the flowers. I thought if I cut the flowers . . . I don't know. If I just focused on that I'd have space to think. Your mother is always looking at me. I know that's what people do—look, I mean. But she stares like she thinks I'm hiding something. And I used not to care, you know? Like I figured she'd come around. But I can't right now.' Mina kept talking. 'I just don't think I can spend the weekend with her. Not a whole weekend. Not right now.'

His wife's voice jumped like a video clip with a file error, some crucial sentence wiped out.

'Fine, then. I won't go,' he said.

'No, you should. You haven't seen her since Christmas. It's you she wants to see anyway. Not me. I can stay here.' And, as if seeing a flicker in his expression, she added, 'You'll have to trust me eventually.'

'Mina, how will I know you're safe? I can't leave you here all by yourself.'

Being alone in an apartment high enough to induce fatality was definitely a nudge in the wrong direction.

'You're tracking me remember. Anyway, I don't have a gun

71

or a car,' Mina said. 'The only pills we have are your multi-vitamins. I'm not a marine. I can't kill myself with a knife.'

But she was clearly capable of damage, if not death. The pain had spread all the way to his fingertips and up his wrist. 'Mina, I want to trust you. I do—' Oscar didn't mean to look at the door, but his eyes must have slid, because Mina interrupted.

'I'm not going to jump. Women don't jump onto solid ground. You can google suicide statistics.'

Was searching for statistics a good or a bad sign? A symptom of obsession or a desire to understand her condition? This life of second-guessing was exhausting.

Mina continued, 'Women don't choose methods of suicide that damage their faces. It's men who shoot themselves in the head and jump onto concrete. Women take pills and try to drown. Men think women aren't serious or aren't brave enough to die like a man. My theory is that women don't do it because even if you want to die, even if every day hurts, you know that, as a woman, having a messed-up face will make your life worse. And so, in case you survive, in case somehow you fail, you have to keep your skin looking good.' She was out of breath when she finished. That precious face was flushed and screwed up.

'Mina, it doesn't matter. If you're dead you're dead.' The skin on his hand felt too tight. The blood was flaking.

Mina pinched the inner elbow of her right arm. She lifted the soft flesh into a tent of skin.

'Stop it,' he said.

'Oscar, please.'

He thought of the end of his to-do list. Mum, Mina. What good would it do to drag his wife to the north of Scotland? The scenarios flicked across his brain. Mina screaming at his mother. Mina weeping in his mother's kitchen, snot bubbling from her nose. The sound of sheep crying outside and his wife thumping the walls inside. He couldn't ditch his mother. She'd already have done the big food shop. She'd have meals planned.

'You're going to see Phoebe tomorrow?'

She nodded, in exaggerated swoops.

'And you'll call me if anything goes wrong? Anything?'

She flung her arms around him, as if he'd proposed. The blood-blotted paper towel drifted to the floor.

The ceiling was sun-marbled. When had she last woken up alone? The hospital didn't count. There had been doctors and nurses, other bodies breathing in other beds. Urine had glistered from her neighbour's plastic tubing. It was impossible to be alone in the hospital. Oscar had come to visit her every day. He'd brought grapes and books. For the whole visiting hour, his face was twisted with confusion. 'Why did you do this?' he'd asked. But she couldn't point and go, There, that. That's what's wrong with me.

Sure, she had issues. Her mom was dead. Stupid death too—slipped, hit her head, and drowned in their bath. All the while the second-hand Fisher-Price mobile had spun over baby Mina's head. Her grandma had died after a series of strokes. Mina was seventeen. The kids at school had laughed at Mina's cutting and slid needles and razor blades in through the gaps in her locker. Strangers shouted *neeeeee-howwww* at her. But she had a father who'd worked hard for his family, multiple degrees, a good husband, 20:20 vision. People made it through far worse with kindness intact. Those people didn't betray their husbands by trying to die on their wedding night. Those people didn't slice open their husbands' hands.

Be happy, Mina thought. Be happy.

She sat up. The birds stared out from the wallpaper. The parrots' beaks gaped. Their blue eyes goggled at her. Other birds . . . magpies? thrushes? . . . pinched fat strawberries in their beaks. Birds in every room of the flat. She stretched out an arm towards the wall and ran a finger along a smooth

74

wing. The birds' eyes looked knowing, like the eyes of strangers on the subway. Phoebe. She was seeing Phoebe today.

Oscar ran his tongue over his lips. They were dry. His hand throbbed. It felt crusty. He sat up and his head brushed the top bunk. Flakes of blood salted the sheets. The overnight cabin smelled musty. The top berth had been reserved for Mina. In her absence, it was empty.

The train had stopped rocking. He eased out of the bunk and went to the window to see what station they were at. When he opened the blind, he saw fields. In the dim light, they were the soft blue-green of bread mould. It was a colour he remembered well from college. None of his roommates could ever be bothered to clear out the fridge.

There was a knock on the door. He opened it and a croissant in plastic wrap was shoved towards him.

'Tea, coffee?' asked the attendant.

'Coffee,' he said. He tossed the squashed croissant onto the top bunk.

An announcement came through a concealed speaker system. 'Apologies for the delay. There is a cow on the track.' Wasn't this sheep country? Oscar supposed he'd be stuck there for a while. He dropped into plank position, his elbows folded, weight on his forearms and toes. His face was close to the blue carpet. The colour was blotched and he wondered if it was the same carpet that had lined these carriages fifteen years ago when he'd taken the train back up from school.

Before he'd gone away to school, they'd lived in a poky north London flat. His mother worked from home, transcribing cassettes of boring adults talking about difficult things. She sat at the large beige desktop. The flat was loud with the sound of the keys, and Oscar had to be silent, always silent, so that his mother could spell out the words of strangers. In the evenings her friends would come over. The women would smoke tobacco and pot, filling the house with a double stink. One of them always wanted to sniff the top of his head.

After he'd gone away, his mother had bought a cottage up near Inverness where she continued her work, receiving recordings first by post, then by email. Oscar's watch told him he'd been in plank position for four minutes. His abdomen trembled. He held it. The ache gripped his legs. Pain endurance is power. Pain endurance is power. Pain endurance is power. Endurance is power. Pain is power. Endurance is pain. Power is pain. Pain is power.

'Please excuse the delay. The cow is proving uncooperative. We are working with the farmer to resolve this as quickly as possible.'

He dropped to his knees. The carpet was rough. Eventually the train shuffled forward, the cow removed.

His mother was under the station clock, staring up at its iron hands. Her own were thrust into the pockets of her waxed jacket.

'Mum,' he called.

'My prodigal one.' She grinned and opened her arms. She'd called him that since he'd gone away to school. When she was a little melancholic or Pinot-tipsy, 'my prodigal sweetheart'. He hugged her, his lips dabbing her cheek. Somewhere along the line, holding his mother had begun to seem strange. Her body was so puny and unknown. He patted her back. The jacket was rain-damp.

'Where's Mina?' His mother looked around him for the shape of his wife among bodies seeping down the platform.

'Afraid it's just me. She has an appointment in town.'

His mother did not ask about the appointment. She'd always been big on privacy. The morning after his wedding, he'd appeared alone at the breakfast laid out for those who'd stayed the night in the cabins. He'd told everyone that Mina

76

was sleeping off the night before. His mother had never pressed him. Almost as soon as he could talk, she'd taught him, 'Ask no questions and I'll tell you no lies. Close your mouth and you'll catch no flies.' She nattered happily on most subjects, but if she didn't want to discuss a topic she wouldn't.

He followed her to the car. As the key rotated, Radio 4 buzzed on. Voices poured into the car. By the time they escaped Inverness, Oscar could tell it was a game show and that the presenter thought himself hilarious. They drove past cows of uncertain stubbornness and black-nosed sheep. The car left the main road, swerving onto the old one-lane track.

Oscar and Mina visited Scotland every other Christmas, when the beech trees were bare and rain mulched the ground. The landscape looked more cheerful now, seams of blue hanging between the clouds. The cottage hovered at the edge of a beech wood whose leaves were going beer-bottle brown. The red door and windowsills were jolly against the old sandstone walls. But he'd never understand why his mother had chosen this part of the world. All she'd said was that it was cheap, and it didn't make any sense to stay in London while he was away at school, did it?

The building was so isolated. Of course, the supermarket delivery driver, the postman, his mum's church group, her Red Squirrel Society friends all came by. She'd told him about the biscuits they ate or didn't and who was gluten-free. But these people seemed as unreal as characters on the side of a cereal box.

She fiddled with a loop of keys. 'Darling, I should let you know that I said I'd host the poetry book club tomorrow. We're reading Larkin this week, whiny little bugger. Wasn't my choice, of course. Give me Hopkins any day. *For rose-moles all in stipple upon trout that swim; Fresh-firecoal chestnut-falls; finches' wings* . . . Well, you know how it goes. So, the girls will be around. They'd love to meet you.'

The door swayed open and he saw again the rubber boots she kept for him, the old hat stand, and the doormat cut to look like a pine forest.

'Are you going to compliment me on my new glasses or what?' she asked.

They were big, round and lemon yellow.

'They're mad.'

She grinned so widely he could see the glint of the gold tooth at the very back. The tooth she'd had replaced before there were resins and which, when he was small, she'd told him was her pirate tooth.

Mina saw the sign sail into view through the Tube window: *Angel*. The station's name was fantastical. Angel! It sounded unreal. Outside, the road was heavy with cars. The sun slanted and the cars glittered. Perhaps there was an angelic dash in the air. The café was empty, apart from a bald man whose head gleamed like sucked candy. Through a tall window, she glimpsed the courtyard that Phoebe had mentioned by text.

'I'm waiting for someone. Is it okay if I sit?' she asked the girl at the counter. Iron tables and chairs clustered in the courtyard. Above them, a tree cradled the sky. Mina chose a seat in the shade. The sound of recorded piano music burbled from the café's open window.

Mina closed her eyes to better feel the sun. A breeze ran through the tree, and the leaves applauded. She did not want to check her phone. It might tell her Phoebe wasn't coming. She eased one eye open. Two women settled at the next-door table. Their heads tilted towards each other. Points of gold danced in the older woman's ears. She nodded again and again as she spoke. What was so agreeable?

Mina told herself that the moment she was sure Phoebe wouldn't come Phoebe would arrive. She wondered how long it took to push out all hope. Was the memory of hoping a form of hope? The question was overblown. This was, after all, just tea with a woman and a dog.

It was so long since a girl had made Mina feel like this.

Mina's first crush was the first girl to get breasts in their year at school. She had worn her top three buttons undone. A mole hung perched above her cleavage. It was the colour of a park bench gone dark with rain. Mina had spent three years wanting to kiss the mole, to feel the gentle bud of it on her bottom lip. She never spoke to the girl. The girl, now woman, had recently been profiled in *Forbes* for a feature on young professionals. Staring at the magazine, Mina had tried to map where the mole was hiding.

The second was Mina's roommate in freshman year. This girl talked in her sleep. She wore fake eyelashes to class but didn't shave her legs all winter. 'No one's going to see them,' the girl always said. The roommate had nightmares and afterwards she'd crawl into Mina's bed, wearing only boxer shorts and a loose T-shirt. The hairs tickled Mina's legs and made her think of coral fronds reaching out for her skin. It was that year that Mina had first thought of her own topiary as optional. The bed was boosted two feet to make room for Mina's books, shoes, and cereal bars underneath. On the thin mattress, they spooned precariously. Later that girl found a girlfriend to cuddle in the night, and Mina wondered, Why not me?

The third was studying jewellery at the art school—a tall girl with two lip rings. She made tiny glass abstracts that seemed too delicate to wear. She'd asked Mina to model a pair of earrings, and Mina had felt those careful fingers raise a blush on each lobe. The feeling had been so intense that she'd fidgeted, jiggling toes and drumming fingers. The girl had had to ask her to sit still. Mina had been so full of longing that she was sure if she said anything at all the girl would

79

run and run and never look back. At a party hosted in that girl's room Mina had met Oscar.

She'd told him about all these women over a dinner of pizza in his dorm room. He'd smiled indulgently. Sometimes, as they fucked, he described another woman touching Mina. He described the things that that other woman might do with lips and blindfolds, as fantastical as bodice-ripping. In cafés, he'd lean towards Mina and ask, 'Her?' nodding towards a swishing skirt. Mina had never done anything about it so it wasn't quite real to either of them. She guessed it never would be.

Phoebe must have forgotten the date. Mina thought of the quiet filling the apartment. She'd go back. She'd meditate. Wasn't that what crazy people did when they were trying to become uncrazy?

'Hi!' Phoebe was followed by a hillock of fur. As it got closer, Mina saw the flapping tongue. Phoebe looped a leash around the chair. Should Mina stroke the animal? It looked suspiciously up at her. 'They take orders at the counter,' Phoebe said. 'Can I get you anything?'

'I'll get it.' Mina wanted to say thank you, thank you for showing up today when you must already have so many people who want your time, your attention.

'I invited you out.'

Mina gave in to the pleasure of being bought a drink. Phoebe returned with Mina's green tea and a latte, bouffant with foam. She settled in her chair, lifted the cup with both hands, and pecked at the froth. 'They do the best matcha lattes here. Want to try?'

Mina did, kissing the soft milk. The foam collapsed as her lips touched it.

'Good, right?' Phoebe said.

Mina was presented with a full view of Phoebe's face. It had the burnish of skin seen underwater. Phoebe belonged among reeds and minnows on a clear day, soaking in lake-light.

As their drinks cooled, they handed across biographical information like a game of Go Fish—matching factoids. They were both more tea-drinkers than coffee-chuggers. Mina's dentist had told her that coffee, tea and soy sauce all stained the teeth. 'It was like he wanted to take all the joy out of my life.'

Phoebe asked, 'Do you remember the stickers they used to give you for going when you were a kid? You know, with pictures of teeth or dinosaurs. They should have that for adults.'

'Adult stickers?'

'Or loyalty cards or those bottles of booze they give you on planes.'

'That doesn't seem very dentisty.'

'Maybe a mint liqueur?'

Phoebe seemed different than at dinner. Her face was smiling, but her hands curled on her lap. When Mina didn't reply immediately, Phoebe laughed, and the sound was like dropped pennies spilling over the pavement. Her eyes hovered here and there over the top of Mina's ears. Was it possible that Phoebe was nervous?

There was a pause and Mina noticed that the piano music had changed to the husk of a singer's voice.

'Anyway, how's Oscar?'

'Oh, he's visiting his mother.'

'I never realised they were close.'

Mina paused, unsure how to explain her husband's relationship to his mother. He spoke to her on the phone regularly. He worried about her living alone, although the woman seemed glint-eyed and happy.

Phoebe added, 'I mean, he spent most summers at our place.'

How had Oscar not mentioned this girl? Oscar always spoke of Theo as his oldest friend. All three must have run through long grass, batted tennis balls, got lost in the woods.

'How long have you known Oscar?' Mina asked.

'Umm . . . I must've been ten so he would've been thirteen.' Phoebe smiled into the memory. 'He was such an awkward kid. He had this baby-giraffe look that made you want to pet him.' She blushed the faintest pink. Mina might have missed it if she'd been less interested in Phoebe's face. Phoebe gave an awkward shrug. 'You know what I mean,' she added.

Mina nodded but, to her, Oscar had always seemed so certain. Sometimes happy, sometimes sad, sometimes angry, always certain. She tried to see her husband as a delicate beast. A thought shivered into existence.

'Did you ever? Were you two ever? You know . . . I don't mind. But I'm curious. He never told me much about growing up here.' She'd been so certain she knew Oscar. She'd found him his hairdresser, bought his underwear, balled his socks, fallen asleep to the thud of his snores. But there was this gap in her knowledge, an empty folder with Phoebe's name on it.

'Oh. No. Nothing like that. Theo would've killed me. Though I guess he wants to kill me now anyway.' She slumped. 'But, like, where am I supposed to go? London is so expensive. I'm a culture and lifestyle blogger. I can't not be in London.'

Mina didn't quite understand what bloggers did or how they survived. Phoebe continued, 'Boarder since I was eight. Supposed to make you independent. Look at me now, living on my brother's sofa.'

What to say to that? Mina couldn't tell Phoebe what independence was or how to get it. Her husband barely trusted her to be alone. Mina had not been to boarding school and the words conjured wizards and beautiful boys in starched cricket outfits, long hair falling over their eyes.

'God, I shouldn't have let you get the teas.' Mina looked

into the bottom of the cup where five specks of green lay, having escaped the pot. No fortune revealed itself in the leaves.

'Oh, don't. One tea isn't going to make a difference. But I can't quite believe this is my life. Do you know what I mean? Sorry, I'm waffling. You don't want to hear this.' Mina did. Mina wanted to hear everything. But Phoebe leaned forwards and said, 'I'm being disgustingly self-centred. Tell me about you. What are you working on?'

Mina thought about the happiness list. *I'm working on being happy* seemed like a statement reserved for yoga retreats and drunken confessions. Instead, she began to talk about the monograph she was supposedly writing. Did Phoebe know how hard it was for a woman to make it through a myth alive?

'Monograph,' Phoebe asked.

'Like a long essay. Sorry, I'm used to academia speak.'

Phoebe said, 'Tell me about one of them. One of your survivors.'

Mina flicked through her brain for one Phoebe might enjoy. There was Lavinia, whose hair catches fire, but survives to marry and bear the sons of Rome. Meh. Lavinia had about as much personality as one of the deer munched upon by her husband-to-be. Psyche might count. Maybe Phoebe would like Psyche.

'Psyche is a princess so stunning that even Venus, the goddess of beauty, is jealous. She can't bear to have Psyche live so she sends her son, Cupid, to kill the girl. But Psyche is so hot that Cupid falls for her. He sneaks her into a mansion deep in the woods. She doesn't know who he is or what he is, only that she's been kidnapped. Each day the sun sets and a warm body slips into her bed. It holds her, it touches her, and its lips by her ear say that she must never see her lover in the light. She fears he is a monster. Finally overcome by curiosity, she lifts a lamp to his face. It's Cupid, chiselled jaw and all. She immediately falls for him. He's furious that she disobeyed and flies off in a sulk. Psyche searches the world for him.' Phoebe sipped her tea, her face too unknown to parse. Mina sped along past the trials Psyche faced. 'Finally, they reconcile. She's beautiful and good. They get married and she is made a goddess. Ta-da! Happy ending. But I guess I wonder . . . Are you still you if you become a goddess?'

'Psyche and Cupid, that's cute,' Phoebe said. 'A marriage of mind and heart.'

It took Mina a moment to understand. But in the Greek Psyche's name meant something closer to breath than to brain. She tried to explain. Just then the dog began to whine. His keening was high-pitched, like a radiator bleeding.

The poetry club arrived in Range Rovers. They wore cardigans and art jewellery. Oscar supposed women like this were to be found all over the world, buried even in these craggy hills. They squeezed his arm and told him he was a good boy for visiting. He nodded, though he sensed they did not expect a reply any more than they expected the spaniels who followed at their feet to chit chat about the weather.

He excused himself to jog over sheep tracks in the marshy fields. When he returned, they had driven off, leaving behind only cake crumbs and a pile of mugs in the sink.

His body felt pleasantly used and stretched. Burrs clung to his socks. He picked the seeds off one by one and lined the green fuzz balls along the grain of the pine table.

In a minute, he'd get online and email a few more decorators.

'Could you refill the bird-feeder?' his mother asked. She was standing with her back to him pouring olive oil over pimple-skinned chicken. 'I know they don't really need it at this time of year but they expect it now. The seeds are under the sink. The feeder's round the other side of the house.'

Oscar found the bag of sunflower seeds. He lifted it with his left hand. The right had not quite healed and was inadequately covered by the pink plaster he'd pasted across it. He still couldn't quite absorb that Mina had done this to him. It was an accident, yes, but not the sort of accident that happened in other people's marriages.

The trees stroked lilac shadows across the ground. Inverness cut a golden stripe into the horizon line. A shimmering strip of dinners being cooked, TVs nattering, a whole city settling in for Saturday evening. So, this was what his mother saw when she looked up from her desk. This and, apparently, birds. The shutters were open. He peered inside. A stack of papers lay beside her laptop. The hunched lamp was off. The air smelled of clean water with a dash of salt, perhaps rising from the firth. A cow moaned goodnight. He thought of those clocks with a dial for different time zones— London, New York, Tokyo, Beijing. No clock would ever bear the name of this damp hill.

As he was thinking, he must have moved the bag of seeds because pain stung across his right hand. He let go and the bag thumped to the ground. Mina. Mina had cut him. The thought ached. He should text her, but he didn't want to. Not now. He had nothing useful to say to his wife. God, there must be some new therapy they could try—mindfulness, sophrology, CBT. People were always saying yoga saved their lives.

His hand itched. It wasn't like she'd tried to stab him. Only, well, he hadn't expected his wife to cut him. It had been going so well. She'd seemed happy. He'd thought this experiment could work. He told himself to man up. His mother had asked him to fill the bird feeder: he could do that.

The feeder was a tube of wire mesh covered at both ends with green plastic. Careful of his palm, he wrenched the cap. It stuck. He tried again. This time it came away. Sunflower seeds swarmed into the feeder.

His mother had put the chicken in the oven and was opening packets of crinkle-cut carrots. 'Thanks, darling. The arthritis in my wrist's been playing up again.'

Was that why the carrots were pre-chopped? She'd always said those were a rip-off. 'Again, Mum? How often is this happening?'

'I told you about it.'

'No, you didn't.'

'I told you I was taking on less work because my wrists were sore.'

'That wasn't a temporary thing? You're not working?'

'Oh, don't look like that. I'm fine. My wrists just get sore.'

'Mum, do you need help? Is there something we can do?'

'Don't look at me like that. I have a bit saved up. Just come and refill the bird feeder every now and then, if you're that bothered about your old mum.'

How long could she live all the way out here? It would be so much easier in a standard-issue two-parent family. People don't care for their one-night stands into old age.

'Mum, are you seeing anyone? A man, I mean. It wouldn't be a bad thing if you had a boyfriend or a gentleman caller.' He put his hands up, like she was going to shoot at him.

She splattered oil over the carrots. 'A gentleman caller? How old do you think I am?'

'You know what I mean.'

'Mina has an appointment in town, does she?' his mother said.

Fair play, Mum. Fair play, he thought.

Mina dreamed. The dream was full of feathers. As if a pillow as large as a train had burst. Fraying feathers clung to her mouth, her hair, battered her eyelids. The first thing she thought when she woke up was, Where did the feathers go? The second was, Why is my phone buzzing?

'Oscar?' she asked, although the display had already shown her husband's name.

'Are you okay?'

She lifted the device away from her ear to see the time: 3 a.m. 'Did something happen?' she asked.

There was a pause. She listened for her husband's breath beneath the crackle.

'Nothing happened,' he said.

'Why are you awake?' She was the one who woke up in the night. He was the one who slept through car alarms and lightning storms.

'I was thinking about you.' Oscar's voice was soft.

'I dreamt of feathers.'

'That's good. Feathers are nice.'

'I suppose. How's your mom's?'

'It's fine. You had a nice day with Phoebe?'

'It was okay. She invited me to see an art thing with her tomorrow. She's reviewing it.'

'So you won't be lonely.'

'No. I won't.'

'You're okay?'

'I'm okay.' And she was. The blanket hugged her. 'Are you?' she asked.

'Of course.'

'I'm sorry for before. With the knife.'

'It wasn't your fault. It's okay.'

The more they said 'okay', the more the word deformed. The *o* inflated, sounding top-heavy.

'So everything's okay?' she asked.

'Yes. I'll see you on Monday. Sleeper gets in in the morning.'

'Okay,' she said.

The Barbican was brown concrete and ribbed with balconies. It put Mina in mind of a crouching animal. Somewhere in the guts was Phoebe. Mina ran her hands through her hair, flattening it. She tucked it behind her ears, then untucked it. It felt bristlier today, as if anticipating trouble.

Phoebe was in the lobby. No dog. Mina stopped before she was seen. It was special, the moment before the greeting, before smiles, before faces became performances. Phoebe leaned against a pillar, playing with a ring. It was overlarge and hung loose around her finger. She lifted and dropped it. Twirling it.

Mina approached and Phoebe looked up. Her face shifted into the welcome. Mina was the one expected, the one waited for. That was a pleasure too.

'Thanks for coming with,' Phoebe said. 'I always try to go to these things twice. It's busier at the weekend and it's good to see how people react to stuff.'

'Do you always write about art?'

'Not always. But I suppose a lot of the blog is art as lifestyle.'

What was the difference between having a lifestyle and having a life? Maybe everyone had the second and only some people the first. She looked at the deep pink where Phoebe's lips met. Mina would subscribe to a blog about what made a person like Phoebe.

Phoebe pulled an expression that might've been embarrassment or might've been bashful pride. 'It's a bit gimmicky. I go to see an exhibition and then I do a themed post. I link to clothes and food you can buy.' She put on a deep mock-professorial voice. 'Costume and Consumerism.'

When Mina didn't respond, Phoebe went on in her normal voice: 'Like, for example, everyone knows Georgia O'Keeffe was big on flowers and deer. So, for the post about her I found this flowery shower curtain, and an enamel pin of this cute deer skull. Anyway, the exhibit was cool. It had all this early work on cityscapes and stuff about her marriage to Man Ray, you know, the photographer. So for the blog, I linked to all this Polaroid and vintage-camera stuff.'

'You really are a nerd.'

'What?'

'Like your brother said the other night. He called you a nerd.' Mina felt stupid for remembering.

'Hey, at least I'm using my degree.' Phoebe sighed. 'Though I don't know if they really care about the art. What people really like to see is me being happy. Being happy next to an object they can buy. Take a picture with me.'

Phoebe looped an arm around Mina's neck and lifted her phone above them. Their faces glowed on screen. The eyes were large and the mouths small.

'Smile,' Phoebe said.

Mina attempted to smile in a way that looked blog-worthy.

'I'll send it to you.'

'Thanks. But I'm not sure your followers will find my face that interesting.'

'Well, tell me some cute Latin words. Maybe for love or beauty. That sort of thing.' Phoebe shrugged. 'I can probably find some mugs or tote bags with them on. Though it'd be better if you made forks or kettles.'

'What?'

'Simple stuff gets the most click-throughs. My followers

can't really afford fancy holidays or their own homes so what they really like is super-nice normal stuff. If you spend a little bit more on this kettle or that mug, your life, too, will be a little bit better. They have to buy a kettle anyway, so they feel like they can afford it. And if they have the perfect kettle, perfect cup, perfect filters, then they have the perfect coffee.'

Mina nodded. Phoebe's fist opened and shut each time she said 'perfect'. Phoebe must've been considering this for a long time.

'So, anyway, it's my job to tell people how to make their boring lives perfect. And I get advertising revenue for it. Or, at least, that's the idea.'

'Is it working?'

'Well, last month I made at least enough for four perfect cups of coffee.'

What was Phoebe living off? There was the brother's sofa, obviously. Could there be alimony? It must be strange to live off the cash of a person you hated. But was an ex-husband's money so different from a husband's? Oscar had paid for the plane tickets to London. Mina felt a zigzag of guilt. She should be with him, in Scotland, not buying tickets to see a show with a woman she wanted to stare at more than any painting. But he'd said she should try to be happy. And she was trying. She would save up the sweetness of this day and bring it back to him.

'Hey, is that a tattoo?' Phoebe took Mina's arm. 'Can I see?'

Mina pushed up her sleeves. Phoebe's fingers traced the blossoms and Mina held her breath to stop herself shaking.

'They're lovely,' Phoebe said.

'I got it done the year I turned thirty. A bit old for it, I guess. I'd been meaning to get one for ages but nothing ever seemed right. Then I saw these peonies. Well, not these ones, a bunch pressed up against the window of some ground-floor apartment. It was February and everything was so fucking cold. They must've been grown in a greenhouse. But just looking at them . . . it made me think of summer.' She loved the way they started as tight fists and by the end of their lives were loose and sloppy, drunk, even.

'Maybe I should do a Mina-and-peonies post, then.'

'I guess.' Mina's face was hot. 'So, what's this exhibit about?'

The artist featured was an Icelandic guy with a blond beard. It was exactly the sort of beard you'd think an Icelandic performance artist would have. He'd hired pyjama-clad young men to sit on the floor and play guitar. In other rooms, videos of his work were projected onto the walls. Phoebe made notes in a pad that sighed as she flipped the pages. At times, she glanced up at Mina, and Mina glanced back.

'This is my favourite,' Phoebe said. 'A few years ago at MOMA, he got this indie band to play the same song for six hours.'

'That doesn't get dull?'

'No. No, it doesn't.'

The room was half dark. Couples were pulled together on the floor. Phoebe stepped around them, picking her way over hands and handbags. They sat down in a clearing in the fleshy forest. Onscreen, men in suits sang, strummed and drummed. The singer held his lips over the microphone. For a moment, his mouth met the mesh of metal. His eyelashes were thick, like a doll's. Music thrummed through the floor and ran up the undersides of Mina's knees and the small of her back. Phoebe adjusted her position and her arm rested against Mina. Mina thought that the sound must be moving through her into Phoebe or from Phoebe into her. Tiny vibrations. People walked in and the screen's projection lit their faces.

'It's good, isn't it?' Phoebe whispered.

Mina thought she'd happily spend six hours watching the

space between their bodies expand and contract with their breath.

The crowd at MOMA stood. They clapped. They waved cellphones. The Londoners surrounding Mina were silent. Onscreen and in life, visitors left and arrived. Bodies replaced bodies.

The words of the song were about sorrow or loss or not getting over someone. It was mournful and vague in the way of all the music Mina had loved when she was fifteen. Maybe that was the point. Grey flecked the musicians' hair. These middle-aged men hadn't just played for six hours. They must have been playing for years, their spines aching as they bent into their sound. They wore yellow earplugs. What would it be like to be so loud you deafened yourself?

'There's a bit where the rhythm guitarist cries and the lead singer looks at him and smiles. It's lovely.' Phoebe's breath was warm on Mina's ear. 'But I'm not sure we'll see it.'

Sometimes one of the musicians would stop and let his body hang while the others continued without him. The camera blurred and focused and blurred again. Had the same cameraman filmed for six hours? Had he found new things to see in the men's faces?

The screen was reflected as a silver rectangle curving across Phoebe's pupils. Mina stretched her pinkie so it brushed the edge of Phoebe's hand. Phoebe kept motionless. And so the two hands lay just touching, like two leaves fallen from the same tree. The tired men sang about sorrow. Light glimmered across Phoebe's hair.

Uptick, uptick, uptick. She could feel the flicker her fingers would make. A great arrowhead of joy.

Oscar dropped his bag on the sofa. His shoulders ached from the return ride in the narrow bunk. Mina sat at the table, her back to him, staring into her laptop. A mug rested by her side. There was something different about his wife. In the alignment of her neck or the tilt of her head?

He called out hello. She remained fixed to the screen. 'Mina,' he said, louder this time. She presented a wide smile. Her lips were orange-red.

'You're wearing lipstick,' he said.

'Yeah.'

How long had it been since he'd tasted the wax of lipstick?

'Do you want coffee? I made a pot. But it might be cold by now. I could microwave it?' Mina stood, already on her way to the kitchen. Oscar stepped into her pathway. He pressed her mouth under his. Her lips were smooth. She smelled slightly different. Could it be the lipstick, or a shifting of pheromones? He could feel the pressure of her mouth beginning to smile. Mina pulled away. 'Don't you want your coffee?' she asked.

'One minute. Shut your eyes.'

She did. He kissed her left eyelid. The skin there was so soft. Her heartbeat flickered behind the thin membrane.

'Keep them shut,' he said.

'Okay.'

The lashes spiked along the tops of her cheeks. Her chin tilted up at him. He paused for a moment, looking at the face he knew so well. This face trusted him. She bit her lip. She'd be waiting for the next kiss to land. He'd keep her safe. He dipped down, moving closer to her, taking in the wife-smell. Slowly he landed a kiss on her right eyelid.

'There, you're balanced out,' he said. 'We can have coffee now.'

'No, my turn.' Mina tiptoed up to him. He closed his eyes. Her kisses were fast—two tickles on each lid. His breath eased and a tingle spread across his forehead.

They'd discovered the eyelid thing during their first hungry months of love. It was their thing. And then they'd stopped. He couldn't remember why. They should do this more often.

As Mina clattered about with the coffee pot, Oscar looked at her screen. He was startled to see Phoebe's face. She was pouting up at the camera, her cheeks sucked in. Below, there was a second photo of her in profile, kneeling in front of a humungous dog. The animal's tongue hooked out to lick Phoebe's mouth. Vaguely nauseating.

'Have fun with Phoebe?' he called.

'Yeah. It was nice.'

'Can't believe she's a blogger. Always thought that was for idiots and egomaniacs.'

'It's a business. I think it's quite brave to keep putting yourself out there.' Mina returned with a coffee cup in two hands, handle facing outwards. He was always amazed by her Teflon fingers. She could withstand any heat, it seemed. She looked calm and well rested.

He took the coffee. Her oval face was tipped up to him. This was the way things were always supposed to have been. The way they used to be.

He reached for the coffee cup, but she stopped him, taking his hand in hers. 'Your poor hand,' she said. Over the weekend, the skin had knitted a brown line. She touched it hesitatingly. 'I took a slice out of you. I can't believe I did that.'

'It'll heal,' he said. 'What doesn't kill you, right?'

'Can I kiss it?'

He nodded, and she pressed her face into the cup of his hand. It ached where her mouth bumped him. 'It's not a big deal,' he said, and patted her head. He'd never been good at big shows of emotion. He didn't want the drama of repentance. 'Let's just forget about it.'

She blinked up at him with wet eyelashes.

'Mina, let's paint the flat together.'

'What?'

'It'll look much better with a coat of fresh paint.' It would be easier to pay someone whose job it was to paint. Someone who wouldn't make mistakes. But they could do this together. Mina could help. Maybe giving her something to do with her hands was the answer, something simpler than all that academic wrangling.

'Okay,' Mina said. 'If that's what you want.'

'It is. Let's do this together.'

Mina sat on the patient's chair. A blue strip of paper covered the plastic seat and it slipped about underneath her. The chair reclined like the one her dentist had. The technician smiled at her and said, 'Give me a chance to look over your paperwork and we'll get started.'

A thin gold band pierced the top of the technician's right ear. The small braids of her hair were looped into a tight bun. Had the technician always known she wanted to examine women's bodies and find their failings?

The technician pulled on a pair of gloves. Her nails were short and round, their outline visible under the latex. The curve of a ring contoured the left ring finger. Mina had never noticed if women were married until she was. Each ring-wearer had promised to be with another person forever. It was strange to be informed of such a large thing by a little metal and rock. Married people always seemed invisibly accompanied by their beloved. Though Mina supposed every person brought with them a spectral cast: families, lovers, friends, cats, past-selves.

'Have you had a pelvic ultrasound before?'

Mina shook her head.

'Okay, it's nothing to be worried about. I'm going to insert this into your vulva.' She held up a dildo-like device attached by a spiralling cord to a larger machine. 'There's a transducer, a device like a very small camera. We'll be able to see what's going on inside. It'll come up on the monitor over there. Any questions?'

Mina felt she should have questions before she let a stranger stick a long plastic rod into her vagina. But she didn't. What was there to say?

The technician smiled. 'Great. If you remove your trousers and underwear, and put them on that chair over there, I'll go outside for a minute and when I get back we can get started.'

This struck Mina as unnecessarily coy. Surely whether the woman saw Mina's backside as she slid out of her jeans was meaningless, given the penetration to follow. Alone, she shucked off her clothes, sat back in the patient's chair.

When the technician returned, she covered the dildo in a silvery gel.

'If you part your legs slightly that'd be great. Sorry if it's cold.'

It was shivery but not painful. In fact, it was almost soothing, as was the woman's firm hand on Mina's knee. Heat rushed to Mina's cheeks. It felt improper to find it pleasant, disrespectful of the woman and her professionalism. Luckily, the technician was looking away from Mina's face and at the screen. A display of abstract blobs appeared in grey. The technician rotated the dildo and the view changed to yet more misshapen shadows. Mina tried to make out anything meaningful. It looked a bit like videos she'd seen of coral polyps. The only sound in the room was the whooping of a crow outside and sometimes a gentle squishing from Mina's vagina.

'What's that?' Mina asked, feeling awkward.

'These are your ovaries.'

'You're inside my ovaries?'

'Not quite. We get a better view of them using this device than we could doing the scan from outside.'

'So, um, does it look okay?'

'Well, it's as your gynaecologist suggested in her notes. You've got polycystic ovaries.' The technician spoke as if she

97

was confirming something Mina should already know. Why hadn't the gynaecologist told Mina this? She had received no note.

'Can you say that again?'

'Polycystic ovaries.' The technician pressed a button on the keyboard and the image onscreen froze. The dildo was retracted. 'You have cysts growing in the walls of your ovaries.' The technician touched the screen, her finger covering one of the blobs. 'Basically, these are collections of fluid.'

A coldness, like a sprinkler system turning on, drenched Mina. Until now, the appointment had felt ridiculous. How many times had she seen a doctor to be told that the problem was probably stress? Here was an image. A visible thing was happening to her. Blobs were growing inside her. When had they started? Why? She stared at the onscreen shadows. As Aeneas, great hero, ventured towards the land of the dead, the Ferryman warned him, 'This is the land of shadows, of sleep, of weary night.' Mina had the odd notion that the shadows that clustered at the edge of the river Styx might have looked like this. If she was hospitalised, would Oscar bring her grapes again? Would she want grapes? When had grapes and sick people become a thing? Thoughts popped like bubbles of soap until one rose to the top of her tongue.

'Are they, um, cancerous?'

'Oh, no, nothing like that. It's totally unrelated to cancer. Your gynaecologist will talk to you about it in more detail. But please don't worry. This is nothing to panic about.'

'So?'

'I'll send the results over to her, and her office will call to schedule an appointment.'

'Oh-kay.'

'Really, don't worry. Like one in ten women have it.'

How was that possible? Mina had never heard of it. She prodded her stomach above where she thought her ovaries

98

were. The skin was squished but revealed no secrets. She looked up at the screen that must have shown so many babies and saw her cysts. Really? This is what grew inside her? Really? Today would be a downtick day.

There were so many types of white. White with yellow undertones. White with green undertones. White with peach, blue, fawn undertones. The internet disagreed about the best type of white. One faction thought yellow-white was warm and welcoming. Another thought it was overdone. It had never occurred to Oscar that white could be overdone. The fashionable people liked white with grey undertones, which the rest of the internet said was dirty and cold. None of the paints were called anything useful. They were labelled Stone and Cloud and Wool, names that made him feel like the paint was mixed with mud and sleet and grass.

He'd bought sample pots while Mina was at her appointment. She was back, and they were painting test sheets. He dipped his brush into the liquid and striped a long stroke of white across the white paper. Mina finished a sheet, and lifted it carefully, pinching it at the corners. Gravity billowed it out like a sail as she carried it over to the newspaper they'd laid across the floor. She placed it below the other completed sheets to dry.

'What do you think? Grey-white or yellow-white?' he asked Mina.

She shrugged and swirled her brush in the water glass. It pinged against the sides. Round and round her wrist went until the water clouded over. 'They're just white.'

'Just white? What did Virgil think of white?'

Mina slouched, her hair falling across her eyes. He'd thought this project would be fun for her. She'd always loved getting the apartment ready for their parties, choosing the decorations, coming home with themed napkins.

'You have to wait for them to dry.' Mina tore off a sheet of paper with a great ripping noise. She grabbed the butter knife, wedging it under the lip of a new pot. She screwed up her face, pushing down with both hands.

'Let me,' he said.

The lid popped up before he could grab the can.

'Did you know the old word for the inner labia was nymphae? They're your little nymphs.' Mina said. The smile she gave him seemed to be a feat of muscular strength rather than any depiction of joy.

'I don't think I have little nymphs. Though yours are lovely.'

'Fair. But you know I'd forgotten that it was the creepy teacher we had in third year who told us. No one had any idea where to look.'

'Huh.'

She made a long sweep down the middle of the sheet. 'There are cysts in my ovaries,' she said, and plunged the brush into paint.

'What?'

'I have to wait to talk to my gynaecologist. But yeah.'

'You said the appointment went fine.'

'It did. Like one in ten women have them. It's nothing.' Her voice was flat.

'Why didn't you tell me about this?' He put down his brush.

'I'm telling you. This is me telling you.'

He pulled out his phone and started googling. He scrolled past diagrams of wombs spread out in pink butterflies until he got to the list of symptoms.

'You aren't fat or hairy.'

'Thanks. I'm glad you noticed,' she said.

'But you aren't.'

'There are things growing in me and that's all you can say?'

He kept reading. It was a long list. Type 2 diabetes, an excess of male hormone, those weren't great. She didn't seem diabetic. Co-morbid with cardiovascular disease, and obstruct-ive sleep apnoea. Then there it was: depression. Polycystic ovarian syndrome was co-morbid with depression.

'Co-morbid' was a strange word. It sounded like the group noun for a cluster of sad teenagers. But he thought he under-stood the gist: two bad things happening at once. It was simple. His wife had tried to kill herself because of a hormone imbalance.

'Read this.' He held it out to her.

'I already did. And yes, yes, I noticed the depression thing. But do you know what? There's no cure. No really clear causes either. Though one of the suggestions is it might be brought on by stress. So, there is that. It's probably all stress. Stress. Stress. Stress.'

She said 'stress' like she was saying 'fuck' or 'goddamn'. He went to hug her. She stepped back.

'You're all . . .' she paused, as if trying to think of the right word '. . . painty.'

He looked at his hands, which were splattered with all the varieties of white.

'I have a headache,' she said. 'I'm going to take a bath.'

Mina dripped from bathroom to bedroom. The wallpaper birds glared at her as if they knew about their planned eradi-cation. Oscar must have finished the samples by now. She shouldn't have snapped. A draught blew across her knees. Mina tucked the towel more tightly around her. Her hair stuck damply to the sides of her face.

Could her ovaries really be why she wanted to die? It sounded suspiciously like the ancient Greeks blaming hysteria on a wandering uterus. Then again, it was better than any explanation she'd had. Mina was trying so hard to be happy and good and it wasn't working.

She flipped open her laptop. It had too many windows

open. And each of the windows had too many tabs. She wasn't like Oscar. She couldn't maintain an inbox with zero unread messages. The number was in the thousands now. Mostly spam. But probably some worthwhile things had got lost too. She opened a blank email and typed, *I want to die. I want to die. I want to die.* Her fingers slammed down on the keys in a way that felt almost as good as screaming.

'What're you up to?' Oscar asked, his voice conciliatory.

'Nothing much, just email.' She Xed out. And from the next tab blossomed Phoebe's face.

He lay on the bed next to her. 'Is that Pheeb?'

Tiny Phoebe grinned up at them. 'It's about a trip she took to a flower market. It's only open on Sundays apparently.' Next to the photos of Phoebe were image grabs of Dutch masters, flowers bursting out of vases.

Oscar took the laptop and scrolled to Phoebe standing in front of buckets of peonies.

Mina said, 'It's weird. You think this flower's so personal and particular to you, then you remember that everyone loves peonies. Though they're out of season now. This is from June.'

Oscar gave her a strange look. 'Do you want to go?' he asked. 'I'm sure we could find time this weekend.'

'I'm sorry,' Mina said. 'For before, I mean. You were trying to help.'

Oscar massaged his eyebrows. 'Perhaps you should think about going back on your meds.'

'They don't work, you know that.'

'Different ones, then.'

'Oscar, it's only been a few weeks,' Mina said. 'Give me a chance. Everyone online says there's supposed to be mood swings at first. But they'll balance out.'

'What if they don't?'

'Please, Oscar.' She knew she sounded like a child. A child begging to be allowed to stay awake another hour into the night, as she had done so long ago. Her grandmother had always shaken her head and pulled her by the hand to the narrow bed in the room they shared.

'Okay,' Oscar said.

After he'd showered off that morning's run, he checked in on his wife. Mina was still in bed, head fallen between pillows. It came to him again, the image of her as a body, as a rotting thing. He needed to pull himself together. He squeezed antiseptic gel onto his palm. Amber crystals ridged the line of the cut. Something was going wrong with the healing.

Watching her body curled like a shrimp, it occurred to him that his wife was a liar. She hadn't told him that she was planning on leaving her life. And she'd tried to do it twice. Oscar could remember the first lie he'd ever told. His mother had bought him a new green umbrella. A bigger boy broke it. When Oscar came home he said the umbrella was lost. Fear had clutched him when he saw his lie had been successful. His mother couldn't tell. It was as if the world he lived in and the world his mother lived in had separated. Reality was not solid. It was as squishy as Play-Doh.

He stroked the side of Mina's head. 'I'm going upstairs to call Dad. Should I wake you when I come back?'

'Love you,' she said.

'You too,' he replied.

He took the winding staircase quickly, fumbled for his keys and opened the door to 5B. It was directly above 4B where he and Mina were staying. Mina was somewhere below his feet. Oscar paced across the shadowed room and pulled open the curtains. Dust rushed into his mouth and eyes. He blinked past the pain until the room refocused. The same acidic yellow pine furniture as downstairs. Even the same awful orange sofa. Just dirtier.

He leaned against the window frame and called his father.

'Hi, Dad.'

There was a pause at the other end as if his father was trying to place the voice.

'Oscar.'

He began: 'I've been emailing that ramen place in Williamsburg about the shipment that got delayed and I think it'd be a good idea to offer them a discount on their next order.'

'If we have to. What else?'

'Dad?'

'Mm.'

'I think it would be a good idea if Mina and I repainted the flats ourselves.'

Another pause.

'It would be good for her—us. After talking to the estate agents and looking into building costs, I don't think a full refurb makes sense. A slap of paint and we can get these on the market.'

A pipe somewhere in the building let out a displeased gurgle.

'A decorator would be faster,' his father said.

Oscar tried to sound certain. 'They're overpriced. And as long as we do a respectable job, it should be fine.'

'If the paint job looks unprofessional that'll turn buyers off.'

'We can do a good job,' Oscar said. 'It might take a bit longer but handling sales long distance has been working out.'

'Fine. Do what you think best.' The voice already seemed to be moving into the distance.

'Thanks Dad.'

Dust spun through the empty room. Each mote was firefly gold in the evening light. His throat burned. He ran a hand along the wallpaper. It was bubbled and warped. Between two panels the paper had come loose entirely, leaving an oval slit. He dug a finger into the gap. The space was cold and damp. Disgusting. He pulled, and the paper came off without too much effort. He always took a certain satisfaction in peeling an orange in a single coil. He imagined this room peeled in one easy spin. He kept pulling the paper, following it sideways, until he met an empty bookcase. He tugged at the shelves. Nothing. He tensed his core. Nothing. He kicked the side. Dust puffed upwards. He couldn't let this shit get to him. He had to proceed calmly. He pressed his head against the wall to see how it was fastened. But his view was blocked by a curve of paper stuck between wood and wall. The space was too narrow for his fingers. Carefully manipulating the edge of his credit card, he edged the paper out. It fell.

As he picked it up, he realised it was photo paper with *Fujifilm* watermarked across the back. He flipped it over.

In the photo, a fat-faced baby looked up from its crib. Red trains were printed on its blanket. A very average baby blanket, the kind probably made in the thousands. Not a big deal, but trains had chugged along his blankie. Blankie, which had shrunk and faded and been abandoned.

Oscar exhaled. He wiped the photo with his sleeve. It was blurry and out of focus. Oscar looked again, squinting at the room. The photo hadn't been taken in the room he'd grown up in. The walls there were a lavender that was more cheerful than attractive. The walls in this photo were dark with splotches of colour, not unlike the room in which he stood. And then it was obvious. The blobs could be birds.

Had he been here before? His nails dug into the scab on his palm. Pain swooped up his arm.

October

October was soggy. Rain rubbed the world grey, the way a broken pencil lead will gradually darken the inside of a pencil case. Mina felt smudgy too. She stretched out on the bright orange couch, her face pressed into the cushions. The wool was bobbled. With one hand she picked at the fuzz, while with the other she scrolled through her email.

Dear Mina,

Thank you for recommending Boris. He seems like a lovely young man.

However, I do not think his manner with Alfie is as successful. Alfie has been asking when you will be available again.

I hope your research is progressing well.

Warmly,

Alexandra Davies

Dear Ms Davies,

I hope to be back in New York for the New Year. I'm sorry to hear it's not working out with Boris, though it's always nice to be missed! Can Alfie hold out that long for me? If he's feeling uninspired, then he may want to check out Adrian Goldsworthy's In the Name of Rome: The Men Who Won the Roman Empire. *It's in English, but I always think it's nice to remember why you're studying a language.*

Very best,

Mina

The Romans were great at war. The wars created the empire that fed the poetry, yet they never moved her. But teaching was not always about what moved you personally.

Guilt spun in her gut at the thought of her research. She opened her computer to the monograph, if that's what it was. At the moment it was a catalogue of women, some underlined passages and scribbled notes.

Mina had never been able to decide if Iphigenia was one of the women who survived. King Agamemnon offended the goddess Artemis. The only way to earn her forgiveness was to sacrifice his daughter. Iphigenia was his youngest, a lovely and loving princess. She was taken to the altar. Then the story split. Sophocles has her die. A deal is a deal. A sacrifice must have blood. Herodotus has her rescued and slipped away to become a priestess of Artemis. Euripides goes further and has her retrieved from hiding by her brother. Did Iphigenia survive? Was blood required?

How would Oscar think about the task? He'd make a plan. Read the stories she loved, then come up with a theory. But she didn't know how to plan around the feeling that her bones were made of granite. It was all her neck could do to hold up her skull.

'We need to decide.' Oscar's voice came from the centre of the room. She rolled her head towards him. He stood, his arms braced, against the table. If she sat up she knew she'd see the paint semi-finalists. The grey-white champion versus the yellow-white champion. On the table were piled books about interior decoration and colour theory, bought by Oscar. Fingers of paper stuck up from between the pages, marking what he'd found.

A fly buzzed above her head. The plump blue body swerved into Mina's vision. She waited for it to divert to the window or the ceiling light. The path spiralled closer to her face. Could she bear the tiny, sticky feet landing on her cheek?

Mina thought of the sadness in her ovaries ripening into fat figs. If the sadness was coming from her body, there was no point in trying to understand it.

A second buzz joined the fly's. 'It's your phone,' Oscar said.

'I know.'

'Aren't you going to get it?'

'It'll be fine.'

Oscar came towards her, holding out the device. 'It's Dr Helene,' he said.

'Oh, God.'

Mina grabbed the phone. 'Dr Helene.'

'Hi, Mina.'

Mina apologised, probably too many times. How had she forgotten the call? She made noises about time zones, although really it was just that the call had slid to the bottom of her mind, like an old take-out container rotting in the fridge.

'One second, I'll set up Skype.' She carried the laptop to their bedroom and propped it up on a pillow. She was aware that she was wearing one of Oscar's old T-shirts from a marathon run years ago. It was not the garb of a woman who had her life together. At the other end of the video, Dr Helene looked only slightly Cubist. She was wearing the same neutral tones she always did.

'How have you been feeling?'

'Fine,' Mina said.

'How's London?'

'It's okay.'

For a while, they talked about polycystic ovaries and what that might or might not mean. Mina made the mistake of mentioning that she'd read it was genetic.

'Do you want to talk about your mother?' Dr Helene asked.

'Not really. I don't think there's much left to say.'

What new conclusion could be reached about an event that had happened so long ago? Everyone had a family tragedy. Some big and some small. And, anyway, Mina had grown up with a woman who fed her, who loved her, who held her hand as she crossed the street. What did it matter if that woman was her grandmother and not her mother? One of her favourite things about Oscar was that he'd never tried to build a case about who she was on the basis of her parents.

'I don't think it matters whether she had polycystic ovaries, do you? I mean they're ashes on my father's bookshelf.'

When Mina was a teenager, she'd questioned the story of slipping in the bath. She'd fantasised about slit wrists or a bottle of Jameson followed by a drunken stupor. It was all too plausible that the woman left alone with a new baby in a small apartment with cockroaches that crawled up through the toilet had wanted to drown her sorrows in hot water and warm whiskey. Her father had stuck to the slipping story. His face had crumpled when she'd tried to bring it up. She'd wondered what might have been different if her father had come home earlier. But she was over it. Perhaps her mother had had postpartum depression, perhaps she'd had a drink problem, perhaps she'd slipped. It didn't matter.

Dr Helene looked fuzzy and distant. The list of reasons to be sad was seemingly endless. Dead mother, bullying, messed-up ovaries, the general grind of living. On and on they went. And yet all so small when she thought of the children who walked out of war zones to grow up to be dentists and doctors, to be kind and good and fair. Whereas she, spoilt creature, could sit here on this bed talking to a woman paid to be sympathetic. Stupid. Stupid. Stupid.

'And how is the transition going?' Dr Helene asked. By which she meant the transition from pills to no pills.

'It's fine,' Mina said.

'And the mood log?'

'A mix,' Mina said. 'Ups and downs.'

'But there have been ups?' Dr Helene leaned forward encouragingly.

Eventually, the session ran out. Mina closed the call, shut her computer, and got off the bed. In the main room, the fly had stopped humming. Had it escaped?

'How was it?' Oscar asked. He was holding some sheets up to the light.

'Fine,' Mina said.

'Yellow-white,' he said. 'Better to do something than spend all this time deciding.' He looked tall and certain, his posture perfect. Oscar had eyes that changed colour in the light. They could be summer-burnt grass or pine-trunk brown. The evening light caught the flecks of gold.

'Thank you for being here,' she said.

He pulled her into a hug and pressed a kiss onto the top of her head.

Mina shrugged on Oscar's dressing-gown. She had her own but she'd always liked his fuzzy robe better. It fell over her knuckles so that she felt like she was disappearing into it.

She stepped over the platoon of paint cans that lined the hallway. The litres of yellow-white had arrived yesterday.

Oscar sat at the kitchen counter. He was playing that Japanese game on his phone again. He pulled his lips together in concentration. A peep from the phone indicated the mini-game was done and he looked up at her. 'I got a call from Dad. He needs me to go back to the States for a couple of days. He's booked me onto a flight tomorrow. An important client wants a meeting.'

The lemon she took from the fridge was soothing to the touch, but scentless. Her throat was sore and her sinuses were clogged. The damp felt as if it had seeped into her skin. 'Isn't that kind of short notice?' Mina asked.

'Well, they're our biggest client . . .' Oscar paused. 'Do you want to come?"

'Won't it be expensive to get a ticket now?' Mina lined up the knife with the centre of the fruit. If she concentrated on doing this task, everything would be fine. She was a thirty-two-year-old woman whose husband was going on a short trip. That was all. There was no need to get upset. Her lungs felt too big for her ribs. She imagined them bursting out, bits of blood and tissue falling everywhere. Breathe, she thought. This is an overreaction. Just another mood that had got disordered and needed putting back on the correct shelf.

Oscar tapped the edge of the kitchen counter. His fingernail beat a nervy rhythm against the wooden slab. 'We can look for ticket discounts,' he said.

'But?' Juice squirted from the lemon onto her fingers.

'The plan is that Dad and I are going to share a hotel room, so that might be a little difficult . . .' Oscar trailed off. 'Though I'm sure you could crash with Abby or Miranda.' She was confused. Then she remembered that it wasn't possible to just go home. They were sub-leasing the apartment.

Tickets would be expensive. Mina had always thought of the money as their money. Yes, her contributions were uneven. Her adjuncting work had always been precarious. Some semesters she'd been able to pick up three or four classes at universities across the city. In others, one or two. But she'd always contributed everything she had. Now she wasn't working. Soon the savings would not be theirs but his.

It made no sense for her to join. She wasn't needed. Abby or Miranda or any other friend would ask how her research was going and she'd have to smile and smile and smile, and say, 'Oh, really great.'

'I'll be fine,' she said, setting the electrical kettle to boil. It chugged earnestly. Oscar was watching her, but she wasn't sure what to do with her face.

She was dependent on this man. He was a good man. If she made him a dating profile, women would want him. They would admire the ridges of muscle. They'd love his work ethic. If she made herself one? No one would want that. The guys in her high school had had this graph. On one axis was hotness and on the other craziness. And then there was a 45-degree line pointing north-east. Above the line was undatable; under the line was datable. The hotter you were, the crazier you were allowed to be. They plotted the names of

113

all the girls in their class. Had Oscar's friends had a graph like that? What would they have made of her?

'I wanted to come to your next appointment.' Oscar touched her shoulder.

'It's okay. I was okay when you went to your mum's, wasn't I?' She poured in the boiling water and the lemon bobbed to the surface. She sniffed. The steam carried a citrus tang.

He tapped the table again, in that same nervous beat. It felt like he was tapping on her skull. Eventually he stopped and walked over, put his arms around her and kissed her shoulder. He said, 'Promise me you'll be okay.' His lips nibbled the tattooed petals on her arms. She let him take her back to bed and unroll her from the dressing-gown. She tried to look at him like a contented wife looked at her husband. But thinking about her facial expression made it hard to think about anything else. Eventually she suggested they try another angle. The relief of letting her expression relax was a pleasure itself.

Afterwards, her lemon water had gone cold. She gulped it.

'I thought, before I left, we could go to that flower market. The one on Phoebe's blog.' His voice was kind, like a man apologising to his child for missing her school play by offering to buy her ice cream. She knew Oscar thought the equation was simple: Mina likes flowers, so flowers make Mina happy. Perhaps that was how it worked for other people.

After exiting the Tube, they found themselves surrounded by concrete towers and smaller yellow-brick buildings. An English flag, greened and weather-flayed, hung from a window. The air was clammy, like laundry forgotten at the bottom of the machine. Mina followed the blue dot of their bodies moving along her phone map. Was this really where the flower market was?

Around the corner, Columbia Road materialised. The street

was stitched with flowers. Blues and pinks and yellows shone against the October sky.

'Sunflowers, armful for a fiver,' men bellowed, from behind their stalls. Their gravelly voices would've been fit to hawk hot dogs.

'See the size of our lilies today, two for seven.'

The street was thick with people. Couples folded hands together. Girls snapped shots of succulents. Olive trees stood erect in their terracotta pots. Thrusting out from beige buckets were enough roses for a wedding.

Mina's body glanced against the passing crowd. A huge bunch of tiger lilies licked her face as their owner tramped past her. Surely it was not warm enough in England for all this glory? They must have come from overseas.

'See anything you like?' her husband asked.

A fluffy dog squatted on the street to take a shit. It looked like Benson's smaller cousin. She examined the stall to her side, careful to avoid the vendor's gaze. She wasn't ready to buy yet. Mina's eye caught on the pink daisies. They were fifty times the size of the white polka dots that crop up in parks and the pink was sherbet-gaudy.

Pink daisies always made her think of senior year. She'd shared a pink clapboard house with two other girls. The paint had been gentled by the sun to the faint blush found inside a lychee's skin. On Sundays, she and Oscar would go to the store and choose a watermelon. They'd take their time. Mina would caress the sides of the melon and rub the scar where fruit had broken from vine. By the checkout, they'd choose a handful of pink daisies, the cheapest flowers—their guilty extravagance. They'd leave with a watermelon so heavy that the store's plastic bag would bulge under its weight.

At home, Oscar would crack open the big-bellied fruit. Mina would scoop out the inside, gobbing melon into the blender the previous renter had left behind. She'd crack ice from trays. Oscar would add a slug of vodka from the bottle they kept on top of the fridge. They'd set out the daisies in a jar and sit at the rickety kitchen table drinking cold pink drinks, with their pink flowers in their pink playhouse, while mosquitoes raised pink mountains on their legs. She'd imagined their grown-up lives were about to begin.

A woman in rubber boots shoved past her. Everything felt too bright. Mina paused and closed her eyes. Behind the lids she was able to find a calm corner. When she opened them, Oscar was paces ahead of her.

'Wait,' she shouted.

'What's wrong?' he asked, when she caught up with him.

'Nothing,' she said. His face changed, going strange. There was something off about it, like those wax models of celebrities. She tried again, 'It's just I thought our life would be different, you know?'

She put a hand out towards him. He didn't take it.

'I love you,' Oscar said. The silent *but* hung in the air, like a slowly deflating balloon.

She sniffed and looked again at her husband. He was wearing the forest-green sweater they'd chosen together. There was a nick in the shoulder revealing his white T-shirt. It was as bright as sunlight breaking through leaves. He must not have noticed. Oscar did not like to keep clothes with mistakes or imperfections.

'Can you just try,' Oscar said, 'a tiny bit harder?'

'I am trying.' The salt water that was filling her eyes dissolved the flowers into smudges.

'Okay, except you're in a flower market. A flower market! And you're crying at nothing. At literally nothing. Nobody gets the life they thought they would.'

Had he been rehearsing this speech in his head?

'What I mean is, nobody's life is perfect. But most people

116

manage.' Oscar lowered his voice. 'How am I supposed to leave you alone when you behave like this?'

'Like what?' she asked.

'Oh, you know perfectly well. Like this. Mina, I have to go to New York.'

'I'm not stopping you.'

She tried to act as if this was ridiculous. To have any sort of life, you had to at least fake being all right. She could not ask her husband to stay, stroke her hair, and clean away each ferocious thought. If she said she might not be okay, then he and Dr Helene and everyone else would say, 'Take this pill, take that pill'. And she'd take them each day, waiting for them to stop working. She had to be fine.

'But you are. You're crying,' he said.

'Oscar, I told you I'm fine.'

'But you're obviously not. Mina, do you have any idea how tiring it is to always be wondering if you're okay? I need you to meet me halfway. I'm doing everything I can. What else do you need?'

'This isn't all about you. Don't be so patronising.' Rage flapped its ragged wings. And she saw herself as if from a great height—this small tattooed woman with the bleached hair crying for her husband's affection. This small woman dressed to look like a rebel but just begging to be held. Pathetic. Pathetic. So cringingly grateful. There was a lot to be grateful for. These flowers, her health, their marriage, every lucky turn her life had taken. But it was impossible to be forever grateful, forever saying thank you, thank you, thank you, yet to wake up and feel miserable for no reason on earth.

'I'm not trying to patronise you. I'm worried about you.'

'Well, you are.'

'Mina, what do you want me to do? Just tell me what you want me to do.'

She said, 'I'll be fine by myself. I'll be fine. I told you I was fine. You don't need to watch me. It's pointless. You can't possibly watch me for the rest of my life. Are we going to be in the old people's home and you won't go to bingo without me in case I hop on a jet to Switzerland? What do you want from me? What am I supposed to say?'

'I don't know.' Heads turned towards his raised voice. There were too many people and they were too close. She could feel them watching. 'Just try to be happy, Mina. Do that for me?' The words were sour.

'Fuck off, Oscar.'

'Mina—'

'Maybe you should have married someone else. Some nice girl who knows all about paint colours. Some nice girl who can play house while you're away at work. Isn't that what you wanted? Maybe we never should have got married.'

'I can't . . .' He paused. 'I can't talk to you like this. I'll see you at home.'

He turned and began walking. His back became just one more green thing, until he vanished among the blooms.

'Sunflowers, armful for a fiver, three for a tenner. Have you ever seen 'em this big? Andrew—bet you haven't seen anything this big in a long while?'

Mina was distantly aware that the man must be shouting to an assistant, co-worker, or stooge. No one seemed to be acknowledging the height of the blooms. The vendor told some iPhone-toting girls they'd have to pay a pound a photo.

Oscar might be hit by a truck. And her last memory of him would be of his back, rigid and unforgiving. She stared into the crowd trying to see him. He was gone.

It wasn't fair. She had a mental illness. You shouldn't yell at someone who was sick. Except you did. She'd yelled at her grandmother as she began to forget people. It stung to be forgotten. The only grace was that Mina knew her grandmother would forget the rages too.

118

She tried to find a path through the crowd. The pavement was littered with petals. 'Littered' was the word. They looked like so much colourful trash. How had they been destroyed? A child? An unloading accident? A lovers' fight? Looking at the yellow drops of flower-flesh, Mina tried to put the bouquet back together in her mind. Shoes had bruised the gold to brown. She stared with such concentration, the petals seemed to wobble. How had she become the sort of person who could go to a river of flowers and come out with nothing? She looked up at the sky. She dared it to rain.

When she got home, Oscar was packing. On the table, a tall drinking glass was filled with peonies. Each was a bud, the flowers yet to come.

'Thank you,' she said. When Oscar gave a half-smile, she noticed the faintest wrinkles around the corners of his mouth. It was strange to realise that all the years they'd been together had begun to groove those cheeks.

'They're your favourite,' he said.

'How did you . . . You can't get them this time of year.'

'Just saw them in this shop on the way home. And I thought the plan was to get you flowers after all.'

'They're beautiful,' she said. And they were, the petals the pale pink of strawberry juice.

He smiled with half his face. 'Is it me?' he asked.

He placed his skipping rope into the corner of his suitcase. The foam-grip handles lay side by side like a sleeping couple.

'Why would you think that?'

'Well, if your wife tries to . . . on your wedding night, it's hard not to take it a little personally.'

'No . . . that wasn't it.' Madness had hit her the way lightning strikes a tree. She hadn't called it down.

'Why?'

'I can't remember. I told you.'

'You must remember something.'

She supposed she did: months of cake-tasting, spreadsheet-making, guest-list counting, budgeting. She'd joked to Abby that the greatest gift of death was that you didn't have to plan your own funeral. When she'd tried on the dress she'd felt beautiful and blessed. Squeezing into the dress on her wedding day, she'd wondered how she ever thought a corset was a blessing. She remembered standing below the pine-cone bower with her feet hurting. She remembered that the ceremony felt as fake as a poorly acted school play. She remembered feeling everyone looking at her, and knowing she should be happy, that she'd been planning this day for so long, and that she'd laid her head on Oscar's arm so many nights wishing for this day. And yet she'd been numb.

She strained to remember further into the night, trying yet again to force her brain to give her something concrete. Perhaps if she could make herself remember the exact moment. She pushed against the blankness in her brain. Had she taken the pills with water? She had the glimmer of a memory that bathroom-floor tiles had been cold against her bare feet. Had her make-up blurred? Or was she imagining that? What had she thought she was doing? What had she said to Oscar? What had he said to her? Why didn't she have an answer for him now, some simple explanation? This happened and therefore my mind did that.

Oscar was carefully slotting socks into the corners of his suitcase, tucking them under the shirts. His hands were so long and delicate.

'I wanted to marry you,' she said, 'so much.' It was true.

They spoke very little after that, careful not to bruise the tender peace.

Mina went to the gynaecologist's office alone. She wondered what the woman would say that the internet hadn't already explained. The gynaecologist repeated the technician's assurances about the unfatal nature of polycystic ovaries. Mina nodded—okay, okay.

They went over the notes. Her menstruation would be irregular, but it shouldn't pose a health risk.

'So, basically, the answer is do nothing?' Mina asked.

'You're thirty-two?' The gynaecologist frowned.

'Yes,' Mina said, and thought, You're seventy? Sixty-eight? How old is Anna Wintour?

'And you said you're not trying for children? Is that a final decision?'

'I hadn't thought about it,' Mina lied. The world would not let a woman ignore this question. What she meant was that she had come to no conclusions, other than that in the immediate future she couldn't see herself taking care of a mouse, never mind a child.

The gynaecologist's perfectly plucked brows rebuked Mina's wishy-washiness. 'You may struggle to conceive, so we recommend you decide sooner rather than later.' Her fountain pen flew across her notebook. The nib flashed its golden arrow.

'When you do wish to conceive, we recommend you come to us straight away.'

The arrogant pen swashed down the page.

'So, this condition makes a person depressed, hairy, overweight, and possibly diabetic, and you recommend I should have a baby soon?'

'You aren't overweight.'

The gynaecologist had a trim, muscular figure that managed to imply she was one of those people who were capable of reading serious books while using an elliptical machine. Okay, fine, so Mina was average weight. But no gym would sweat off the whispery voice that kept suggesting the world would be a better place without her. And now they were saying this voice might be a twisted part of her reproductive organs. But, hey, at least so far, she wasn't too heavy, which she should, apparently, now deem a medical blessing. Mina pinched the soft patch of her inner elbow.

'Some patients have concerns that are helped by speaking to a therapist. I can refer you to a therapist.'

'No, thank you,' Mina said. 'I'm all right for now. I'll call you if I decide I want to have babies.'

Standing on the street, she wondered if it was too late to call Oscar. She realised she could check. The stalking app worked both ways. She opened it to be told her husband was offline, which must mean he was in the air. It didn't tell her if he hadn't texted because security had been a bitch or because he was still upset with his weepy wife.

Mina texted Phoebe: *Busy?*

They made plans to meet the next day. The promise of Phoebe's presence seemed to speed Mina's step, like one of those airport walkways that boost each traveller along.

She took the bus home, sitting on the top deck. At each stop she peered down at the parted hair and bald patches of strangers. She decided to do something to make it up to Oscar. She could start repainting the flat now. He'd be pleased to see the work begun. Each room would be white and clean, ready for strangers to fling mortgages at. And then she and

Oscar would leave this place and go back to New York. Their friends would ask what they had done, and she would describe how she'd painted the flats, how good the pain had felt in her muscles, how it had refreshed her to move away from academic life, and now she was ready again to begin work.

On her phone, she asked the internet how hard it was to remove wallpaper. The answer was that it was quite difficult, but the success rates seemed higher than suicide. Was it still gallows humour if you were trying not to die? A YouTube video of a man in blue rubber gloves explained how to remove wallpaper, using a stainless-steel scraper, a perforating tool and fabric softener. The tools were puzzling to Mina, who had grown up in a rented flat, the white walls softening to grey over the years. But the man, smiling under his moustache, promised it could all be bought at your local hardware store. Where was hers? Google told her close by. She got off the bus a stop early.

The clerk guided her to the tools. As she walked home, implements clanking joyfully, it was almost possible to pretend she had gone out only for tools and not to be told of all the ways in which her body was wrong.

She pulled back the couch and stared at the expanse of wall. The birds clutched their strawberries, gazing back with mad indigo eyes. Two-thirds fabric softener, one-third water, the man had said, and Mina drenched the flock. She wedged the stainless-steel scraper under the seam of the wallpaper. It took a careful twist and flick of the wrist to prise it up. Then she ripped. The paper was sticky. The smell of gluey lavender filled her nose. Rip. Rip. The shreds made her think of pulling the skin from her own lip. Ripping and ripping. Her nail broke, bending under the force. She put the finger into her mouth—a mistake: bitter soap bloomed across her taste-buds.

She pulled over a chair to reach the top of the wall. The chair wobbled as she jerked her arm. She tore birds in half.

Beaks and wings scattered. Goodbye, birds. Goodbye. Paper coasted to the floor.

She'd once had a therapist who'd told her to imagine a perfectly peaceful place. The exercise sent her into despair. She couldn't make such a place feel real. The therapist should have told her to imagine the joy of tearing a wall to shreds.

She should have started with 5B, not in the flat they lived in. It was too late now. Birds drifted under chair legs and onto the couch. She would show her husband that she was trying. Her arms ached from the effort.

By now, Oscar's plane would've landed back home in America. Was America home? Mina thought of her grand-mother, who'd never returned to Shanghai. Grandma said that during the Cultural Revolution her China died. Mina missed the spare ribs that Grandma used to get delivered, demanding that they be cut so that each big bone became three grand-daughter-ready pieces. Mina ate those ribs even after she became vegetarian. She would've done worse to keep her grandmother happy.

She jumped off the chair. Her feet landed in the slurry of paper. She picked stray scraps off the couch. She'd need to buy something to cover the floor. She scrubbed the mugs she'd left to soak in the sink. She tossed the coffee grounds. She thought of the list of things that made her happy: hexagonal tiles, sharpening pencils, black jeans.

Mentally, she rewrote it: tearing off wallpaper, waking up late and realising there was one less hour to live through, sharpening pencils. Phoebe's mouth floated into her mind. Phoebe's mouth made her happy. Perhaps it should be Oscar's. But that mouth had so much history. It had been tasted too often to conjure any emotion as simple as happiness. Didn't they say that if you eat the same food every day your taste-buds numb to the flavour?

No, that wasn't quite right. She loved that mouth. She loved the way it turned down at the corners when he smiled and the rigorous whiteness of the well-flossed teeth. But that mouth was part of the body that had left her in the street because she was crying. He'd apologised. It wasn't a big deal. There was no need to start crying again.

Oscar plugged his phone into the socket next to the hotel bed. The room had twin beds, one shower, one TV, one telephone, and two Bibles. His father stood at the sideboard. His shoes were laid out on one of the free maps from the hotel lobby. A brogue obliterated all of Lower Manhattan. His father dabbed on black polish. Oscar had polished his own shoes before his flight and they made a neat pair by the door.

His father was tall. Six foot one. Taller than Oscar, actually. Perhaps it was the hamburgers that had supplemented his father's California childhood. The height was easy to forget because, although they talked on the phone almost daily, he hardly saw the man. The longest they'd spent together was the trip to Tokyo they'd taken at the end of Oscar's third year at Umeda Trading. In Tokyo, his father's Californian switched into a jangle of Japanese. What did they call it? *Perapera*—the onomatopoeic word for fluency or chatter. *Perapera perapera.* Yes, that was what it had sounded like. Meanwhile, Oscar had been trying to wedge into his head phrases for *It is good to meet you, I commend myself to your care. I am sorry. I have made a mistake. I am sorry my Japanese is not very good.* If he'd been the child of married people, his voice would have known the correct ways to lilt. They'd travelled to Tokyo so that Oscar could be added to the Umeda family register. The register was required for bank accounts, inheritance, every little thing. His father had suggested it would be easier if Oscar changed his name to Umeda worldwide.

He wasn't a Shepard any more. Shepard had been written on his school assignments, his passport, even his socks. His mother spent hours sewing in name-tapes, swearing under her breath as she pricked her fingers. The clothing had to be christened, because Oscar Shepard was all that would distinguish it from a thousand other boys' sweaty cotton. At the time, he hadn't wanted to go away to school. But Mum had said he was lucky to have a dad who could stump up the fees.

'Dad?'

'Mmm?'

'Thanks for letting us paint the flats ourselves.'

His father sighed and held the shoe to the light. 'I don't want to be hard on you. I was young once too. But you have to stay focused. Hungry?' his father asked.

'A little.'

His father removed a fat-bellied rice cooker from his suitcase. It bleeped jovially as it was plugged in. Next appeared a Ziploc bag of rice. The grains had the semi-transparency of seashells. His father placed a bottle of tamago furikake seasoning on the TV stand. Sesame seeds, deep green shreds of seaweed and crumbs of dried egg showed through the glass bottle.

'I brought these for breakfast, but I'll put some on now.'

'Thanks, Dad.'

'Breakfast is so overpriced in hotels,' his father said. They didn't need to save eighteen dollars on breakfast. The golden script that flowed along the linings of his father's brogues and the many-dialled watch that spun on his wrist argued otherwise. But while Kenichi Umeda dressed in silk and cashmere, he loved squeezing in a dollar or two more of profit.

His father dropped handfuls of rice into the rice cooker's metal bowl. He carried it to the bathroom. Oscar heard the gush of water as his father rinsed the starch off the rice.

The phone lit to tell him the battery had returned. He logged onto the hotel WiFi. Mina had sent a photo of a blotchy beige rectangle. Modern art? A phone error? He scrolled up. *De-wallpapering!!* And a happy emoji. Before he could take in that this was a photo of the apartment's wall, he saw the sentence above it. *Gyno said having kids prob hard.*

A kid. What would their life be like with a kid? He saw that cab ride back from the bridge a second time, and in this version a small person perched between them. A child with curly hair and Mina's dainty cat-like nose. A child he'd have to feed, clothe and shelter from the world and from its mother. They couldn't have children. It was only logical so why did he feel like he was losing something? He couldn't reply, *Don't worry, you're obviously not fit to be a parent.* He was so tired of coming up with the nicer way of phrasing things.

His father kneeled by the rice cooker, pressing buttons. Oscar had to invent something kind to say to Mina. But this was exhausting. He'd think of something tomorrow. On his phone's to-do list, he made a note: *Nice message to M.*

Eventually a column of steam rose from the rice cooker's vent and the pillowy smell of rice filled the room. From the roller suitcase his father extracted a rice paddle, two bowls and spoons.

'Eileen Johnson, what's she like?' his father asked.

The head buyer was neither attractive nor unattractive. Her eyes were capped with what seemed to be green contact lenses. They were too bright to be natural. She maintained aggressive eye contact. His impression had been of a woman who knew what she wanted.

'She's quite demanding,' Oscar said.

The rice cooker sang the 'Twinkle, Twinkle, Little Star' melody. His father got on his hands and knees to attend to it, filling the bowls with rice. Oscar wondered if he should have jumped to serve or whether that would have been rude. Neither the Japanese app nor the evening classes he took in

NYC had instructed on the etiquette of touching another man's rice cooker. His father handed him a bowl.

'Do you think she's upset?' his father asked. 'Have they tried to send anything back? Anything in their communications about a problem?' He chewed, and his lean jaw moved from left to right.

'No, no. I don't think she can be unhappy. She would've just stopped future orders by email. Or made an underling call us.' Oscar took a bite of rice, which was soft and delicate. The sweet-salt of the furikake blended with the chubby grains.

His father sighed. 'I guess we'll find out in the morning.'

For a while they ate in silence and then his father said, 'You know my friend Imada at the Nagata brewery?'

No, I don't, Oscar thought, because you say my Japanese is too weak. 'You've mentioned him,' he said.

'He retired. Wants to spend time with his granddaughter. And the kid who took over, just forty-two, would you believe it, says he can't keep up our old deal. Little asshole.'

His father had special relationships with so many of the suppliers, drinking buddies who gave them the best price. Even passing the Japanese Language Placement Test wouldn't teach Oscar how to replicate that. But he had to start somewhere.

'That's the way things are going. All those online order forms. Nobody wants to have an actual telephone conversation any more.'

Oscar's body was on Greenwich Mean Time. He choked down a yawn.

'You can sleep,' his father said.

'I'm fine. It's just jet lag. So, what's the new guy's name? Do you think we should keep working with them?'

'We'll see.'

Oscar always stretched before bed. He tried not to feel self-conscious in his boxers as he dropped into a plank. Today he would try to hold it for five minutes. He liked the plank because it proved that sometimes staying in place is as hard as moving. Harder, even. It was the sort of strength he was training for. He had to be strong enough to hold his position. At the three-minute mark his abdominals quaked. At the four-minute mark, they seared. Without moving his feet, he adjusted his weight from left to right to left and back to centre. It was the smallest of respites. At five, he dropped to his knees.

Phoebe suggested a pub lunch. Mina had never had a pub lunch. The last time she'd been in a pub had been in Providence for St Patrick's Day. Someone had ordered her a green beer.

The Moorhen was not Irish. The walls were the soft yellow of hollandaise. The bar was long and beaded with amber bottles, which caught the sun. The couples who sat drinking or nibbling roast carrots were young and as groomed as the dogs that lay in the shadows of their tables.

The waiter led her through glass to a terrace. Phoebe sat, Benson at her feet. Behind and below her was a stretch of canal. With his hind leg, the dog scratched himself. The paw flickered and blurred. His ears shook with the violence of it. His collar tinkled. The October day had a pinch in the air and she was jealous of his enormous fur coat.

'Benson, remember me?' Mina put out her hand to be sniffed. Knitting-needle teeth were visible behind the round lip. She reckoned he could bite down to her lifeline if he chose.

'I ordered us both Buck's Fizz,' Phoebe said. 'I know they're uncool, but the ones here are great.'

'I don't think I've had that before.'

'Orange juice and champagne. Or in this case, I suspect, sparkling wine.'

'Oh. Mimosas. Wonderful.' Mimosas were poured from pitchers every New York Saturday.

From the canal came a squall. Two geese writhed their necks, like beaky snakes.

'You live near here?' Mina asked.

'No. Well, kind of. Theo does.' Phoebe's long fingers teased the dog's caramel coat. 'I suppose if I live anywhere I live here. But tonight I'm banned between seven and midnight or I'll become a pumpkin.'

'A pumpkin?'

'Theo's planning on bringing a girl over and doesn't want me spoiling the mood.' Phoebe patted Benson. 'Not you either, poppet. Theo doesn't like you very much, does he?' The dog rolled over, mouth open, tongue hanging drunkenly to the side. 'I don't know if I would've adopted this hand-some guy if I'd known I was getting divorced. It's hard enough to find a place to crash when your husband got most of the couple-friends. And there are allergies, small children, smaller dogs . . . Benson wouldn't hurt a fly but . . .'

'Do you want to talk about it? The divorce, I mean.'

'Not really. I've already paid my lawyer far too much to listen to that nonsense.' Phoebe turned away to look at the weed-veiled water. A barge's prow pierced the sheet of green, pushing up black wavelets. The boat's sides were painted with gigantic ferns. The artist had been more enthusiastic than skilled and the plants curved manically.

'Did you know ferns were originally sea-plants? They had to evolve their way ashore,' Mina said, and immediately felt dumb. Why was she telling Phoebe things she'd learnt in elementary school?

The mimosas came. Mina sipped to fill the silence. Phoebe knocked back half of the drink. The attractively typeset menu displayed only two vegetarian options. They talked about the news, which was gloomy. Politicians were terrible. Somehow that swerved to overpriced pet-sitters. Phoebe's hands waltzed as she talked. Once in a while she'd stop, lean forwards, her eyes meeting Mina's, and ask, 'Right?' And Mina nodded.

The simple conversation was delicious. Benson settled his chin on Mina's foot.

After her second mimosa, Phoebe said, 'Sorry, I'm in a strange place in my life. The short version is that my husband, ex-husband, fell in love with a paediatrician who runs marathons for leukaemia research.'

'He's an idiot,' Mina said, and waited for the long version.

Phoebe finished her drink, ran a finger around the rim of the champagne glass, and said, 'It's cold out here, isn't it? What's taking the food so long? Should we get another drink?' The waiter, when Phoebe waved him over, promised the food would be there in five minutes.

He left, and Phoebe leaned forwards as if telling Mina a secret that no one else in the pub deserved to hear. 'For most of uni, I was dating this girl, Camilla. Milly that's what everyone called her. And my parents hated her. I mean they'd never say it was because she was a girl. We're not that sort of family. But they were always asking about her nose ring, like if it meant anything? And then I started up with Brendan and they fucking loved him. So when he asked me to marry him, I thought why not? I wanted to get on with my life. I wanted the choices to be over and the real thing to start. Brendan snored. All he ever wanted to do was come home and watch Sky Sports. But I hate the idea of him slobbering all over that woman. Is that awful?' With each sentence, Phoebe gave an ashamed dip of her head.

'Probably a normal amount of awful. Some things aren't meant to be.' Mina tried to picture Phoebe with this older man. She envisioned a moustache snuffling against Phoebe's delicate neck.

All her adult life Mina had been with Oscar. It was impossible to imagine life without him. She would never be able to finish a bag of spinach.

Phoebe said, 'Ugh. You're too good a listener. Now I've overshared.'

Mina wasn't sure if that was a compliment or not, so she just made a helpless expression.

'I promise I don't normally go on about myself like this.'

'I like listening,' she said.

'That's nonsense. Everyone likes talking about themselves. Tell me something about you.'

Mina considered her options. I want to run my tongue along the dent in your collarbone that your top has made visible. Nope. Sometimes I want to die and sometimes I want to buy a box of tomatoes and stand by the fridge eating them out of a paper carton and I don't understand how I can hold both desires. Nope.

'Sometimes I wish I hadn't taken Oscar's last name.'

'Why did you? I mean, lots of women don't, these days.'

'I didn't want him to be alone with it. You see, he had his mom's name growing up.' Mina stopped, embarrassed. Phoebe would know that. They would have scraped their knees on the same trees. Maybe she even wrote him Christmas cards, addressing Oscar Shepard in wobbling gel-pen script. Mina braved onwards. 'It wasn't till he'd been working for his dad that he got it changed to Umeda. I don't get it myself. But Oscar's weird about his dad. I wanted to keep him company.' When he'd asked her to take his name, he had been repotting the cacti. There was soil spread over the table. The little green bodies languished on newspaper. He was lining the glass bowl with pebbles. The way he placed one stone beside the other with such care made her say, 'Yes.' And she hadn't ever taken it back. 'I guess I don't regret it, really. It's just I never planned on taking a man's name.'

'There's so much I never . . .'

Mina's risotto came, crescented with mushrooms. Phoebe ate pink-hearted roast beef. Mina wanted to remember this meal. She wanted to remember the hot porcini on her cold lips and the way Phoebe's eyes glittered in the cold air. As a child, Mina had kept a diary. The entries were all meals. Tuesday: dumplings. Wednesday: steamed fish. Thursday: chicken nuggets. She supposed that was why so much blogging was about food. It was a child's diary turned multimedia.

The bill was more than Mina had calculated. Champagne and orange juice had addled her mathematics. Putting down the bankcard, her fingers clenched. This wasn't a good use of funds. But Oscar had said she was to be happy. It was only one lunch.

Phoebe stood to go. Dread punched Mina in the stomach. She didn't want to go back to the empty apartment. She just didn't. She couldn't be alone, her only company a phone that Oscar seemed content to ignore.

'Stay at our place,' Mina said.

'What?'

'We have a sofa that's probably as comfy as your brother's.'

'I don't want to impose.'

'You're not imposing. Oscar's away for work. You can keep me company. Unless you have plans, which I guess you probably do.'

Phoebe tucked a loose curl behind her ear. 'Uh, I don't have anything on. If you're sure. I'd need to grab a change of clothes. But my brother's place is only a fifteen-minute walk or so—up Highbury Fields way. Are you sure it's okay?'

Mina reassured her yet again that it was fine. It was ridiculous for Phoebe to sit around waiting for her brother to finish fucking when Mina was perfectly happy to have her over. Phoebe smiled. Mina glanced at the crooked tooth and felt her own mouth crook upwards in response.

As they walked, Phoebe pointed out the place that had the best coffee, the place that had the best cheese, the pub in which her best friend had been broken up with. Mina felt a zip of jealousy that she was not this best friend. Although how could she be?

Benson jerked forwards into a coven of pigeons, dragging Phoebe behind him. The birds exploded upwards. Phoebe yelped and hid her face with her hands. The pigeons settled on top of the bus stop. But the hands still masked Phoebe's face.

'It's okay,' Mina said. 'They're gone.'

'Snakes are fine,' Phoebe said. 'Or mice. Or rats. But pigeons? They fly. I always feel like they're going to touch my face.'

Mina wanted to hug her, but said instead, 'I don't know. They always make me think of my grandma. She used to feed them. Which I guess is a bit of a thing: old lady plus pigeons. It started because of the Meals on Wheels delivery. That's this service they have in the States where these people bring food to the elderly. Do you have it here?'

Phoebe nodded. Mina described how each meal on wheels came in a cardboard tray with a day's serving of butter, a single serving of milk, a single piece of fruit and a micro-waveable entrée. These her grandmother ate at the kitchen table. But she'd ignore the single slice of plastic-wrapped bread. The slices stacked up inside the decrepit refrigerator. The machine had been older than Mina and had a heavy door.

'I suggested we donate the bread to the homeless. But Grandma thought they might be insulted. She thought bread wouldn't do them much good. She wouldn't let me eat it. She'd heard something on the radio about pre-sliced bread lacking nutrition.'

Nor was Mina allowed to toss it out the day it arrived. Even the suggestion caused her grandmother's lips to pucker. Her grandmother did not throw things out. She did not dispose of restaurant flyers or old shoes. Inside its packaging the bread seemed cryogenically frozen. It lasted for months. Each day, when Mina got home from high school, she checked for dots of mould. Mould rendered the bread irredeemable and therefore disposable. Mina tried to talk to her father about it, on one of the rare evenings he was home. He said that Grandma grew up in the war. That was why she could not toss out good food.

'Then I was doing the vacuuming. Grandma's back wasn't great by then and my dad was always working. Anyway, I was vacuuming, and *Mary Poppins* was running on TV in the background. And I looked up to see the pigeon lady sitting on the steps of some British church. I guess you would know which one.'

'Not a clue,' Phoebe said.

'Well, that's what gave me the idea.'

On a Saturday, they went to the park. Her grandma wore a straw fedora bought on sale at Century 21. It was tilted back on her head, like an old-world gangster's. Mina tore open the tricky plastic wrappers and her grandmother threw the bread. 'That's when she told me.' Mina tried to capture the half-humorous tone her grandmother had used. *'Before I retired, I never saw pigeons. I was busy busy busy. Now, pigeons everywhere.'*

Her grandmother died. The bread had stopped coming. Mina became too busy for pigeons. But the birds remained. 'Ugh, sorry, you didn't ask for my life history.' She chewed the inside of her lip.

Phoebe said, 'Your grandma seems like a cool lady.'

'She was,' Mina said.

Phoebe stopped in front of a brass-knockered door and dug around in her bag for a key. The house was one of many in a long terrace. It seemed somewhere that Mary Poppins would have worked, full of scuffed children and Christmas pudding. But the many doorbells indicated it had been split

136

into apartments. Phoebe slipped into the hall, Benson at her heels. Mina followed them up a narrow staircase to Theo's apartment. Inside, a guitar was strapped to the wall. Iridescent abalone chips jewelled the neck. In front of the lifeboat-sized TV there was a leather couch. Phoebe slept on it. Every night her cheek pressed down on the black seat. Mina let her fingers skim the slippery surface.

Three large suitcases stood in a corner: one waxed canvas and two nylon, as if divorce was only a very long vacation. Mina sat on the couch while Phoebe unzipped the canvas suitcase. As she bent down, her tight jeans traced the ω of her ass. In the right pocket a coin pressed its outline in the taut denim. It was a truly lovely rear end. Odd that such a thing existed, given all asses were fundamentally quite similar, just two slabs of flesh side by side. But there it was: Phoebe's beautiful behind.

Perhaps it was Mina's absorption that meant she didn't hear feet coming up the stairs or the key in the door.

'Pheeb,' Theo said. His tie was pulled loose and lay lop-sidedly on his shirt.

'Theo, hi, I was just picking some stuff up. I didn't think you'd be home now.'

'I forgot a file.'

'Good news. I'm getting out of your hair for the night. Mina's taking me in.'

'Great.' Theo pulled out his phone and stared briefly at the screen. Mina looked for the sibling resemblance and found it only in the tender pink of the earlobes and the narrowness of the upper lip. On Phoebe the lip was a coy prelude to the modest swell of the lower. On Theo, it was just half an unre-markable mouth.

'Hi, Theo,' she said.

'Mina, hi, sorry, I've just got this work thing. I can't really talk about it.' He stepped over the coffee table to a translucent plastic box by the window. The lid came off with a violent snap. He grabbed a file. 'Look, I have to get back. But, it was, uh, great to see you. Say hi to Oscar for me.'

Seconds after he shut the door behind him, Phoebe said, 'Dickhead. Look at me, I'm a big important barrister.'

Mina wondered if he'd tell Oscar he'd seen her with Phoebe. Why hadn't Oscar called to say he'd arrived safely? He hadn't even texted.

The buyer's office was located in a tower so high that Oscar's neck ached looking up at it. In the one short month he'd been in England he'd lost the habit of height. London had a few tall buildings. New York was a porcupine. This tower was one of its many quills. Beyond the rotating brass door, Oscar and his father had to supply a security guard with their names and ID before being issued with a badge each. It allowed them to swipe through another set of barriers to the elevator banks. A screen the size of a paperback book was embedded in the side of the elevator. On it, Oscar read the wind speed, humidity and temperature of the city outside. Animated clouds bobbed along a digital sky.

His phone vibrated. It was probably Mina. He visualised a lead wall lining his skull and repelling the non-work-related emotions trying to batter their way inside. He switched the phone to Do Not Disturb. But then, because he couldn't stop himself, he flicked open his phone's tracking app. There at home was the little icon of his wife. Inside the bubble was her profile photo, the same one she used for Facebook. Mina in her wedding dress. At home. Safe. Nothing to worry about.

The lift led into a reception room. Screens attached to the walls glowed with dewy peaches. The displays flicked to a white man holding a whiter lamb. Oscar thought the man was probably an actor. His father approached the receptionist to explain they had an appointment with Eileen Johnson.

Oscar's stomach clenched as the screen flicked to a shot of a man on a yacht drinking red wine. They'd been steadily ordering the IPA. There had been no mess-ups in shipment. Had there been a deterioration in quality? How could he reassure Eileen Johnson?

The receptionist led them through a narrow hall to a conference room. The window gave a view onto New York's glassy glory. From this far up the city looked like a sculpture and not a place where humans lived. He could just about see the river that had eaten one of his wife's flip-flops. He pushed the thought away.

'Sit,' Eileen Johnson commanded. She was seated at the head of the table, a MacBook flipped open in front of her. A half-drunk cup of coffee rested by her hand. The hand itself was large and heavily ringed in gold. His father took the chair nearest to her. Oscar took the one beside it. Eileen Johnson narrowed her too-green eyes at them.

He put out a hand towards her. 'Oscar, we met before.' Eileen Johnson didn't reach out to shake it. That was just as well because the Band-Aid was peeling. He tucked the hand into his pocket. Oscar continued, 'And this is our CEO, Kenichi Umeda.'

'Please call me Ken.'

Eileen Johnson shut her laptop. 'We've been loving the pale ale. Loving it. The owl thing is cute. But not too, you know, too cute.' The brewery's logo was a wide-eyed owl with a tubby stomach. The bird was on their bottles.

Oscar replied, 'That's wonder—'

Eileen Johnson interrupted, 'The thing is Japan was a big deal decades ago. Decades. They eat sushi in Nebraska now. Thai food was five years ago. Mongolian is the thing now. Or Nepali. So I wasn't sure about your product. But, you know, the people in Nebraska, they need groceries too. Japan is just the right amount of accessible. And we've been thinking it's

139

going to have a second wave. A second tsunami, if you will.'
She snorted at her own joke. Oscar gave the smile he always
gave when a client mentioned ninjas, samurai or tsunamis.
His father nodded and said nothing. 'But it's also got to have
something new. Something to get people talking. So, what
I'm thinking, what we're thinking, is that in the spring we're
going to do a big Japan thing. Cherry blossoms and so on.
And we'd like you to be part of that. We want products that
feel novel. Exciting, but not too challenging. Not too strange.
In most households, women buy the groceries. Cute would
be good. Something like the ale, but new. Different. Something
we can get excited about. We're rolling this out across the
country. So we need to get organised. Get ready. I assume you
can prepare me some options.'

She widened her eyes. The green irises became islands in
a milky sea.

'Yes, of course,' Oscar said. 'What sort of time frame were
you imagining?'

A few ideas began to simmer in the back of his head. But
he wanted to check prices. His father would need to check
which craft breweries had the capacity to meet the grocery
store's vast demand.

'A month,' she said. 'My secretary will email you.'

The meeting had taken less time than it took the flight
attendant to hand out Oscar's meal on the plane. But clients
were clients and big clients were big clients. He didn't want
his face or his father's to be forgotten. It was better that they
stick in her mind.

As he and his father waited for the elevator, Oscar pulled
out his phone. He didn't have to type in his password. Mina's
messages hovered onscreen.

Are you alive?

?

?

140

?
?
Yes, he typed. *Busy sorry.*

They stepped out into the sun. Across the street in Bryant Park, office workers used plastic utensils to cram lunches down. As they walked past a woman forking up a terrarium of salad, Oscar asked his father if he wanted to get lunch in the hotel.

'Is there somewhere fast around here?'

'Yeah.' Oscar paused. 'Are you in a hurry?'

'I'd like to go back to the hotel and take a nap.'

He'd never thought of his father as a napper, but the man was getting older. 'There's a Japanese bookstore with lunch bentos on the second floor,' he suggested. He guided his father past bright spines, figurines, manga, and posters of wide-eyed magical girls to the food corner. Inside the black plastic bentos were golden tempura prawns, rectangles of white rice, and katsu pork. His father grabbed a bento and a green triangle of matcha cake. Oscar chose two salmon-stuffed rice balls.

His father spotted a table next to a group of technicolour-haired teenagers. They were jabbering about exams and someone named Chloë. Their purple and green drinks glittered with ice.

Oscar said, 'That was promising, don't you think?'

'Any ideas about what to pitch?' His father snapped open the disposable chopsticks, rubbing them together to remove the chance of a splinter.

'A few.'

As he chewed his rice, Oscar tried to construct the customer Eileen Johnson was trying to reach: a woman who wanted a drink that felt Japanese. Given the chain's demographic, this was a woman with some disposable income and who was into health foods. Perhaps he could try the sweet-potato IPA. Sweet potatoes seemed to be cropping up in every vegan, Paleolithic, clean-eating health book. He was unsure about the gender implications. Only 25 per cent of beer drinkers were female, which some in the industry saw as a law and others saw as an opportunity for expansion. Oscar suspected the owl ales attracted more women.

Would Mina buy a drink because it had an owl on? Maybe. He pictured her on tiptoe, reaching upwards, the hem of her dress rising. Mina, do owls make you happy?

Normally when deciding what product to pitch, Oscar would choose a few possibilities and throw a party. He'd see what was finished and what was ignored. He'd note what his guests asked about and what they Instagrammed. His stock of drinks was in mini-storage. Transporting them to England would be difficult. Mid-air leaks were not ideal.

His father had moved on to the cake. He paused, fork holding a scruffy pyramid of sponge. 'Would you like some?'

'I'm fine.' Oscar avoided refined sugars when he could. They fucked up insulin levels and muscle development. He got out his phone and typed in the notes:

(a) Source drink selection.
(b) Shortlist—consult industry ppl?
(c) Pitch

It was a simple list but it was good to have everything written out.

His father cleared his throat. 'I was talking to Ami, and she was thinking it would be nice to see you. You could work on the pitch at our place. And we should start thinking about next quarter generally. It would be easier to go over the books in person.' *Our place* meant the new house on a cutesy island near Seattle. He'd never been. The couple had moved there last year. For work Oscar visited their flat in LA, a place with huge windows that let in the disconcerting blue of the Los

Angeles sky. He'd kept the trips short. What was it people said? House guests, like fish, go off after three days?

Oscar's flight back to England was on a flexible ticket. They hadn't been certain what exactly Eileen Johnson needed or how long it would take. He could move the flight back. Could Ami really want to see him? Oscar's father's wife had always been polite. At his wedding, she'd kissed him on both cheeks. She'd signed his birthday cards. But she couldn't like to be reminded of her husband's bastard son.

'I should probably get back to Mina,' he said. 'She's already started stripping the wallpaper.'

'She can manage without you for a few days.' His father frowned.

Oscar had a sense that just as you might use up your sick days, he was using up his son-days.

When he'd hated his father, it had been less complicated. By Oscar's fourteenth birthday, he was away at school. His father had arranged to pick him up and take him into the village for a meal. Oscar had already seen his mum for the exeat and she'd given him an envelope with twenty pounds inside because he was 'too old for toys'. He couldn't remember what he'd spent it on. But holding the envelope, he'd been struck by how light adulthood felt.

As Oscar had waited for his father, he'd played Snake on his Nokia. The pixellated serpent had grown so long it almost filled the screen. Baush, from the year below, stuck his head in the door and said, 'Your dad's with the housemaster.' Oscar looked up and lost the game. Not a good start.

The country fathers drove down in Range Rovers. The city fathers had their sons to stay in London, and the sons bought uppers from their friends in day school and came back with tales of neon nights. Oscar's father was neither of these. His father stood under the halogen lighting looking foreign. He stared like a tourist, his skull rolling around on a skinny neck.

In the taxi, his father asked about his classes. They were fine. Oscar mentioned he'd made the D team for football. And his father, a man Oscar was sure didn't know the difference between a penalty and a goal-mouth scramble, frowned.

'The D team?' he asked. 'As in A, B, C, D?'

Oscar nodded.

'Okay, then,' said his father. 'The D team.'

Oscar didn't bother explaining that many boys didn't make any team. The D team had matches at other schools. Afterwards they sheltered from the rain eating the Mars Bar minis that the games teacher gave out only on match days.

The lunch had been booked at the place that the school recommended parents took their sons. The menu written in chalk on the wall suggested chicken and potatoes or roast beef and potatoes or pork chops and potatoes, all with the obligatory carrots and peas. It must have been Sunday. Some details of the day had got lost. Probably there were some other boys there—no one Oscar cared about. Then Theo's family clattered in, mother, father, Theo and the red-headed sister, gnome-like with goggling eyes too large for her face. Theo shouted, 'Shepard!' and Theo's mother came over. Oscar's father had stuck out his hand, awkward and too formal. Oscar could still remember the sweat of wrongness that came over him as their hands touched. Theo started on how he'd been away for the weekend and he'd left his notes for Geography at home and could he copy Oscar's? They were doing something about river-systems and oxbow lakes, or perhaps that was the year after. Oscar's father asked about Gloucester. But he kept saying it weird. Even when Theo's dad said it right, Oscar's father continued with his 'Glow-sester.'

Theo's family went for their own meal. Although Oscar

had his back to their table, every ten minutes he heard Theo's father snort into laughter. Oscar's father did not eat the potatoes and that struck Oscar as effeminate. He ate all of his own in thick sweeps of gravy, even though his stomach hurt. Very quickly they ran out of things to say to each other. In the cab on the way back Oscar had asked, 'Why do you bother coming?'

'It's your birthday.'

'Well, don't bother,' Oscar said.

And the next year his father hadn't shown up. Or the one after that. It was the end of birthdays. Though the cards still came, signed *Dad & Ami*.

Oscar thought of his tasks. He visualised a crane carefully placing the long iron joists of a skyscraper in position.

I.   Make this sale. His father had a cellar: in peace and quiet he could work quickly.

II. Sell the flats. He could handle some of that long distance surely.

III. Get Mina sorted. Would Mina be okay? By herself? She'd been fine while he was at his mother's. She herself had said it was impossible for him to watch her forever.

Triage. He had to triage. The term, borrowed from French military hospitals, had always appealed to him. Let the healthy soldiers take care of themselves. The flats would be fine. Abandon the soldiers too wounded to save: Mina. And tend those you can: this job. Of course he wouldn't abandon Mina. He'd be home soon. By then he'd have figured out what to say about the baby issue.

His father sighed. 'Look, there's something I've been wanting to talk to you about.'

'What?'

'I don't want to get into it here.' His father looked around

145

at the teenagers slurping taro smoothies. Oscar was so tired of deciphering the crinkled foreheads of everyone around him. What message was he supposed to read in these scrawls?

'Let me check with Mina,' he said.

'Great. I'll tell Ami you're coming.'

Mina had somehow forgotten the apartment's disarray, until they walked through the door. Wallpaper hung like an open wound. Everything smelled of fabric softener.

'Sorry, it's a bit of a mess. We've been redecorating.'

Phoebe walked up to the gap Mina had torn in the wallpaper. Her hand followed the rip until she was crouching on the floor. Leaves of paper curled, abandoned, by the gash. Mina rushed to collect them. They'd dried out in the hours she'd been away. Phoebe caught one as it escaped Mina's grip.

'Relax. You're a guest,' Mina said.

'I want to.'

'You don't have to. I didn't invite you over to clean up. Please. I'll vacuum tomorrow. It'll be easier.'

The dog charged into this stand-off. He rolled over. His tail knocked more paper into the air.

Phoebe rubbed an indulgent hand on his belly. 'Who's a useless boy? You are, yes, you are.'

They ordered Chinese, which came in steam-clouded plastic. She ate Buddha's Delight. The deep-fried tofu was greasy. But the oil was delicious and the tofu seared gold. She wondered what Grandma would've made of the English girl sitting beside her, noodle dangling over her lip onto the pointed chin. She probably would've shrugged and rolled her eyes as she did at cell phones, video games, the president, and everything else the last decades had spat up.

As they ate, they watched an animated kids' movie full of adult jokes. Mina had missed it in cinemas. The idea of seats roiling with toddlers had felt like too much. It was probably for the best that she was officially not good mother material. The light from the screen made Phoebe look ghostly. The edge of her hair flickered, like a burning thing. As they sat knee-to-knee on the couch, Mina realised that it was far too small for Phoebe to sleep on. It was more a loveseat than a proper couch. Phoebe would have to take the bed. Mina would sleep better in this small space than she could alone on a big mattress thinking of Phoebe crammed on these stiff cushions. As the drama of the movie wound tighter, Phoebe leaned forwards as if trying to dive into the laptop. It worked out okay, as Mina knew it would.

'No, you can't do that,' Phoebe said, when Mina offered the bed.

'I can't?'

'I'm not kicking you out of your own bed.'

It became obvious that they'd share the bed. This was the sensible solution.

Mina said, 'I'll brush my teeth while you change.'

The electric toothbrush pulsed against her molars. Mina rolled it over her tongue. She made a second circuit of her teeth. Her face felt greasy. She scrubbed the cleanser across her cheeks and chin. Her mouth, too, was hot. Women shared beds all the time. It wasn't scandalous. It was the stuff of commercials and chick flicks. Women became sisters after only a few good jokes. This was nothing.

Her phone buzzed—Oscar. She looked at his name for a second before picking it up.

'Why didn't you text me when you landed?' she asked, keeping her voice low. There was no need for Phoebe to hear this.

'I was working, Mina. Look, I'm sorry I didn't message you sooner.'

'You're upset. You're using my name.'

'It's your name,' Oscar said. 'Look this is stupid. I'm just calling to ask if you'll be okay if I go to Dad's for a few days to work on the pitch for Eileen Johnson and the stuff for next year.'

'How long is a few days?'

'I don't know. Just a few days.'

Part of her wanted to scream. He wasn't supposed to just leave. London was supposed to be a trip they took together. 'But I thought we were going to paint the apartment together?'

'I'll be back in a few days to help you finish it. I just need to concentrate on work for a little bit. I just need a little space. This contract is really important.'

How could she scream with Phoebe right outside? Anyway, Dr Helene said it was important not to create a crisis just because you felt like you were already in one.

'Okay,' Mina said. 'Go.' Her face in the mirror was pale, the eyelashes stubby. She looked too boring to be crazy.

'And you'll be okay?'

'Mmm,' Mina said.

'I might not call as much because I'll be trying to focus. Will you be okay?'

'It's fine,' Mina said. It wasn't. But there didn't seem anything else to say. Beyond the bathroom wall Phoebe was waiting.

'Mina, I just want you to be happy. Try to be happy for me?'

'Okay.' Wasn't that what she was already doing?

He hung up and Mina rinsed her toothbrush. Happy. She smiled at the Mina in the mirror. It didn't look convincing.

Phoebe would be wondering where she was.

Mina called, 'Are you decent?'

Phoebe was wearing blue pyjamas with white trim and pearlescent buttons. Across the pocket, white thread wrote the initials PW. Her feet poked out from satiny folds. The feet were covered in freckles, as if she had been dancing in copper sands. This white-faced girl had perfect freckled feet. Mina felt like she'd seen a secret. She must've been staring because Phoebe laughed and said, 'Oh, these. I know the PJs are a bit much. I got sent them as promotional material by a company that wanted me to feature them on the blog. They're silly, but feel. They're silk.' She held out a sleeve to Mina, who grasped it between thumb and forefinger. The fabric felt almost indecently smooth. The back of her hand skimmed Phoebe's knuckles.

Phoebe got into bed on Oscar's side. There was no print of his body except in Mina's memory. She hit the light.

In the dark, Mina tweaked her pillow and flopped onto her back. In the side of her vision, she could see the contours of Phoebe. Be happy, Oscar kept saying. And Mina let herself dwell on what might make her happy. Rolling Phoebe over and pressing herself against the other woman. Tasting the goodness of her, sucking the freckled toes. A devouring hunger rolled in her belly. Stupid, Mina thought. She would never kiss Phoebe. Such a thing was impossible. Mina could imagine configurations of hands, mouths, breasts, buttocks. But she couldn't think how to bridge the small gap of space between two faces. Mina had never initiated. It was Oscar who had put his mouth over hers as they'd sat on the school steps, watching groups of drunk kids flap past. Before that, other boys had put their mouths on hers. Some approached with puckers and some swooped forward open-mouthed, like whales trawling the ocean. For all the girls she'd watched over the years, she had never been able to take the simple step of leaning forwards.

Then all at once, lying next to this beautiful woman, Mina missed her husband. She missed him in her ribcage. She checked her phone again and there was nothing. Nothing at all. Not a *Goodnight*, *I love you* or *I miss you*. Mina had fallen in love with Oscar because he made grocery lists. In college, no one she knew made grocery lists. They ate cheap pizza or wandered the aisles of the store, leaving with grapes, Brie and baguette, aiming at sophistication and ending up with stomach aches. His handwriting had been so neat and even, listing exactly what he wanted. And then he'd collect exactly what they needed. But she supposed he didn't need her any more.

Phoebe squirmed in her sleep and the wiggle took the bedding. A breeze gnawed the left side of Mina's body from her neck to her calf. She rolled closer to the heat. Phoebe's back was to her. In the shadowed room, Phoebe's hair was not red. It was only undulation. Very slowly, Mina moved towards Phoebe, until her face met a curl of hair. Silently, Mina tensed her lips and pressed them against the strand, feeling the lovely dead cells against her mouth.

Oscar strapped into the plane seat. It was the middle one because the ticket had been booked last minute. They hadn't been able to get seats together so his father was a few rows ahead. What did his father want to talk to him about? Were they selling the flats to expand the business? Perhaps they could hire Oscar a translator so that he could handle more of the Japanese work. Or maybe his father would finally listen to his suggestion and set up a sales team to do online orders. Mina could recover at her own rate without worrying about the academic job market.

'PLEASE PLACE YOUR MOBILE DEVICES IN AIR-PLANE MODE. PLEASE STORE LARGER ELECTRICALS IN THE SEAT IN FRONT OF YOU AS WE PREPARE FOR TAKE-OFF.'

Once larger electricals were permitted again, he opened his laptop and wrote:

Possibilities
SWEET POTATO BREW
Pros
Seems to be playing well in bars
Not challenging
Halo effect from perceived health benefits of sweet potatoes?
Cons
Too similar to already stocked product?
Autumnal associations

Appeal to female shoppers uncertain
Conclusion
Maybe

Oscar had majored in Econ. He'd learnt statistical modelling and utility curves. Neither was particularly useful for his father's business. He'd known nothing about the alcoholic beverage industry or Japan. In college there were kids who joined the Asian frat or the Japan club. They had karaoke nights and watched anime. They wrote essays about feeling not quite at home in Asia or America. Useless. He'd grown up on green beans, not green tea, and he was fine with that. Only after his father hired him did he hit the books.

There were lessons to be learned from history. In the tenth and eleventh centuries, the type of sake you drank indicated your social class. What you drank declared who you were. Oscar was pretty sure Americans weren't so different. Americans who drank sake thought they were sophisticated. In the nineteenth century, sake culture encountered beer. Beer became the way to say you were modern and Western. A Tokyo housewife recorded with great pride in her diary that she'd served München beer and bananas at her dinner party. In other words, you don't have to give people an authentic experience. They just have to feel like they're getting it. He had to make people feel special.

'Excuse me, could I get through?' The window-seat's occupant had returned from the toilet. Oscar folded away his notebook and stood. 'Sorry, sorry,' the man said. Oscar allowed him to squeeze back into his window-seat.

'It's fine.'

The man viewed this nicety as a segue into telling Oscar that he was going to visit his son, who was creative. The other son was a doctor. Did Oscar know that the man had married his wife after two months? They'd been together forty years.

152

They'd come to America from Athens. Had Oscar been to Athens? No? It was very crowded. On and on.

Oscar and his father drove from the airport onto a ferry, off the ferry, and down curving wooded roads to a clapboard building. Timber boards stacked up, like the white spaces on lined paper. Oscar pulled both their cases from the car. If a neighbour peeked out of their window, they would have seen a dutiful son entering his father's house. Oscar wished he could watch his own life from the window of another's house. It would look so orderly.

Ami padded into the front hall to meet them. Every time he saw her, she was wearing a pastel cardigan. This one had seashells embroidered in peach thread. Added to this were pink suede slippers with a roll of sheepskin emerging from the ankles.

'Sorry for arriving at such short notice,' he said.

'We're delighted to have you,' Ami said. Ami's California drawl matched her husband's. She pronounced Ami like Amy. She, like his father, was *nisei*, second generation, a child of immigrants. Technically Oscar was *sansei*, the third generation to live outside Japan. But the word felt inapplicable. The language didn't belong to him. He was learning it from cartoon rabbits.

She suggested that she show him his bedroom, beckoning the way. As Oscar walked past the open door to the kitchen, he saw a large rice cooker presiding over the counter top. His father must keep the other for travel. Ami turned, as if hearing the pause in his steps.

'I was admiring your rice cooker.'

'We got it cheap. Your dad knows a guy who orders them wholesale. It makes cakes too. Do you like sponge?' she asked. 'I should totally do you the sponge. It's so fluffy.' Ami was pretty. She was certainly prettier than his mother. Ami was pretty the way a vase or a flower is pretty. Her face looked as if it had been designed with appeal in mind. When she was younger, she must have been cute. He shook away the thought. This was a weird thing to observe about your not-quite-stepmother. There was no word for the woman whose husband your mother had borrowed.

The guest room had windows on three walls. Through two he could see the green embrace of pine trees. Their shadows rippled across the floor. The third looked over a garden into a field. Beyond that was a strip of silver water, and beyond that, mountains. It struck him then that this airy house and his mother's cottage had strangely similar views, as if his parents were following the same dance steps at great distance.

'That's Ichiro,' Ami said, pointing towards the window. At first, he thought she meant the mountain. Then he saw that she was pointing to the field. A white animal ambled among the yellow grass.

'Is that a . . .' Oscar paused because it certainly wasn't a horse.

'He's a llama. We moved here so we could adopt him.' Ami straightened the already straight coverlet. As she petted the cotton, she described a documentary she'd seen about the raising of llamas. She hadn't been able to stop thinking about it for weeks, months even. But, of course, in LA, it hadn't been possible to keep such an animal. She was a kindergarten teacher and had small humans to care for. But she visited llama farms. She considered the difference between the Ccara and Tampuli breeds. 'And then finally we adopted Ichiro.'

'Congratulations,' Oscar said. Was that the right thing to say when someone made a ridiculous choice? He supposed so. It was what people said at weddings after all.

'Thank you. When we got him he was so teensy.' She made a pinching gesture. Then she laughed. 'Well, not that teensy. I'll show you a photo later.'

She left him to get settled. Oscar stood by the window,

watching the llama pick its way across the grass. It did not appear to be moving with any great purpose. It looked like a horse drawn by a child who'd only ever seen rabbits.

Oscar let the thought of Mina enter his brain. He was not a stupid man. His brain had always done what he told it to. If there was a problem, he worked at it and eventually it was solved. Guilt was not a useful emotion. He thought of her in the taxi back from the bridge and the way she'd held onto that stupid rubber flip-flop. It had been dirty with the imprint of her foot. He thought of her lips smeared with vomit. How she used to kiss him all over his face and the top of his head. He thought of moving to New York together after college and how scared he'd been, and how much he'd wanted to be in that city. It was a city without his mother or father and they were going to make it theirs. Mina had danced around that empty apartment, saying, 'We're home. We're home. We're home.' He thought of the first time they'd fucked. He could barely hear her over the sound of the sheets rustling against the dorm-issued rubber mattress. He could just make out her voice breathing, 'You, you, you.'

The figure of Ami appeared at the field's edge. She held out a hand to the animal and it bent its head to the cup of her palm.

It was just Mina and the apartment, and her fingers going sore from stripping this wall. Days. It felt like one unending day that snuck around the globe. As soon as she felt she'd made it through, the day arrived again. The progress was slow. The wall was wet. And perhaps she had slept too much or too little. The remaining birds glared at her with their scratched and scribbled-over eyes.

The time on the oven clock was wrong, off by both minutes and hours. Mina could have forgiven it that. But every time she looked at it, it didn't seem to have moved. Could the hours possibly have stretched so long? Oscar had been gone for five days. On the tracking map, their dots were ridiculously far away. To see them both, she had to zoom out so far that his icon covered the entirety of the island he was staying on.

Are you okay? she texted.

Fine, he replied.

When are you coming back? she texted.

Soon.

How soon is soon?

I just need to deal with some things. A few more days, maybe another week.

It was only five days. She was a grown woman. But she hadn't spoken to anyone since Phoebe stayed over. Oscar didn't call. Her calendar was all downticks. The sharp Vs stabbing downwards.

She opened her laptop to think about the women who survived. But her mind paraded the fragile bodies of those who hadn't. She downloaded twenty articles from JSTOR, but as soon as she started reading, her brain slid away from the words. She told herself that life was just a series of moments. She just had to make it through this one.

There was a noise, short, like a sudden exhalation of breath or a cat landing. She looked around but saw no creature capable of breathing or jumping. A few hours later, she heard it again. More time passed, and looking in the right direction, she saw it. The bunch of peonies Oscar had bought her was moulting. How had she never realised petals made a sound as they fall? They seemed like they should be silent but of course they had weight.

She texted Oscar: *Did you know petals make a sound when they fall?*

No reply.

She missed the trust she used to have in the pills. She missed the reassurance of them, and the daily swallow. She missed the way she rarely thought of them, the way you never think of how the toilet works until it clogs. Persephone swallowed pomegranate seed after pomegranate seed and that way became a wife. Were those her last pomegranate seeds? Or did she eat them by the fuchsia handful, damned to Hades as she already was? Or perhaps she didn't mind. As godly husbands went, Hades wasn't bad. He didn't fuck around as much as Zeus or Poseidon. He had a cordial relationship with his mother-in-law. Perhaps it was Hades she should pity. He sat alone every summer. While fruits and flowers and music festivals burgeoned, he had only the dead to talk to.

That morning he and his father had gone over the suppliers which would be able to meet the demands of a major grocery chain. Now his father was conducting long phone calls in a Japanese so swift and technical that Oscar, waiting outside the door, understood only every tenth word—go, come, there, how much, here, when, month.

Oscar wished he could call Mina and talk through the pitch. But it was impossible to say, 'Hey, can you stop being depressed for a minute and be my partner again?'

His father had given him access to the cellar and he'd carried some options into the light of the kitchen. He lined them up on the polished oak table in two rows, like a football-team photo. The taller sake bottles raised their pale necks at the back. Beer bottles squatted up front.

He recognised some of the brands. The pepper ale was as familiar as Mina's face. It was one he'd pitched hard early on. Others were new to him. He'd never drunk chūhai. The cans were adorned with images of peaches, cherries, lychees. Chūhai were popular with Japanese women. He'd tried this type of pre-made cocktail only once. The sugary peach that masked the cheap sake had irritated his throat and tongue.

He could parse only some of the kanji. He slid out his phone and opened the camera app. If he took a picture, he'd have the time and privacy to examine the brands and practise pronunciation.

CLICK.

After muting the phone, he moved closer. For each drink, he wanted a close-up of the label. As he centred the frame on each can, he became fluid and fast. Each shot took only a second. He reached over the chūhai to grab a blue bottle of sake.

'Oscar?' Ami's voice was behind him. He turned quickly, putting the phone down on the table.

Ami stood just inside the room, looking oddly misplaced, like a hat accidentally left on a subway seat. He wasn't sure what it was about her posture or her silence that gave the impression. He wondered if she'd lost something, and if he should offer to help her find it.

'I didn't want to interrupt.' She adjusted her face into a serious cast. 'But I wasn't sure if I'd get a chance to talk to you like this. And I thought while your father is busy . . . I suppose I just wanted to ask if you've ever thought about working somewhere else?'

'Somewhere else?'

'Someone else I guess would be a better way of putting it. Not working for your father.'

He'd taken the family name. Wasn't that good enough? Maybe she resented sharing it with him.

'Does he have a problem with my work?' Was this what his father had wanted to talk to him about?

She turned to the window where the llama pointed its ridiculous ears. 'I'd ask my own son the same question. It's not personal. I'd want him to consider his options.'

Oscar wondered if all women were so irrational or only the ones in his life. The llama couldn't work for his father. The llama didn't have a wife to support.

'Do you not want me working for him?'

Her expression was tinged with pity, like a girl explaining you're nice but not really her type. Oscar's phone buzzed where he'd laid it on the table. The sound was a heavy throb.

The sake bottles stood calm. His wife's ghostly hands were unable to shake them, try as she might.

'Do you need to get that?' Ami said.

Mina's name beamed up from the screen. Next to it was a mouse emoji. She'd snuck the emoji into his contacts. When he asked her why a mouse, she'd said rat was her year. Rats, she said, were smart but difficult. He was rat year too, but he'd never gone in for that sort of thing.

If he didn't pick up what would Ami think? Would she tell his father that Oscar, too, betrayed wives?

So he took the call, nodding to Ami as he stepped out of the kitchen into the hallway. Mina filled his ear: 'When are you coming back?'

Oscar flattened his voice so that it would sound calm and she would hear her own hysteria. 'I've been busy.' The phone was hot against his cheek. He held it slightly further from his ear.

'I thought we were going to paint this apartment together. I bought a ladder.' She sounded so sad, her voice almost keening.

'I'll be home soon,' he said. Despite the big bed and the lavender-scented sheets, Oscar had been tired all week. He didn't know where his body-clock was set to—London, New York, or just some aeroplane, full of endless rounds of naps and foil-wrapped meals. 'What's wrong?' he asked.

'I miss you. Can't you do whatever this is back here?'

Oscar had the uncomfortable feeling of shirking. He'd never liked skipping class, though he had once or twice with Theo back in the day, wandering to the woods to smoke and listen to CDs on Theo's Discman. In college, he'd always been the first to drop his paper into the hand-in box. And yet, as a husband, he was procrastinating.

'There's something I need to figure out with Dad.' Oscar sat on the staircase and rested his head against the wall. It

160

was white. All the walls of this house were white. He didn't know if it was grey-white or yellow-white, if it was called Wax or Jasmine. It beamed only the idea of white.

'Oh. Is everything okay?' she asked.

'It's fine.'

'You sound angry.'

'I'm not angry,' he said.

'You sound angry.'

He added, 'Sometimes even sane people get tired.'

There was a time when she was his rest, when they'd lie in bed, her back pressed against his belly, his arm looped over her, and he'd whisper his worries into the nape of her neck.

He lay back. The stairs jabbed his vertebrae. Above him, the bulb rested in its tasteful Art Deco globe.

'It's so fucking lonely here without you. Why are you being like this? You've never been like this before.'

'Mina, you weren't like this before either. I don't know what to tell you.'

'Just come back, please. I love you. I need you.'

Some memory of his former self leapt up and out of his body to save her, but his body stayed sprawled on the staircase. He would go to her eventually, but he was so tired. He would rest here with the absurd llama and the white walls. Then he'd figure out what to do about his wife. 'I should go. I don't know, why don't you invite Phoebe over? You had fun with her at that gallery, right?'

A few minutes after he'd hung up a notification popped up on his phone. More than a notification it was an instruction: *Mina's location services are not available. Ask them to correct their settings.*

This was what doctors called a Cry for Help. But he couldn't bring himself to call her back. Maybe she was right. Maybe they never should have got married. God, he'd stood up in front of all of their friends and told them he was getting married. He'd seen couples squeeze hands under the rented tablecloths. Afterwards, there had been a tumble of copycat weddings.

He'd drunk a lot of toasts at the wedding. His father had supplied the booze and the bar had been generous. But he hadn't felt drunk. They'd walked from the reception hall. Their closest friends were staying in other cabins nearby. The bridal cabin was the largest and the furthest from the reception hall. There had been plenty of night air to open his brain cells.

The room had smelt of candle wicks. It was a good smell. Mina's stockings had got torn and she slipped them off over her thighs. The thong had been new and oddly tricky to remove. When he did, he threw it over his shoulder and it landed as soundless as snow. Mina's dress was old fashioned, with a corseted waist and the thrill of bustles and ruffles that seemed designed for plunging his hands inside. Her thighs were honey-gold in the low light. He remembered that they had rocked gently under his hands. He remembered saying, 'I want my wife.' She'd laughed, hadn't she? He'd fiddled with the buttons, but there were too many. They were lined up along the back of the dress in a string, like a pearl necklace, and were fastened with tight loops of silk. So he'd left it on. The taffeta petticoats, flipped upwards, had tickled and teased his chest. At one point, she'd reached up and stroked the long ridge of his nose. 'Forever,' she'd said. Her eyes were shut and her head flung back. At one point, he'd felt the cool rub of the wedding ring against his neck.

Afterwards, she went to the bathroom. She was gone a while and he lay on the bed. Outside the window, he could see the lights on in the other cabins. It was March, and rain, which had held off for the ceremony, had begun to fondle the trees. He wondered how many of his friends were fucking, making love, sleeping. He thought briefly of his mother alone in her own cabin. He worried, it was absurd, but he worried that she'd be jealous. He had thought how strange it was to have everything you wanted. He might've dozed. Just for a moment, slipping into contentment, like it was a sudsy bath.

When he woke, there were no window lights on outside. And his wife was not in their bed. He found her in the bathroom. Her face was squashed against the toilet seat. There was vomit everywhere. It filled the gaps between the tiles and clung to her carefully ringleted hair. He'd had to step in it in his bare feet. With horror, he felt that it was cold. Cold vomit meant it had had time to cool. He shook her, and her eyelids had opened, the pupils as large as blueberries. He hadn't understood then. He'd thought it was food poisoning. Or alcohol. He'd thought it was an overflow of too much joy. And still he was afraid. He called 911.

He'd taken his wife out of her wedding dress. Button by button. Under the bright light of the bathroom, he saw that the white dress had white peonies embroidered into the fabric. The threads were barely raised above the silk. Button by button, he revealed the smooth triangle of her back. Button by button, he ended his wedding day. As he reached her waist, his fingers began to hurt. The skin was red where the dress's struts had pressed into her ribcage. He pulled her out of the heavy garment. He washed her face with the guest-cabin towels. He held the water under her nose until she gargled and spat it into the toilet. Her eyelids kept rolling shut. Then, as he heard the emergency services rapping at the door, she tried to keep her neck straight. Her mouth opened and closed, trying to make words. But none came out. She stuck a hand out towards him. And he knew, he just knew, she wanted him to hold it. How could you stay married to a woman like that? But how could you leave her?

I love you, he typed into the phone.

Okay, she replied.

Oscar had been in America for a week and on the West Coast for five days. He'd fulfilled his usual orders. But he hadn't found the right products to send to Eileen Johnson. He'd drawn up spreadsheets with their products and regional sales figures. Nothing felt right. He kept thinking about Mina. He was there in order not to think about her. And yet there she was, ricocheting around his brain, like a poltergeist. To make matters worse, the cut on his hand was oozing a brown-yellow gunge. The internet said that sort of thing came from scratching. But he didn't scratch, or not in the day, and there was nothing he could do about his sleep self.

Oscar needed to go for a run to clear his head. The island was a place where the elderly retired and the rich built summer homes, leaving them empty, like crystal tumblers saved for special occasions. He ran past these houses to the shore. The air smelled the way all those taxi air fresheners hoped to, of sap and generations of pine needles deep in the soil. Brambles lined the track. The workout wasn't as vigorous as he'd have liked, because he kept stopping to consult the map Ami had drawn. Her landmarks were mysterious. Crow Lane was a real street name, but BIG TREE was just that: a very big tree. The fir sloped so it shadowed the house beneath. At the shore, busybody pelicans bulged their fat chests.

Perhaps it was time to try a less numerical approach. He looked at his phone: two bars of signal, each only a few millimetres tall. But those millimetres should be enough to reach New York.

'Jimmy, you there?' Oscar asked.

'It's early.'

Oscar looked at his watch. 'It's noon where you are.'

'Exactly.'

They'd known each other in college. Oscar had gone to work for his father, Jim had got his bartending licence. He was the one Oscar tested new products on and he made them move. The skinny bartender was somehow always at the centre of grinning group selfies. To his right and left were always beautiful women holding drinks in unusual colours.

'Can you tell me who's been ordering that sweet-potato IPA?' He'd persuaded Jim to persuade the bar owner to order a crate.

Jim launched into an anecdote about this cute Iranian girl with eyes that knew things. She'd sat at his bar all night drinking straight out of the bottle. Her friends had been there but he could feel her watching him. Oscar let the story spin out.

'So women order the beer?' he asked.

'I guess.'

But Jim paid more attention to the drink orders made by cute girls. This was not exactly an unbiased accounting.

The pelicans took flight. They moved together, like dandelion seeds blown across the water.

'Do guys ever order it?' Oscar asked.

'Yeah, a couple. You know, I think we're out, actually. I can check later.'

'That'd be brilliant.'

Oscar made it home with no wrong turnings.

He placed the sake bottles on one side of the table, the beer and chūhai on the other. Each bottle gave a heavy clink as he moved it aside. Pure sake was too searing for the puritanical regulations of most American states, which would not allow spirits into a grocery store. A beer with 3.2 per cent ABV or under would be ideal. That would pass the grocery test in the majority of states. The sobriety of American shopping aisles had confused him when he'd first arrived from Britain, where all beacons of drunkenness stood proudly together under the banner of Beer, Wine and Spirits.

The chūhai was lower in alcohol, but harder to classify. It was a mixed drink and was likely to fall foul of the intricate grocery-store laws, which differed from state to state. Better to stick with beer. In most states, if a drink was classified as a beer, it could be sold down the aisle from dog food and loo roll.

He filled a glass with water, as he'd need to clear his palate. He wrote the date in the top left corner of a clean page of his notebook.

'I don't want to interrupt,' Ami interrupted. She was holding a blue bowl in both hands as if she was making an offering at the temple of an obscure god. She laid it at his elbow and he looked down to see goldfish crackers. 'Snacks. It's not good to drink on an empty stomach.' She pulled up a chair beside him and picked up a fish. 'I shouldn't be having these, not at my age. There's too much salt. My doctor told me to avoid salt, oil, red meat, coffee.' She talked fast. The sleeves of her cardigan were pushed over her elbows.

'I'm sorry,' she said. 'About before, what I said about working for your father. I didn't want you to think . . . I don't have any children, you know that. We wanted to but.' She paused. 'That doesn't matter. What I'm trying to say is, I haven't had a lot of practice at that sort of advice.'

'It's not a big deal,' he said. She must have thought so many times how much simpler her life would have been without him. As a boy, he'd certainly wished her dead. He'd thought that was all it took to play happy families. One mummy. One daddy.

He asked which was her favourite beer, and she pointed at

one with blossom emblazoned on the front. He popped it open and she poured it into two glasses.

'Does Mina like London?' she asked, as she took her first sip.

He should never have left Mina alone in London. He should never have let her go to that appointment by herself. Weird that there might never be a child with his face and hers. He hadn't focused on it long enough to wish for it. But he'd always assumed there would be a kid he'd teach to recite two times two is four, three times three is nine, four times four is sixteen. He'd figured they'd sign up to the YMCA and he'd hold a little body while it kicked water and held onto his neck, always knowing it could rely on its father. 'I think so,' he said.

Ami said, 'I loved it. I loved those houses in Notting Hill with all the different colours. And those kids on Carnaby Street in their corduroy flares and those flowery shirts. They looked so wild. You just wanted to pluck them and put them in a vase. We almost lived in London, you know.'

She looked down at her drink. Oscar grabbed a handful of the goldfish.

Ami undid the loose knot of her hair so it flowed down her back. 'I suppose Ichiro wouldn't have had much space in London.'

'No,' he said, 'I suppose not.'

The drink was sweet.

'What do you think?' he asked Ami. 'Would women buy this? Would your friends buy this?'

Ami tilted her head. 'I'm not sure.'

He spun the bottle around to the nutrition label, scanning for エネルギー enerugii, energy, i.e. calories, and winced. That number would not be female-friendly. 'But you'd drink it?'

Ami shrugged, and a shoal of wrinkles appeared in her neck. He'd never drunk with his own mother. They had tea and custard creams. Though one of his early memories was of an empty white-wine bottle on the side table. His mother and some woman lay on the sofa. The woman's head rested in his mother's lap and his mother was stroking her hair. The woman had been crying. He hadn't seen an adult cry before.

Oscar downed his drink. Then he swilled water over his molars and the top of his mouth. He dug the bottle opener's beak into another beer. It gave a satisfying pop. It was one of the best parts of a drink, that hiss. A mushroom of foam rose to the surface. Oscar knew the brewery but he'd never had their red rice ale. The liquid was as red as strawberry coulis. The taste was yeasty. Fruity too. It would be good with fried noodles, he thought. Or a fry-up. Or a burger, even.

'Aniseed,' Ami said.

'What?'

'That's the after-taste.'

'Let me write that down,' he said.

Somehow the conversation drifted to the first drink Oscar's father had bought Ami—a vodka lemonade. And from there to how he'd come to her small apartment to smash every roach using his own copy of the phone book. That somehow, even in the hard years, he'd found a way to buy her tickets to the zoo.

They were halfway through a peach-jelly drink that Ami had discovered at the back of a cupboard when his father came downstairs.

'I haven't made dinner,' she said. 'I've been helping Oscar with his research.'

Oscar held up the notebook. His father stood looking at them. He was wearing a blue golf shirt. Had he been playing golf? Oscar didn't own any golf shirts. Oscar owned clothes for life and clothes for exercise and he didn't allow them to cross-pollinate. As he stared at the shirt, he felt his face get warm. He touched his cheek. When this happened with friends, he always said, 'Oops. Asian glow.' But it would be weird to say that now. It would sound like he was blaming them. Look what you did to me. Oscar laughed for no reason.

'I'll cook,' his father said. Ami laid her head on her arms, like a kid slumped over her desk.

'You should visit more often,' she said. 'I need a drinking buddy.' Her eyes glittered. One arm lay extended outwards and each knuckle was the size of a hazelnut, but the fingers themselves were narrow splints. How had her hand looked when she was young? When he was a child, Ami was only a figure judging them from a distance, like a CCTV camera. She yawned and swirled her glass.

'You're a lightweight,' he said.

'Takes one to know one.'

Oscar wasn't sure how much time passed before his father returned carrying two plates. Fried eggs on toast and a handful of greens.

'I don't know how much salt and pepper you like,' his father said. The edges of the eggs were curled and crisped.

'Thanks, Dad.'

After Oscar's father put Ami's down in front of her, she grabbed his now empty hand and kissed the back. Oscar's face heated up as if he'd been spying. He looked away and out of the window. The sun was a yolky yellow at the edge of the sky. Oscar split the yolk on his plate and watched it spread to match the sunset. His tongue was booze-numbed, but the egg whites were flaky and the butter was sweet. They didn't talk as they ate. Every now and then he heard the rush of a car on the road. He was glad to be staying put.

When are you coming home? Mina texted Oscar.
Soon.
That's what you said yesterday. When?
Soon.
I miss you, she typed.
I miss you too.
No, but I really miss you.
No reply.
Mina wrote, *What if there was an emergency?*
Is it an emergency?
No.

How do you tell if it's an emergency before it's already too late? She'd wanted to understand the floor plan of her sadness. Here it was. She managed half an hour on the wall, flecks of paper getting under her nails, until she gave up.

After a break for hummus and bendy carrot sticks, she tried again at research. Her mouse flicked to JSTOR to download yet more articles about surviving women. She couldn't decide if JSTOR's seemingly unending database of academic thought was a horror or wonder. Every time she typed in the words, she expected to see a review or thesis outlining everything she wanted to say but better. Other times she wondered if it was possible to construct any argument at all. Take, for example, the beautiful Ariadne, sorceress, priestess, and keeper of the Minotaur. Ariadne who fell for Theseus, son of Poseidon, sinewy and strong. Ariadne taught Theseus how to escape her father's labyrinth. She rode with him on swift ships away from her home, her father and all she knew. She survived her father. She survived the escape. She must have felt she had earned her hero's love. Yet on the island of Naxos, he abandoned her sleeping form. What would it have been like to wake up to a blue Mediterranean sky and no lover? What happened to her afterwards? In some tales, she was killed by Artemis, in others by Perseus. In some versions, she hanged herself from a tree. How long did you have to live for it to count as survival?

'As it's a special occasion. I thought I'd break out the daiginjō.' His father proffered the bottle with a sommelier's poise.

'Thanks. You didn't have to.' Oscar smiled.

'Nonsense. I wanted to.' His father explained how this brand used only Yamada-Nishiki rice. 'The strain predates the war. None of this bio-engineering anti-pest shit. Emperors drank sake made from this rice.'

It was not a brand they sold to Americans. Few would know to value it. It must've been from his father's personal stash. The sake cup was the soft white of the feathers Oscar bounded across, running to the shore. He closed his eyes to catch the drink's bright notes. His palate was dulled from the champagne had Ami served with the first course. Even so, he was impressed by the complexity of flavour.

Ami brought out the cake. Strawberry slices formed a 33. The numbers were so close they were spooning. Smoke drifted up from the single candle. Ami passed him the knife. 'For the birthday boy.'

He recognised that triangle of steel and his hand clenched. The black handle with the dots of steel was the doppelgänger of the one in the London flat. He took this knife. Stupid to be upset. Mina was far from this steel edge.

'Go on,' Ami said.

He lifted the knife and saw a small inscription, a German brand, a good one. This was more expensive than the cheap implement in the London flat. A false twin.

The cake was frosted. As he pressed the knife, icing cracked, like a lake in spring. The cake was too big for three people, but he cut and served and made the required appreciative noises.

'Is this the famous rice-cooker cake?'

'Nah,' Ami said. 'I saw the recipe on TV.'

'Did you see this?' his father asked, holding up his phone. The president's face shone in an expression of contorted rage. For a while Oscar, his father and Ami talked about the people on the news as if the politicians were mutual friends. Unfortunate and idiotic friends, but people they all had in common. People they shared. The conversation was easy, nice, even.

There was a pause during which he realised his brain was a warm buzz. The empty champagne magnum was on the table, brandishing its torn golden flag.

'I'm sorry,' Ami said. 'I'm sorry. I'm sorry.'

At first he didn't understand what she was sorry for and he looked around to see if the champagne had spilt. Her face was red, not just drink-pink, but red around the eyes. Her mouth twisted, and the wrinkles sliced deeper.

His father leaned over and rubbed her shoulder. He made the noises you'd make to a lost animal or a small child. 'Sssh . . . sssh . . . sssh . . .'

Oscar stood, but then he didn't know what to do so he sat again. A crying woman was a strange object. He never knew how to interact with one. Mina, he just held. But this person? The strangest thing was that Ami was smiling tentatively behind the tears.

His father looked up. His hand was on Ami's neck. Ami wiped her eyes with her index fingers. There weren't many tears, just a smear of liquid and a shine on her short eyelashes. 'It's silly. I was just thinking about the cake.'

'It's delicious,' Oscar looked down at it. 'Really good. Nothing to cry about.'

'No, not this thing.' She waved a hand over the assembled crumbs. 'About all the cakes we didn't make you.'

Why should this woman be baking him cakes? 'It's fine.'

'I . . . We were going to live together. You'd live with us. Your dad planned it. I knew by then. I knew, and I was so angry. I was fucking angry. On top of everything else, this woman was going to have a baby.' She glared into the grain of the table.

His father kept making that 'Sshh . . . sshh' noise.

'I held you and you were such a cute baby. You tugged onto the ends of my hair like this.' She made two tight fists. 'I wanted to chew you up. To nibble on that cute little leg. But she was always there—your mother. Watching us. I just wanted her to go away. I thought maybe we could just pretend she'd died. I'm sorry. I shouldn't be saying this about your mom.'

'What do you mean I was going to live with you? You were going to adopt me?' Oscar asked. He didn't want to think about Ami chewing his leg.

'We'd been trying for a while by then to have a baby so your dad offered to raise you and take care of everything. But your mother refused. Said she didn't like the idea of a son on the other side of the world. Your dad came up with a second plan. We'd go to London. He didn't tell me what was going on until he'd bought the flats. Wanted to have all his chips in place. She'd live upstairs and you'd be downstairs with us. Your mom could be a career woman or whatever. He even did the wallpaper the same so you'd feel like it was one big home. Birds. Your dad said your mother liked birds.'

'Wait. The flats? You all were going to live in the flats?' He looked to his father for confirmation, for sanity, for context. How would the visas even work? But Ami kept talking. His body got hotter and hotter, as if he were sitting too close to a fire. He swiped at his forehead with the back of his hand.

'You were so cute but . . . there was your mother. She didn't

174

even want a baby. She wanted to be some hotshot journalist. And yet she had you. I guess I wasn't very nice. But I couldn't share you with that woman. A home with that woman. I . . .' She wasn't crying now, just looking at her hands. 'I told your dad he had to choose. It was you or me. I'm ashamed of it now . . . but I don't know if I could have said anything different.'

'Journalist?' Oscar asked. His mother was not a journalist. His mother laughed at the TV journalists whose inane questions she typed up. Whenever she said, 'The press,' she rolled her eyes.

The chair's spindles dug into his back and he had the urge to stand, to pace, but he stayed put.

His father said, 'When I met your mom she was writing articles for this women's magazine, but she told me she wanted to be a serious reporter. Investigative journalist, that's what it was. She was uncertain about raising a child. So I suggested an arrangement.' He said these things as if he had had nothing to do with the situation, as if he were merely reporting the facts.

Ami sucked the tines of her fork. There was no cake left on her plate.

Oscar's mother had never said anything about journalism. What was his father trying to imply? What did *uncertain* mean? That Oscar might've been aborted?

Oscar closed his eyes. He felt the cake gumming the roof of his mouth.

Abortion was normal, sensible, even. He was the result of infidelity, of an inadvisable fling. He was an inadvisable child. His mother must have considered it. He clenched his hands under the table, then unclenched them. This was the sort of thing Mina would make a big deal of. But he wasn't Mina.

His mother had held career ambitions beyond typing up other people's words. But who did the things they'd planned?

He'd grown up fine without Ami's birthday cakes. At the end of a run, you had to force your body to slow, to ease the breath in and out, and that was what he did.

His father gathered up their plates. Oscar scooped up the empty flutes. He inserted the champagne bottle into the recycling.

'Oh, bubbles in the brain,' Ami said. 'I've ruined everything.'

'No, you haven't,' Oscar said, because it seemed the thing to say.

They were silent as his father plastic-wrapped the remaining cake. The cling-film pressed down and smeared the icing. The centre sagged. The cake disappeared into the refrigerator. His father shut the fridge door slowly, carefully.

'It was an idea. It didn't work out,' his father said. 'I guess I don't always understand women that well. But the rent on those apartments paid for your school. So, in the end, they weren't a bad buy.'

Was this it? The talk they were supposed to have? Big whoop. They had failed to adopt him decades ago. Strange how when people let you down there are rarely explosions. Rarely blood. Just that sense of a dimming of light in the room.

Ami blotted her eyes with the kitchen roll. These people were better suited to raising a llama than a child. His father stood there in that ridiculous aquamarine golf shirt, the Brooks Brothers lamb stitched on the pocket. Ridiculous. This was all ridiculous. Oscar's mouth was sharp with too much sugar from the cake he'd eaten out of politeness.

'This is why you asked me here? To tell me this?' His throat was taut.

'Oscar.' Ami was standing, coming towards him, as if to hug him. And he knew then that he did not want to be touched.

'I'm going for a run,' he said.

'It's dark,' she replied.

'There's a flashlight on the hall bench,' his father said.

'Oscar.' Ami stepped closer.

'I have to go,' he said, 'before the sugar metabolises.' He waved a hand towards the crumbed table.

On the road, his feet beat an even rhythm. But the beam of the torch swung erratically across the road and the grass. The light blinded him so he turned it off. There was enough moon to see by. Every now and then he switched the rubber-coated device from one hand to the other. Just one more pointless weight.

Mina had texted, *Happy Birthday*. Just like the other acquaintances who saw fit to mark his ageing. Probably she was angry that he wasn't celebrating it with her. But it was his birthday. On this day surely it was okay to want to relax?

Mina looked at the calendar, and the way her upticks and downticks flitted through the month. Since Oscar had left she'd drawn a week of Vs.

A big downtick for his birthday. She'd drawn him a card. She'd ordered a book of Japanese fairy tales. On the left pages there were Japanese words and on the right English. She'd thought he might use it to study for that language exam he was so stressed about. But he hadn't been there to receive it.

Right at the end, the uptick. *The Women Who Survive* had not progressed. But the knowledge of Phoebe's coming was enough for Mina's mood to rise, like a bird beating once more skywards.

Phoebe arrived on time, Benson in tow, making good on her offer to spend her free afternoon pulling paper. She worked efficiently, her nose an inch from her spatula. She nuzzled the steel under the wallpaper's seam. With a yank, she dragged off a great paper snake. Old glue stippled its back. Benson ran to where it fell, snuffling around the edges. Mina worried he'd bite it, but after a few growls, he lost interest.

'You don't have to do this,' Mina said.

'It's good to be out of my brother's place.' Phoebe's spatula dug under the next seam. 'This takes me back to sixth form, making the sets for the school plays.'

Small muscles rose and fell in Phoebe's long arms. Each time she peeled away a strip she paused to look at her trophy. The work went faster with four hands. Phoebe's phone twinkled pop songs. Paper flew to the bedsheet spread across the floor. The dog watched them. His head rested on his front paws in resigned confusion. Mina made tea. Phoebe took hers in a style she called builder's, full of milk and sugar, and drank as she worked. By midday, the wall was stripped. The plaster's complexion was pockmarked blue, white, grey and pink.

Phoebe flopped onto the couch and kicked off her shoes.

'Redecorating might be the new Soulcycle,' she said, and swung her feet up onto the padded arm, so that she took up the couch's full length.

'Soulcycle? Never tried it.' Mina dropped to the floor by the couch.

'You just cycle in a gym with the lights off while they blast electro and someone shouts at you. It's a thing.'

Even before she'd left New York, Mina must've been falling away from her friends. No one had dragged her to this torture. She said, 'So wallpaper removal is your official fitness style forecast?'

'For it to be official,' Phoebe made air quotes around *official*, 'I'd need a sponsorship deal, preferably one which meant I got buckets of cash rather than buckets of paint. But don't your arms feel good?'

Mina curled her biceps.

'There you go.' Phoebe reached and squeezed Mina's muscle.

Mina clenched harder.

'I have a favour to ask,' Phoebe said. 'Could you watch Benson tonight?'

'Does Theo have someone coming over again?'

'Not exactly, but I have a thing.'

'A thing? Yeah. I can watch Benson.' Mina wondered if a *thing* was a way of saying a *date*.

Phoebe looked uncomfortable and pulled a tangerine cushion over her stomach, hugging it. 'If I leave him at Theo's he chews up the furniture. I mean, Benson's a poppet but he gets lonely and bored.'

At the sound of his name, Benson approached. He balanced his two brown front paws on the sofa, looking up at his mistress. Phoebe hefted him onto her lap, pulling him so close that the dog's tufted ears framed her face. His huge body blocked his mistress's almost completely. 'Benson's a shelter baby. The rescue centre said his old owners were nice. They only left him because they were moving to Melbourne. But he gets edgy sometimes. I don't think he's sure I'm going to come back.' The dog's eyes, ringed like knots of wood, goggled at his mistress. 'Though I am, aren't I, darling? Of course I am.'

'Really, it's not a problem at all. Will you be coming back to pick him up, or . . . ?'

'It might be easier if I came in the morning.'

Would the night feel less empty with a dog? Mina forced her voice to sound funny and playful. 'Oh it's that sort of a thing, is it?' She cocked an eyebrow.

Phoebe covered her face with the cushion and issued a muffled groan. Theatrically, she flung her arms up into the air and the cushion fell to the floor. She said, 'Okay, so here it is. I waitress. I mean, that's not who I am. I'm not a waitress. I'm a blogger or a creative entrepreneur. But sometimes, well, Monday to Thursday, five thirty to eleven thirty, I waitress.'

Mina blinked away confusion. 'But there's nothing wrong with waitressing. I worked at an ice-cream place all through college.'

'Yeah, you used to work at an ice-cream shop. Note the past tense.'

'Okay,' Mina said. 'You're a creative entrepreneur who waitresses. That's pretty normal.'

'It's normal for twenty-one-year-olds fresh out of uni. Angst is cool when you're twenty-one. I'm almost thirty. I have sore knees. You know, even the trophy wives the guys bring in are younger than I am.'

'You're beautiful and you're much more interesting than anyone's trophy wife.' Mina felt guilty for saying this. She was sure some of the trophy wives were perfectly interesting. She'd never had a conversation with one.

After a lunch of boiled eggs and toast, they began in the bedroom. Mina hadn't yet bought anything to protect the floor and the spare bed sheet was only large enough to cover a patch. They dragged it across the floor to each new work-site. Around four o'clock, the birds began to appear dejected and slightly lost. Perhaps it was a trick of the afternoon light. As they worked, Phoebe described the restaurant. It was a bistro specialising in food from Alsace, that strip of land between France and Germany contested in war after war. The menu was all schnitzel and sausages.

'Is it stupid, do you think, that I reckoned something would come along? That I never found what you'd call a real job? I was hoping the blog would take off. And I thought there was no point in chasing some high-powered thing. We were trying for a baby.' Phoebe tilted her head.

'I think it's cool that you're a waitress,' Mina said. 'You make people happy. You bring them something they want.'

Too soon Phoebe had to go. Again she changed in the bedroom, watched by the remaining flock. Mina was slightly disappointed when she returned in a white shirt and black skirt—no sign of a dirndl or Fräulein-esque puffed sleeves.

Phoebe left, and Mina stared at the brown-eyed dog. It was

better than being alone, she decided. Benson snuggled against her knee. She ran her fingers over his head.

A notification popped up on her phone. It was the stalking app. *Oscar's battery is low. Tell him to charge his phone.*

She sat down on the floor and drew Benson close to her. The fur compacted under her arms and the dog's body was surprisingly slim. What did he think when his owners vanished to Australia?

She missed Oscar, and the way he'd start each day knowing what he wanted to accomplish. She missed the way he knew how to locate the knots in her back. She checked her phone. Nothing from Oscar. Not a word. Not an emoji. Nothing. She opened the app. The little photo of her husband hovered above the West Coast. It was the image from the Umeda Trading website. He looked professional and slightly distant.

Then there was Phoebe. Phoebe, for whom Mina had no words that made sense. Once she'd seen an owl on a camping trip. He'd lingered on his branch, golden-eyed and stripe-feathered. Mina had stared and stared until long after he flew off. That was how she felt about Phoebe.

Mina supposed that before Freud, people repressed their emotions. But she'd lost count of the times one of her New York friends began a sentence, 'So my therapist says . . .' Mapping your emotions was easy. It was cutting a new path that felt impossible.

Benson's doggy breath huffed into the apartment. She levelled her phone with his face. The tail tapped a marching beat. She sent a photo to Oscar. Silly. But was it so wrong to hope for something more than a perfunctory *busy*? She didn't want to beg. She couldn't demand, Come home. Because hadn't she said she'd be fine? It wasn't like she was about to die.

Mina looked up Phoebe's restaurant. It had varnished

tables, parquet floors and gleaming lamps. A long, polished bar was studded with crystal tumblers. Right now customers would be ordering bratwurst and watching Phoebe take the order, her long hair pinned up to reveal the freckleless neck.

'Shall we go on walkies?' she asked the dog.

The sun was low. The shops had closed. Bars and restaurants had taken the stage. The dog strained at the leash, as his nose followed an invisible trail.

Mina noticed the mother and son from some way down the street. The boy's blue cap had caught her attention. A complicated monogram was stitched across the front. Lumpy knees stuck out from navy shorts. He looked like a boy from another era, about to be evacuated to the countryside or head off for high jinks. Had Oscar ever had a cap like that? Had his curls poked out from under the brim? The mother and boy came closer. It was late to be coming home from school, but perhaps he was in a club or a team. All at once, the boy was running, limbs flying akimbo. Mina's breath caught, and she tried to step out of his way. But before the peak of his cap could connect to her stomach, he stopped. Right in front of Benson. He stuck an upturned palm towards the dog. Mina looked on, unsure. What had Phoebe said about Benson being edgy? What would she do if he bit the child? Shouldn't the mother have stopped this?

The mother stood to one side, her hands full of groceries. Leeks protruded from the plastic bags. 'I'm sorry,' she said. 'He's in his dog phase.'

The boy scratched Benson behind the ears. The dog flopped over and the boy petted the belly with almost scientific concentration.

'He's a champ,' he said, in a serious voice, as if it had taken him some minutes to come to this conclusion. His hand continued over Benson's belly. Mina zinged with pride. Ridiculous. Benson didn't belong to her.

The mother sighed, the grocery bags lodged in her elbow. 'Come on, Jacob. We've got to be going.'

Other dog owners nodded to Mina and she nodded back—a member of this club for tonight. She and the dog trooped past pubs, bookshops, tube stops. Flocks of eye-linered girls winged past. Then, for a few streets, no one. The dog's legs lifted and dropped but his tail drooped. It must be heavy carrying that weight of fur.

The road bent into a bridge. Mina looked over the side to see the ruffled back of a canal. Trees bowed over the water, leaves kissing it goodnight. One of the barges had Christmas lights strung around its rail. Mina thought she recognised the area from her previous visit to Phoebe's part of town. Wasn't the restaurant where Phoebe worked nearby? Mina wouldn't go in. She just wanted to see where Phoebe worked.

On a street of closed stores, a van was parked, the headlights on and the back doors open. Benson strained towards the vehicle. Mina pulled back on the lead, and the strap bit her palms.

'No. Bad dog.'

He let out a low, whistling whine.

The driver's seat was empty. A newspaper was folded on the dashboard, the block capitals of the headline mysterious in the low light. *CLEAN ME* was written in the grime on the truck's side. Benson hurried on, hustling towards the back of the van.

Another step and she saw inside. Mina's shoulders leaped towards her ears. Inside the van bodies hung from hooks, limbs strapped together. Animals, she realised, headless and skinned. Cows? Deer? Sheep? She wasn't sure. She had only the sense of limbs, and queasy white and red flesh.

The shadows between the meat shifted. It was a man in a blue shirt, like a hospital orderly's. He lifted a body off its hook. One hand took the feet, or were they hooves? The other

184

grasped the corpse around its middle. There was a moment when he and the meat were dancing, before he dropped it to the van's floor.

Mina didn't think she was better than meat-eaters. She was sure lives, both animal and human, were lost in the farming of cotton and the sewing of clothes and the collecting of the oil that the freighters used to carry even her simple socks across the ocean. She was sure that everything she did probably maimed some creature. It was just that when she tried to eat sinew, she felt a kicking in her stomach, as if the animal was trying to escape.

The man's eyes slid into hers. For a moment she felt that he'd like to eat her. She imagined that mouth, hot and saliva-sticky, clamping down on her arm. If they were pulled into that van, how long would it take Oscar to realise she was missing? She dragged Benson away.

The restaurant and its generous blue awnings appeared around the corner. From the sidewalk, it was impossible to see Phoebe. The diners were bathed in twenty-four-carat light. On the other side of the street was a triangle of grass and benches. There were many buttons of green sewn into London and she hadn't seen any of them patrolled. Mina eyed this grassy polygon. There was a paved path down the middle. Couples walked slowly, so close their coats brushed, while busy single people sliced past. She chose a bench with a clear view of the restaurant. Benson, calm after the long walk, settled at her feet. His haunch rested against her. Mina buried her cold hands in his fur.

She just wanted to glimpse this waitress-Phoebe. But Phoebe must've been working far back in the restaurant because her slim profile never appeared in the windows. Mina's body was sore from the day's efforts. She did a few shoulder rolls that Oscar had taught her. She wondered if this was what stalkers felt like. But stalkers were not entrusted with the care of the stalkee's dog. It didn't seem so wrong to want to see a familiar face, if only for a second, if only from a distance.

Mina skimmed her emails. Nothing from Oscar today. A wedding invitation from a girl she'd taken Introductory Latin with and who now worked for JPMorgan. An invitation to submit papers to a conference on Ovid. Suggested topics included:

Amor: Force of destruction?
Emotions in Ovid
The dearth of same-sex relationships in Ovid
Intertextuality in Ovid: What's new?
The Ovidian aesthetics
Ovid's literary persona(e)
The psychology of exile in the Ovidian corpus
Seduction in ancient literature: a comparative examination
Tales of Transformation *compared (within* Metamorphoses,
   across genres, and/or across cultures)
Visualizing Ovid
Post-classical Ovid (reception and adaptation in all genres)

Past-Mina would have thrown something together. She would have applied for travel grants. The conference was in Shanghai. Supposedly select contributions would be translated into Chinese. Present-day Mina turned off her phone and shoved it into her back pocket.

Gradually, diners stopped arriving. Every time the door opened it was for another group of full-bellied clients leaving. Some hugged and kissed. Few looked over their shoulders.

A woman in a white shirt and black skirt appeared in the doorway. Her face was turned away as she talked to someone inside. But the figure was all wrong to be Phoebe. Then a gaggle of others. Finally, Phoebe. Mina called out a greeting, but it was ignored. She shouted Phoebe's name.

Phoebe approached, confusion crinkling her face.

Benson rushed towards his mistress, tongue waving. Mina, who'd had the leash loosely around her wrist, found herself dragged up and out of her seat. The yank was so hard her shoulder screamed in its socket.

'Mina, hi, is everything okay? Is Benson okay?'

'He's fine. He's here.' She must look like a crazy person. After the first attempt, a doctor with a checklist had quizzed her to prove she wasn't a danger to herself or others. If she was a danger, she would've been assigned another ward, one she wouldn't have been allowed to leave. The exhausting thing about being crazy was the constant need to convince people she wasn't.

'Benson and I just got here,' she said, eliding into that 'just' the hours spent on the bench as the night got cooler. In the scheme of her life, she had 'just' arrived in London. 'I thought it might be fun to walk across the city. To get to know it better.'

'Oh, cool.' Phoebe looked over her shoulder. It wasn't quite a full turn, more of a twitch. 'I told my friends we'd get drinks after my shift was up, so . . .'

'Go, have fun. Benson and I'll be fine.'

Phoebe twitched her head again. 'If you can't take him, if there's been a problem . . .'

'There's no problem. Have fun. It's a beautiful night.' Her hip was half turned away. But something must've shown in Mina's face, because Phoebe seemed to think she needed to offer Mina more. She said, 'It's a new moon, you know.'

Mina asked, 'A new moon is when you can't see it, right?' There were no stars, only the faint light of the city reflecting off banks of cloud.

'Yeah, I have an app that tracks the cycle. They say you're supposed to feed the new moon your wishes. And then you reap them on the full moon. My astrologer friend told me, and I've been trying it. For the blog, you know?'

Yet more apps. Mina wondered if the moon felt stalked. Another group emerged from the restaurant.

'Anyway, I really have to go,' Phoebe said. 'But we'll hang out tomorrow, okay?' She squeezed Mina's shoulder and Mina was left with the dog and the hungry moon.

Mina and Benson watched Phoebe as she walked away. Benson pulled on the lead, but Mina held him. No, she thought, you're stuck with me tonight. Phoebe's was the efficient step of someone who knew where she was going. It was the sort of walk that would be easy to fall into line behind. Then abruptly, she stopped, as if halted by the riptide of Mina's stare.

The figure was lovely, though at this distance unremarkable. What was the exact distance to best see a person? That question was like trying to build a fence around a perfume. Beauty's borders were forever fluxing. How many inches away had Phoebe been when the first shock of her beauty rolled over Mina? Phoebe stayed motionless for a minute.

'Is everything okay?' Mina called.

Phoebe swung around, waving a phone aloft. 'I've cancelled.'

Mina caught up with her, Benson tugging on the leash.

'Let's go for a drink. There's a pub around here that'll be okay with Benson. It's not far.' Phoebe smiled her lovely smile.

'I didn't want to make you cancel.'

'You didn't make me. You're alone in this city and that's rubbish. If I was alone in New York, I'm sure I'd feel like crap. I'd have invited you out with those guys but they're going clubbing, and I've lumbered you with my dog. Anyway, I'm getting too old for vodka Red Bulls.'

Mina found that she'd forgotten the right distance at which to walk with someone. What was the natural separation of bodies? It was like touch-typing. It only worked if you didn't think about it too much. Mina walked next to Phoebe, trying not to think about walking next to Phoebe.

The houses were two or three storeys. A bit like the brown-stones in Brooklyn, only white. They all had little holes dug in the ground in front of them, like moats. Oscar had told her there was an expression that an Englishman's home was his castle. Mina thought someone, probably also Oscar, had told her the name of the moats. A lightwell? Windows opened onto these lightwells, and as they walked, Phoebe ducked her head to peer into a kitchen.

Phoebe said, 'I have this soft spot for a granite countertop. I mean, I hate cooking, but I always think if I had one then maybe I wouldn't.'

Mina had never taken much interest in the countertops of other people's kitchens. Had Phoebe had a granite countertop in the Peckham flat?

'Oh, God, no. Everything was Ikea, flat-pack. But I always thought, Someday. Someday I'm going to be that sort of person. Actually, that wasn't the real dream.'

Mina wondered what the real dream was. It seemed like a contradiction in terms. She was pretty sure that, whatever dream it was, it hadn't included a strange American. Jealousy shivered along the hairs of Mina's arms, which was absurd. A friend's girlfriend had said, in passing, that bisexuals could not be trusted. They'd fuck anyone. Mina had wanted to punch her. She knew plenty of monosexuals who fucked around. Was it because Mina was crazy that she wanted this girl? Was wanting to lick along the tender edge of an ear just a symptom? No. Impossible. Phoebe had nothing to do with the hurtling sadness. That was why Mina wanted her. Anyway, nothing had happened. These were only the crimes of wishing and dreaming. Was it so bad to stand with this girl, stealing happiness from their shared air? Try to be happy, Oscar had said.

There were so many categories to which you could belong, sane or insane, cheater or loyal wife, mono or bi. She saw a thousand versions of herself. The sane, straight Mina, who ground against a different man every night. The depressed faithful Mina, who never thought of anyone's mouth but Oscar's. They all seemed momentarily possible.

'Mind if we take a detour?' Phoebe asked. Mina nodded, not trusting herself to speak. She hadn't done anything. Would never figure out how to do anything, not even under this new moon. She was safe in cowardice. Phoebe's hair spelled incantations in its curls and it would have been the work of seconds to reach out, turn the face and taste the gappy teeth. But Mina didn't even sling an arm through Phoebe's.

More houses, windows mostly shuttered. Phoebe walked quickly, her small bun bobbing as she went. 'Here,' she said. The house was just like all the others on its row. The downstairs lights were on and the walls were painted a green like the top of a pool table.

'No, you have to stand this way.' Phoebe pulled Mina's shoulders, angling her, then pressing her down into a squat. 'So, this was the real dream. One day we were going to have art. I don't mean Picassos, but I don't mean a museum print of *Starry Night* either. Real art by real artists.' She pointed. 'Like that.' On the wall was a painting. It was hard to tell the exact dimensions but Mina thought maybe about the size of a fridge door. It was of a shiny black pair of shoes. They were huge but the shape was that of a little girl's patent Mary Janes slightly worn. Creases lumped the toes, and the strap of one was undone and left to hang. Blobs of paint imitated the shine of light.

'That's cool,' Mina said. Her thighs were getting sore in the squat and she stood. She liked museums enough but none of her friends had art. They had Polaroids, sometimes record covers, vinyl decals. It wasn't a thing she'd thought to want. Phoebe pressed her face against the railings, staring into that house, her lower lip curled under her teeth. It was a look Mina could only call hunger. Gently, she reached out and stroked Phoebe's shoulder. She wanted to tell her that it would all be okay.

O scar, I need you.' The voice on the other end of the phone was slurred. He took the toothbrush out of his mouth.

'Mina?' he asked. How late was it there? Five a.m.? Six?

'Oscar, something terrible's going to happen.'

His chest felt hard and he swallowed the toothpaste. Mint clogged his throat. What had she done? 'Mina, what's wrong with your voice? Are you hurt?'

'Don't say my name like that.'

'Like what?'

'Like that. MMMinaaa,' she said.

It hit him. 'You're drunk.'

'No, I'm not.'

'Yes, you are.'

'Only a few drinks. Just a few. With Pheeebeee.'

'Go to sleep, Mina.'

'When are you coming back?'

'Soon.'

'Something terrible's going to happen.'

'Go to sleep, Mina.'

Mina woke up first. Her head hurt. They'd both drunk too much at the pub. Phoebe was sprawled on the bed, in her waitress clothes. Memories of the night before burbled upwards.

After the third drink, all Phoebe could talk about was her husband's new lover. She had cried. Not a lot. Just a few tears rolling out, like candies from a gumball machine. Mina had wanted to swallow them up. Instead, she'd fed Benson peanuts from the bar.

She'd nodded and touched Phoebe's arm again, feeling as if she was stealing something. If she was a man, she would be an ugly sort. She'd be a user. She'd be the kind of man who waited for his female friends' hearts to break so he could slip the pieces into his pocket. The only difference: she held no hope that this sad girl would tumble into her comforting embrace.

The pub closed and they went back to 4B. Phoebe collapsed on the bed. But Mina hadn't been able to sleep. She'd called Oscar. She'd begged. Weak. She didn't want to be this fucking weak.

She went to the fridge, looking for a treat to give Benson. He'd polished off the can of Grain-Free dog food Phoebe had left for him. Mina had no meat. She dipped her fingers into the margarine. Kneeling, she called to the dog, beckoning with her yellowed digits. He lapped at her hand until it was sticky with dog-spit.

Oscar's voice had sounded so different. She hadn't been able to imagine the faces he was making. Was he leaving her? Was that what this was? Was he expecting her to jump off the roof or otherwise dispose of herself so that he could get on with his work? Had he stopped loving her? Was the slogan right all along: You had to love yourself to be lovable? It was a terrifying idea. Life without Oscar. Nobody would worry about her now. Nobody would wonder where she was. Nobody would ask what she was doing to make herself happy. It would just be her and life, that stubborn thing.

Should she continue stripping the walls? What would happen after she removed all these birds? The naked wall was too rough to be easily cleaned up with a slap of paint. Still, she'd tried to do this for her husband, not that he was here to see.

Phoebe walked in, wearing only boxer shorts and a shirt. Bare legs poured out from the shorts, and Mina saw there was one more freckle just in the inner bend of Phoebe's right thigh. Benson ran to Phoebe. His long tail sighed against the floor.

'Is your mummy a mess? Yes, she is, yes, she is. Poor Auntie Mina had to put up with Mummy blubbing all night.' But Phoebe was smiling now, relaxed and confident. She was the sort of person who knew her blubbering would be forgiven.

Mina was an only child. She'd never be an auntie. Phoebe kissed the dog again and again. Each pucker sounded like a bubble popping.

Mina had a feeling, not *déjà vu*, the opposite. *Après vu*? The sense she'd see this mouth kiss again and again. Outside the sky was a block of cloud. Somewhere nearby someone was drilling. There was no romance here. For a moment, she thought she saw a leering face in the plasterwork, but it was just a long scratch and two gouges. But here was this bright girl and Mina's blood knew what Ovid had known, what the Greeks had known, what every myth and story taught, that sometimes against all better judgement you try to catch the nymph darting by. Or maybe it was nothing so grand as that. Maybe it was just that her brain was a slop bag of chemicals.

'Phoebe?' she said.

Phoebe gave Benson one last kiss right on the tip of his nose and stood up. Mina was already standing so close to her that it required only one step forwards. Phoebe had a slight height advantage even in bare feet. Mina angled her face up. Her lips met Phoebe's. It was a dry kiss. Her tongue stayed behind her teeth. Her eyes were open, but her face was too close to Phoebe's to detect an expression. She pulled away. She stepped back.

'Oh,' Phoebe said.

'Sorry,' Mina said.

'Oh,' Phoebe repeated. And she sat down on the arm of the couch. Benson rolled onto his back begging for a belly scratch. The top of the dog's head received so many of Phoebe's kisses. Mina had taken just one.

She had given Oscar a similar close-mouthed kiss many times. Quick and casual, forgotten as soon as skin parted from skin. This kiss dawdled in the air. Invisible—but not quite gone.

'I never thought of you like that,' Phoebe said.

Mina knew she was not the sort of girl that girls fall for. A woman would see her cracks and stay away. Men might overlook them, but they'd be obvious to a woman.

'You're married,' Phoebe said, 'to my brother's friend.' She scrunched her face. The room smelled of the fabric softener's chemical-bloom. When had Mina lost her ability to plan, to see beyond the impulse, to understand what might happen next? Was this what Dr Helene had meant by impulsive behaviour? Was it sickness? Or just the simple, normal desire to push yourself towards something beautiful? Her mind must be more than just a list of symptoms.

Phoebe circled her right hand around her left wrist so thumb and pinkie met. Then she adjusted so it was thumb and ring finger, then thumb and index. Then the process reversed. Was it a gesture people who knew her well recognised? How long did you have to know someone before you memorised each twitch?

Outside the apartment, the world paced onwards. Inside, Phoebe and Mina and a few straggler birds were suspended in time. Standing above her, Mina saw the birch-white strip of Phoebe's bent neck, the tip of her nose, the edge of her mouth, her lowered eyes.

Mina dropped down onto the couch next to her. She edged closer. There was time for Phoebe to stand or slap. But Phoebe just danced her fingers around her wrist.

This kiss was different—slow and toothy, not a bite but a dragging of incisors over lip skin. The back of Phoebe's neck rested in Mina's palm and Phoebe's curls tickled Mina's thumb. Their bodies tilted to the couch cushions, all elbows and legs and hot breath. From the corner of her eye, she could see the way Phoebe's hair splayed out onto the orange sofa. Orange hair. Orange cotton. Phoebe should have disappeared into it. Instead Mina noticed whispers of gold among the red strands.

Mina had read essays by lesbians. They were eloquent about acceptance and rejection and marriage rights. They didn't tell her what to do with hand and mouth. But so far this was okay. She was okay. Phoebe sighed as Mina's mouth found its way to her neck. Mina thought this was what it was to be a nymph or a river god or any hungry creature.

'Wait,' Phoebe said. And Mina pulled herself up and back and away. Her greed had stained Phoebe's throat. The skin was as pink as if raspberries had been smashed there. Mina waited. She had the instinct to plead but no idea what it was she should be pleading for. Phoebe's discretion, her forgiveness, another chance?

Phoebe said, 'I should go.' She stomped her legs into her jeans. Socks covered the freckled toes. Her bag was swung over her shoulder.

She called Benson to her and, Mina forgotten, he ambled forward. The round haunches rolled jauntily, as if he had witnessed nothing of note. Phoebe clipped the leash to his collar with a vicious click.

'Wait,' Mina said.

'I need to think.' Phoebe already had her hand on the door.

'But . . .' Mina said.

The door shut. Mina walked to the sink and poured her dry mouth a tall glass of water, then a second glass, then a third. She filled herself with the coldness. Phoebe would be in the elevator. Mina ran a nail along her arm and watched a chalk-like line appear. She did it again until there were five, like a cartoon prisoner's log. Phoebe would be in the street. Phoebe would be gone. The time had passed to chase her.

Oscar slept, woke in the light of the new day and began to run again. He beat his sore feet against the road. He'd thought he was there to learn the Japanese side of the business, not to be told a sordid family drama. Perhaps he should be thinking about working for someone else. He could work in a sane, clean office, where everyone fulfilled their contracts, and there was no rumpled bed or crying wife. A place where he wouldn't have to think about being a professional. He'd just be one. He thought of himself alone, no Mina, no weird family situation. And then he pushed himself to run faster. He pushed harder into the wind. He pushed until the wind and pain blew through his head and everything else was gone.

Blue. Green. Pine. Car. His father's house. The grind of gravel underfoot. The slowing of his muscles. Breath. Sweat clung to Oscar's upper lip. He flopped forwards and braced himself against his knees. He needed water. A shower would be great. He rolled back his shoulders. He loved the end of the run, when his head was full of heat and blood and empty of thought. He towelled his face with the front of his shirt, and as he lowered the fabric the front door opened. Bodies filled the space. Ami and his father were side by side. Ami supported her husband's elbow. His father's face was as pale as bread dough, puffy too. Oscar felt he'd seen the scene before. A body leaning on a body never meant anything good.

'Dad . . . Ami . . .'

Ami led his father forward a few more steps. 'Your dad's had a thing. I'm driving him to the hospital.'

'A thing?'

'I'll call you and explain.'

'I should come.'

His father said, 'It's probably nothing.'

'Please, Oscar. Just stay here,' Ami said. And he saw himself through her eyes, the awkward relative getting underfoot in the emergency.

'Let me know if there's anything I can do.'

She propped his father against the porch. 'I'll drive the car out of the garage,' she said.

'Just a spasm,' his father said. His breath was audible in the quiet air.

'Dad—' But then the car was there and Ami was opening the door. Oscar took his father's arm. It was thin, all elbow and bone. His father gripped him, the nail digging into Oscar's skin.

They drove off, the sound disappearing into the breath of wind through the pines.

Hunger hacked at Mina's gut. She stuck a hand onto the cool surface of the counter to balance herself against the rush. Drips coagulated on the refrigerator's back wall. A bag of basil skulked in a corner. When Mina pulled it out, she saw it had gone limp and damp. The wobbling pat of tofu didn't look like an adequate meal.

Outside, the evening's chill clung to her T-shirt. The supermarket was close and she walked quickly. The world smelled of wet leaves on cement. It was a smell Mina always forgot until autumn came again. A soft smell. A kind smell. Despite her hunger she stood for a moment, letting this good scent into her lungs. She wished she could call Phoebe to ask if she too had noticed this smell. Did it smell like this where Oscar was? Mina crossed her arms over her cold chest and hurried to the store.

She walked up and down the vegetable aisle. She lifted a sweet potato, feeling its rough hide. It seemed too exhausting to chew. She ran a finger down a long leek and cupped a broccoli crown. The greenery seemed as inedible as the tree roots that pushed against London's pavements. She ventured into dry goods. The chips, or crisps as the English called them, were packaged in colours appropriate for toy trucks or nuclear warning signs.

Mina lapped the lanes again and again. The strip lights pasted blemishes onto the faces of the shoppers. She turned into the confectionary aisle. The boxes were gaudy gold, purple, orange. In their glare, she almost missed the couple walking hand in hand. A boy and a girl. In their wire basket nuzzled a bottle of wine and a pale baguette. Mina followed them at a safe distance, wanting to remain in the orbit of young love. The girl stopped walking. Mina stopped too, next to a display of milk-chocolate pumpkins. The girl threw her arms around the boy's neck, wrapping tight around him as a vine around a tree. Mina ducked away.

The hunger had not left, but Mina could not tell what it hungered for. Somehow she ended up in the meat aisle. It didn't smell how she thought meat should smell. The stench wasn't life or death, but disinfectant. Here there were no bodies, only pieces—a flock of wings, a phalanx of legs, a huddle of breasts. Eventually, even the sense of body part disappeared. There were only blobs of pink and red. She opened the refrigerator cabinet and touched a lump. It had the same give as a human arm or a thigh. With her eyes shut, she might be touching Phoebe, or Oscar. She removed a sirloin steak. The meat was food-dye red. Wasn't food dye made out of beetles? Through the plastic wrap, she pressed her thumb harder into the squishy flesh. A firm band of fat crowned the top, and this resisted her more.

'Can I help you?' The boy looked like a high schooler. His eyes were the same black as the single hair on his upper lip. There was fear in them.

Mina looked down to where her thumbs pressed into the meat. In the past, people had told her she looked like a vegetarian, whatever that meant. Did he think she was protesting? Or perhaps he thought she was a crazed carnivore about to rip open the packet and chew. 'I'm fine,' she said. 'Just shopping.'

He didn't leave.

'I'm fine,' she repeated. Before he could reply, she walked away, turning so quickly her shoes squeaked. The meat was in her hands. She thought of slipping it behind a bank of chocolate bars, but she didn't like the thought of it festering there so she carried it to the checkout and paid for lipids and blood.

In the apartment, she slid it to the very back of the fridge and flipped it upside down so only the innocent foam tray showed.

She opened her mood calendar and carefully, one by one, she tore out all the pages. One by one she dropped them into the mouth of the trash. Each one she watched drift slowly down. She would not, could not, live a life of downward arrows. And if they kept going down then the least she could do was stop drawing them.

The llama stared at him under white lashes. The eyelashes belonged on a billboard, but the teeth were a gross yellow-brown. Oscar was not a pet person. He thought maybe pet-love was best practised from a young age, like a foreign language or a violin. His mother had never had an animal. She always said she got more pleasure from wild things. At school some of the boys had had rodents, but all the cool animals were off limits—snakes, bats, Alaskan wolfhounds.

Ami had texted from the hospital to say they were keeping his father overnight for observation. That she'd sleep there.

He had angina in July. Think it may be another. Please feed Ichiro his evening treat. Apples in kitchen. Slice first.

Angina. His first thought was vagina, a ridiculous thought, the thought of a child. Yet there it was angina, vagina. Mina would know the etymology. Mina . . . he should tell Mina this.

Oscar googled. It wasn't like a heart attack. It was a heart attack—the smallest kind. Smaller than an infarction, smaller than cardiac arrest. It wasn't a stopping of blood to the heart, just a weakening of flow. Oscar thought of his own heart, beating and beating every second he'd been alive, as reliable as the sun or the stars.

He saw again the way his father and Ami leaned on each other. He wished his wife were there, that she was wrapping her arms around his head, that he could press his nose into her neck and smell her warmth. He'd have to apologise for not calling. He should have called more. It was only that he'd had nothing to say. Why was he thinking about his wife? Shouldn't he be thinking about his father? They always wrote on Facebook when someone posted sad news, *Sending thoughts and prayers*. Better just to do what Ami had asked.

The llama shunted its head between the widely spaced wires of the fence. Steel dug against wool, but Ichiro didn't seem to notice. The teeth were really very long. He might lose a finger. Oscar thought of all the people who died rafting, abseiling, on safari, doing meaningless things for the sake of it. But his father was in hospital. His wife was crazy. If his semi-stepmother wanted the llama fed, he could do that one thing.

He took the smallest slice. The skin was waxy. He put the apple on the flat of his hand. The tongue was slimy. The lump moved under the short-haired jaw and pulsed down the animal's neck.

It was cold in the apartment. The sud-smell from the de-wallpapering misted the air. Her body ached but would not sleep. What time was it? She had kissed Phoebe. She had kissed Phoebe. She had kissed Phoebe. What did it mean? It didn't feel real. Phoebe would never speak to her again. And she'd have to lie to Oscar. Even if he held her again, she'd never be able to relax against his chest. Because the lie would be a wall between them. She'd know that her mouth had drifted and she'd tasted the salt of Phoebe's skin. That salt might stay in Mina's arteries for years. No. No lies. If she lied, then this would be bigger and worse. Maybe he'd mind less, because Phoebe was a woman. Maybe he wouldn't think it was as big a deal. Even thinking that she felt like a shit. She didn't want Phoebe because she was a woman, or at least Mina didn't think so. She wanted her because she was Phoebe. Not that it would help to tell Oscar that. Facts would be best.

Her phone tried to predict each word. After *k* it suggested keep and know but *ki* got it to kiss. For Phoebe, it required the first four letters. Mina was thankful for that reprieve. It made her feel for a moment as if her desires were not so predictable.

It hung in the New Message box—*I kissed Phoebe*. She clicked Send. Oscar knew now. He knew what she had done. The small, hungry thing.

I'm sorry, she typed and then deleted it. *Will you call me?* She deleted that too. She wondered if she should claim the message was a typo. But what could she possibly have meant to write? *I killed Phoebe? I missed Phoebe? I dissed Phoebe? I kissed peaches? I killed peaches?*

No, it wouldn't work. The birds stared down at her from the walls. The phone's light faded from gleam to grey. And he did not call. Although he must be awake.

She could not sleep in her room surrounded by the birds' eyes. And so as dawn came up she crashed on the orange sofa, surrounded by scarred plaster.

The hangover licked Oscar's eyeballs. He had tried to work, but he'd just ended up drinking. He turned on his phone. His wife's message rose up onto the screen.

I kissed Phoebe.

The words sat there as he tried to understand them. Two faces crushed together. Mina's teeth and tongue shunted into a mouth he'd tasted long ago. What next? It was one thing for Mina to cancel a visit to his mother, to cut him even, and another to throw herself upon the sister of his oldest friend. Did you have to forgive someone everything just because they were depressed?

He didn't bother figuring out what time it was over there. He called.

'What the fuck?' he asked.

'I don't know.'

'What do you mean you don't know?'

'You told me you wanted me to try to be happy. And my head just feels full of rocks. All the time. All the time.'

He could see it now—Mina wild-eyed. The way Phoebe's mouth would twist in shock and she'd shove Mina back. The way Mina's hair would fall across her face. His wife craven with apologies, saying she was just crazy, saying she was just full of rocks. He could see how she would cross her arms over her chest the way she did when she was worried.

'It was stupid,' she said.

In other circumstances, his wife kissing Phoebe might've been hot. Now he just wanted peace.

'Mina, what am I supposed to do? What am I supposed to tell Theo?'

'That's what you care about? Theo? I'm sorry. But you weren't here and . . . and . . .'

'Mina, do you have any idea what I'm dealing with?'

'I might if you told me. I'm not stupid. I know you're avoiding me. What happened? You got tired, so you left. Grow some balls. Tell me that. Tell me you don't want to see me anymore.'

Oscar forced himself to be calm. He rolled one deltoid, then the other. Pull himself together. He needed to pull himself together.

'Oscar, are you there?'

If he spoke he'd say something awful. Something cruel. 'I can't talk to you,' he said, 'not when you're like this, Mina. I won't be back for a while.'

Somewhere in the house a landline began to ring. It bleeped with the shrill importance of a baby crying.

'Mina, I've got to go.'

With each step he took, Oscar tried to put Mina out of his mind. The ringing was coming from his father's study in the eaves of the house. It was a small room with a wooden table pressed against the window. There was one chair. One bookshelf. A jar with one pen, two pencils, one ruler, and a pair of orange-handled scissors. He picked up the telephone, and a voice began in polite Japanese. The beginnings of words made sense but the phrasings were too formal for Oscar to imitate. In the politest Japanese he had, he explained that Umeda-san had been taken ill and asked the man to call later.

A picture of Ami stood on the windowsill. She looked very young. A purple beret was tucked over her ears. She was sitting on a stone wall, her toes meeting in a point. She was smiling at those shoes like she and they shared a secret understanding. Had his father already fucked his mother when this was taken?

He thought of the way Ami had kissed his father's hand. The way she had held him.

Oscar had never wanted to cheat on Mina. He found plenty of women attractive. But he hadn't wanted to be the sort of person who made a promise and broke it. Anyway, the logistics removed any excitement. He'd have to find a cheap room, pack protection, and shower afterwards, then be careful not to come home smelling of hotel shampoo. It was so much to keep track of. Yet his father seemed to have got away with it. Oscar pulled the picture of that baby from his wallet. Why hadn't his father stayed in England at least? Why give up so easily? What if it was too late to ask? No, angina wasn't deadly. This wasn't a heart attack, just a heart glitch. His father would be fine.

He went back down to the bedroom. He ordered samples of the red rice beer and a stout that had a coffee-chocolaty aroma to Jimmy's bar and to George's place. George managed a fish place in Williamsburg. There were only two menu options. Despite or because of this the restaurant flourished. The tiny shop appealed to Japanese expats and skinny white girls alike. George's opinion counted.

The hangover bit another morsel of Oscar's brain.

Neither of them wrote to her. Not Phoebe. Not Oscar. On the app, Oscar's little icon hovered smugly across the world. Her arms itched. She wondered if she was allergic to fabric softener. It was as if her body wanted to be clawed away. Be happy, she thought. That was what Oscar had asked her to do. And she had tried. All wrong. But she had tried.

Ovid told the story of a girl who fell into a mad lust with her brother. It was a love that kept her rocking awake through the night. The hunger disgusted her but would not end. Finally, she confessed her love in a note scratched onto a tablet. Her brother was horrified. But she hoped with tears to change his mind. She begged and pleaded. He ran from her. And she was left to walk the earth in hunger and sorrow. Many of the women walked. It was a thing they did, pacing out their miseries as if distance might cure them. And sometimes it did. This girl was found by the nymphs, who witnessed her weeping and weeping. They helped in the only way they knew how. They transformed her into a bubbling spring that flowed from dark soil. Sometimes Mina thought the transformed were the lucky ones.

Mina wept briefly, in a burst as sudden as a sneeze. But her arms and legs did not fold or flow or burst into rivers.

*C*an *you meet me at the Victoria and Albert Museum cafe
at 2:30*

Phoebe's text was a question but there was no question
mark at the end. Did that indicate an assumption of agreement
or an indifference to Mina's sense of grammar? It was a public
place. Perhaps she was trying to stop Mina making a scene.
Did Mina look like the sort of person who would make a
scene? Mina considered waiting to reply. If she waited, Phoebe
would wait. And they'd spend weeks and months in artificial
silence.

Okay, she wrote. It seemed more relaxed than *OK*. *Ay*
added a mellow sway.

Two-thirty was soon. She'd slept until noon. Every time
her eyes opened to the light she'd remembered the tone of
Oscar's voice and dived back into sleep, until finally her body
refused.

What to wear? Out of the window, the smooth sky was
pillowcase white. She touched the top of her arm, where
she knew the inked peonies wrapped and guarded her. But
today they didn't seem enough. She needed another talisman,
but it had to be equally hidden. She couldn't show up in a
red lipstick. She mustn't look over-the-top. Or like the sort
of woman who had affairs often and easily. She'd never
done anything like this. Perfume? Had she packed it? The
vial was in the plastic bag of toiletry miscellany that she'd
shoved under the sink. The glass tube was mostly full. Mina

rarely wore perfume. She was convinced the bluster of city life blew it away. She held the tip of the small nozzle under her nose. Orange and cardamom. The top jammed, stiff with lack of use. She hit it harder with her palm and it sprayed. She let the bottle kiss her wrists and the backs of her ears. With her eyes shut, she felt like she was standing in an orange grove somewhere sun-blessed. She'd never been to an orange grove. They were probably rank with pesticides. In spite of this, she thought of nymphs fleet-footing it through the trees.

The museum's steps were bloated with tourists. Mina's eyes caught on a brace of teenagers. A boy slotted his hand neatly into the back of a girl's jeans. It made them complete in some way, like when two sections of flat-pack are slotted together and suddenly a bookshelf emerges.

Where was Phoebe?

THE EXCELLENCE OF EVERY ART MUST CONSIST IN THE COMPLETE ACCOMPLISHMENT OF ITS PURPOSE, proclaimed the gold letters above the door. Women had been sculpted to hold the words. Most wore thin drapes that clung to thighs and breasts but the central figures, the ones holding up *IN THE*, were naked to their belly buttons. There was nothing to indicate the purpose of these women. Or maybe they were nymphs.

The difference between nymphs and women was vague. They had breasts, thighs, toes. They desired and were desired. Sure, nymphs were of the sea, the woods, and rivers. But it barely seemed to matter. No, the biggest difference was that nymphs did not get old. They were transformed into many things but never into women, mundane and middle-aged. Mina's back ached. Her shoulders ached. Her neck ached. Oscar would have told her the name of each screaming muscle, but he did not want to talk to her.

Mina's eyes fell to Phoebe sitting on the step, her long legs flung out, crossed at their suede booties. A sweater was tossed over one shoulder, as jaunty as a catalogue model's. She scribbled in that little notebook. Mina stepped quietly. She didn't say anything until they were positioned as close as old friends.

'Working on a blog?' Mina asked.

'Nah,' Phoebe said. 'I just like it here and I thought we should talk.'

Mina put out a hand to help her up. But Phoebe pressed her palm on the dirty step and pushed herself upright. Phoebe would rather touch that much-trodden slab than Mina's freshly washed fingers.

'I'm bad at this,' Phoebe said.

'Okay.' Mina didn't know what to do with her hands. She crossed them over her chest. That seemed aggressive so she dropped them to her sides. But then they were dangling purposelessly. Phoebe reached into her bag and pulled out a packet of cigarettes. She put one into her mouth. The lighter took a few clicks before the flame started.

'I thought you gave up smoking,' Mina said. 'Not that it's any of my business.' Had she sounded sarcastic? She hadn't meant to. It wasn't her business.

'Yeah,' Phoebe said, 'I also promised to be married to one person forever and ever and ever, until I died blah-blah.' She puffed a thin streamer of smoke.

'That makes sense,' Mina said, mostly because it seemed good to agree. She had never kissed a smoker and, for some reason, that seemed much more foreign than kissing a woman. What would Phoebe's mouth taste like now? She supposed she'd never know.

'You know the guy who designed the birds on your wallpaper? They have his wife's wedding ring here.'

'Okay.' Mina touched her own. The band was moulded into

a swirl of leaves and few people realised it was a wedding ring.

'But they also have the jewellery his wife's lover gave her. And they call those her most interesting pieces. Like the lover's jewellery was better, as if her husband's wedding ring wasn't right there . . .' Phoebe trailed off.

Mina stepped closer to Phoebe as a river of school kids tumbled out of the museum. She fumbled for what to say. 'Women in those days, I mean . . . they didn't have much of a choice about being married. You can't really blame her.'

'Okay, fair. But my husband did. He chose to be married. He chose to sleep in the same bed. He slept in sheets we chose together. He heard me talk in my sleep. We had a dog together.'

Where was Benson? Was he just waiting for Phoebe to come home? Were his teeth ripping into the furniture, his bounding heart shredded with anxiety that Phoebe was gone forever? Mina sympathised.

'I'm not doing what that skank did to me to another person. I'm not going to be that shitty selfish human.'

Skank. It sounded like the word for some imaginary monster, something with a snake's face and lion's claws—or like a jabberwock or bandersnatch. Was Mina a skank? What did it feel like to be a skank?

'It's not like you think,' she said.

'You're not a married woman?' Phoebe asked, voice sticky with sarcasm.

'Okay, yes.' There was an awkward pause. Mina ran her tongue over the top of her teeth. 'But it's not like that.'

I can't talk to you, those were his words. Not even, *I won't.* But, *I can't.* You, after all these years, have disappointed me too much.

'What's it like, then?' Phoebe seemed confused. 'Aren't you living in his . . .'

210

'It's complicated.' And it was. How big a space meant a departure? It was cold, and someone was shouting in Italian.

'Why?'

'He says he doesn't want to talk to me. He won't tell me when he's coming back from America.'

'Because of?' Phoebe made a sweeping gesture with her hand, covering the space between them.

'No, nothing to do with you.' And it wasn't, not really. Phoebe was so new to her life.

'Why then?'

'I changed.'

Phoebe laughed, her arm reached out and grabbed Mina's shoulder to steady herself. Mina savoured each digit. She had not horrified Phoebe entirely.

'That's what my husband said too. You aren't the person I married. Have you ever heard such complete and utter rubbish? The person I married came home on time and didn't have to be nagged about dishes and gave me foot massages. But so it goes . . . You get married, you change. Or maybe you don't change. Maybe he was always a liar and a cheat.'

'I'm sorry that happened to you,' Mina said. She twirled her wedding ring. 'Though maybe, I don't know, maybe I did change.' She felt like a different person, a person whose contours had cracked and chipped.

'I should show you my favourite thing in this place,' Phoebe said. She ground the cigarette out with her boot and left it there. They walked in under a great green glass chandelier. They ducked past the dead heads of Roman senators into a courtyard. A truck was selling refreshments. Kids crumbled muffins onto the tables. Phoebe turned a corner and pointed to the wall. Two glazed plaques were sealed into the bricks. Each was only the size of a piece of printer paper. One was green and the other brown-black.

211

TO
TYCHO
A FAITHFVL DOG
WHO DIED·V·IAN·
MDCCCLXXXV·

And on the right:

In Memory of
Jim
Died 1879
Aged 15 Years.
Faithful Dog of
Sir Henry Cole,
of this
Museum.

'I've loved these ever since I was little. Was always a dog person. I used to say I'd name my dog Tycho. But somehow I forgot, and then Benson was already Benson.' Phoebe smiled, her crooked tooth showing.

'Why not Jim?'

'What?'

'Why Tycho and not Jim?'

'Tycho's a better name. Obviously.'

'Poor Jim,' Mina said. And she turned away from the panels, only to realise that Phoebe was just behind her. Their noses were nearly touching.

'Oh,' Phoebe said. 'Fuck it.'

Why Phoebe chose that minute to kiss her Mina would never know. In the moment, it was not the first question that came to mind. Phoebe's mouth was warm and the kiss dissolved, like a marshmallow. There was only the slightest hint of ash.

'There are children here,' Mina said, but did not step away. Her hand had found the curve of Phoebe's back.

'So let's go where they aren't.'

After they made it back to the apartment, Phoebe and Mina kissed. Under the bead-eyed birds, they rolled around on the bed, measuring the length and breadth of it with their bodies. Their feet twisted the sheets. Mina was sure she'd remember this. But as soon as she thought it, she wasn't sure what this moment was. Was it Phoebe's hands finding their way under Mina's shirt? Was it Phoebe's lashes and the red that shone through the mascara like the heat within a coal? Or was it the simple sense of body plus body?

She had half expected that Phoebe's form would be familiar. Two women were surely similar. But Phoebe was as foreign as a body could be. The cherry-pit nipples felt new. The swerve of the hips felt new. The long flat buttocks felt new. They looked like two pillows recently slept on. Her mouth fitted exactly into the dip below Phoebe's hipbone. It was as if her own body had known exactly what it needed.

'Stop,' Phoebe said.

Mina stopped. Every muscle in her body tensed.

'Your nails.' Phoebe sat up in the bed.

Her nails. They weren't pretty. They weren't polished or filed. The pink oblongs extended to a white ridge. Idiot. Idiot. Idiot. Girls who liked girls kept their nails short. Everyone knew that. Everyone. But no girl had ever let Mina close enough for nails to matter.

'I can cut them,' she said 'I'll cut them. Wait here.'

The plastic bag of toiletries lay on the bathroom floor. She'd never quite bothered unpacking it. Her hand fumbled through sample packets of moisturiser, disposable razors, tweezers. No clippers. She poured them onto the floor in a tinkling, clanking rush. No clippers were immediately visible.

213

What about the kitchen scissors? She could use those. Would the sliced nails be too rough? Sharp angles were unacceptable. Maybe the clippers were hidden in the rainbow scatter on the tiles. There were no windows in the bathroom and the bulb gave a sallow tallow light. She dropped to the floor, running her hands through the bottles of nail polish, the hotel shampoos, everything that was not a pair of nail clippers. A lip balm rolled under the sink. She noticed then the spider of hair gathered in the corner. Her bleached hair and Oscar's black had balled into this disgusting tangle of marriage. She'd deal with that later.

What about the bathroom cabinet? She caught a glimpse of herself in the mirror and saw the strange soft body, the lace of her bra faded to grey. Mina gripped the edge of the sink. Phoebe would be getting bored. She had to look faster. There was Oscar's toothbrush. He must've forgotten it. The bristles were bent from months between his molars. Oscar's toothbrush. Poor abandoned thing. No, she was losing track. There—camouflaged behind the taps, clippers. Long and silver, with a steely mouth open. Mina picked them up. They were hefty, for toes and not fingers. But they'd do.

Phoebe rapped on the frame of the open door.

'I found them,' Mina said.

'Give me.' Phoebe held out an open palm. 'Sit.' Phoebe gestured to the closed toilet lid. Mina stepped over the chaos and sat. Phoebe balanced on the edge of the bath. The shower curtain billowed around her, gowning her. Phoebe's bare feet rested on the tiles, and if Mina had been feeling less ridiculous, less foolish, she would have reached down and stroked their copper-stippled curves.

'Hand,' Phoebe said. Mina put out her right hand. Phoebe took it. Her touch was careful. She eased the clippers' steel mouth over Mina's thumbnail. One by one, she stripped each finger.

'I'm sorry,' Mina said. 'I'm sorry.'

'Don't be silly.' Phoebe petted the hand she was holding.

'I just didn't think you'd . . . I wasn't prepared.'

'It's fine.'

Mina wanted to ask, Am I doing this right? How many other people have you done this with? Mina felt ridiculous to have reached her thirties and have failed to touch a female body.

Phoebe tilted her head to one side and asked, 'What's the worst sex you ever had?'

Mina boggled at her, but Phoebe tilted her head to the side, pale brows rising. Perhaps because they were in the bathroom Mina thought of Mr Dereham, the drama teacher's husband. They'd never even touched and certainly never had sex. Mina had put her email address on a list for everyone involved in the school play. It was her first email address, ridiculous-nickname@yahoo.com. A week into rehearsal she'd started getting the photographs. They were taken in a bathroom mirror. You could see his wife's Frizz Ease shampoo in the background. His naked body was too awkward to be frightening. Later Dr Helene had wanted to make something of it. Somehow, though, Mina had never been scared of Mr Dereham. She was only anxious that her grandma might glance over at the computer screen to see the crisscross trail of hair under Mr Dereham's belly. Her grandma often came to where Mina sat at the beige desktop. She'd be carrying a plate of washed grapes or a mug of jasmine tea or a single chocolate to keep Mina's strength up through her homework. She did not need to see the sad pouch of that belly.

When Mina finished describing Mr Dereham, Phoebe laughed. 'So stop looking so stressed. This can't be worse than that, can it?' She kissed the back of Mina's now declawed right hand. Mina marvelled. What had she done to deserve such gentleness? She would have to find a way to thank her.

'Other one,' Phoebe said.

Mina put her left hand out and hoped for the best.

Afterwards, naked and tired, Mina and Phoebe lay in bed and talked. The talk was of nothing important, just the peeling back of lives that lovers do. Each episode of life unwrapped revealed another layer of paper to be torn through. Mina recited the details of her years in New York—the dumpling place in Flushing, the library at the university, the silver-backed cat who lived in the bodega. Mina described her grandmother in the hospital bed. Her calves had been so smooth, like a little girl's, and it was strange and obscene. Mina went further back until she was a child lying awake in bed, waiting for the click and shuffle of her dad coming home. Somehow it was possible to talk about her life without mentioning bridges or pills. Eventually, she'd tell Phoebe but not yet. She wanted to bask in the warmth of this moment.

Phoebe told of a mortgage and how the bank manager held himself like a headmaster. But he'd signed the papers for the flat in Peckham. She'd loved the word *Peckham*, and the punch of the *p*. Her husband lived there now, because he was better able to fulfil the mortgage. He'd paid off her stake. It was better this way. There were smaller shames. Strange ones that lasted despite their insignificance. Phoebe had been in a school play and she'd fallen centre stage, but everyone had thought it was part of the show. She said how her brother's friends had found ways to touch her in the garden or the children's playroom or the pantry. Phoebe had grown up in a house with a pantry: how absurd, how lovely.

'Shit. It's my shift.' Phoebe kicked the sheets to the floor where they fell like a surrendered flag. She ran to the bathroom dressing as she went, shirt over her head. Then she was out again. She flourished a make-up brush and eyeshadow artillery. The brush moved double-time over the lids, painting them peach, not that used Band-Aid pink-beige that people meant

216

when they said peach. Phoebe's lids were gold and fuchsia and glossy, as lush as the sun-ripe fruit. They said to the world, *Eat me!* Then she was gone.

Mina made the bed. She scooped the spider of hair from under the sink. She bustled. A message appeared on her phone.

Hired decorators. Starting week from now. Please let in on Mon. Paying by bank transfer.

Should she reply? Apologise again? Tell him about fucking Phoebe. Ask, 'Is Theo your big worry now?' But what right did she have to be angry? None. She thought of Oscar's poor cut hand. Had the scab healed? It must have. Her cuts had always transformed into thin white lines after about a week. Ridiculously, she wished Phoebe were here. Around Phoebe she felt calm.

She didn't notice walking to the kitchen. But it wasn't like it was a vast journey. It was a natural place to pace. She looked at the knife that had cut him. It was a good knife, not too flimsy. It had weight. In the old days, she'd cut her left wrist when it was her fault and the right when it was someone else's. She was left-handed. In both cases it was always along the rail—i.e. along the grain of her veins. And never across the tracks—i.e. across the wrist. Where had she learnt the little maxim for the best way to hurt yourself? Faint scars remained, many more on left than right. She combed the skin with the blunt side of the knife, not pressing, just running it along.

There were things she had to repent. Things she'd once have tallied on that left wrist. The bridge. Cutting Oscar. Cheating on Oscar?

No. This was ridiculous. Self-indulgent. She placed the knife on the countertop, so carefully that it made no sound. Her brain said, *I want to die.* Her first feeling was, *Oh, you again.* In an apartment that had only just held the lovely twisting body of Phoebe, her brain said, *I want to die* again.

The air of this room had embraced Phoebe's arms, legs, back, breasts. She told that hunk of an organ to shut up. But that was like telling tea not to cool or mould not to grow.

Mina tried it out loud: 'I want to die.'

Oscar heard the door and the sound of steps on the wooden floorboards. His legs carried him down the stairs and to the hall. Ami looked worse than his father, flecks of drool stuck just below her mouth. Her cardigan was buttoned wrong and hung in odd loops. His father looked just fine. No different than he'd ever been. He was even wearing his watch.

Ami yawned.

'I need a drink,' his father said.

'No, you don't,' Ami said. 'Oscar, your father is not to drink anything.'

'Oh, you're no fun.' His father hung up his coat.

'Shall I make tea?' Oscar asked.

'Something herbal,' Ami said.

Oscar made fresh mint tea. He didn't like mint, but it was there. The boiling kettle was as loud as a car starting.

'This is the second time it's happened,' Ami said.

'Don't scare the kid,' his father said.

Framed by the window, Ichiro ambled across his field, the most useless brother a man could ask for.

'Ken . . .' Ami said. 'We agreed.'

And so his father began to explain how angina isn't fatal. How it's nothing to be worried about. How he could take an aspirin. Oscar dropped leaves into the hot water and waited as the smell of toothpaste filled his nose.

'I'm retiring,' his father said, 'at the end of this year. Well, that was the plan. That's what I needed to tell you. It's why I'm selling the flats. Ami and I . . . we don't have a lot of needs. There's Ichiro, of course. But if I'm right about the market they should see us through.'

'You're retiring?' The mint leaves floated in the hot water.

'What about . . .' He stopped, because what sort of son finds out his father is ill and asks about his job? Was that what Ami had been going on about? Work elsewhere? Stop stressing out your dad? 'Do you need to eat?' Oscar asked. And then thought that it wasn't his kitchen to offer.

'I'm fine,' his father said, sounding exactly like Mina when the opposite was true.

The deer's walk was stilted. It looked like a robot hiding beneath fawn-skin. Did all deer walk like that? Mina wasn't sure. Come to think of it, she'd probably seen more robots than deer. When she'd seen the animals, they'd been on the side of the road at night, their eyes burning headlamp bright. But she hadn't absorbed the size. This creature was as large as a man. Larger. She thought of the hunter who Artemis transformed into a deer after he spotted the goddess naked. Never had Mina realised that he must've stretched to fill this form.

Benson growled, low and hungry. It was incongruous coming from an animal that looked as if it could've been stitched from a shag rug.

'No, sweetheart, not dinner.' Phoebe said to the dog, and tightened her grip on the leash. Her white knuckles looked almost green.

The deer turned its wet eyes towards them.

It had been Phoebe's idea to go to Richmond Park. Mina had imagined a park like Central Park, full of children and tourists and college students on first dates. In Richmond Park, the trees' imperious stance implied they were older even than the idea of New York. The leaves had turned, and Mina trod over brown, red and marigold. The sound of the city had retreated. She tried to describe the way space seemed to be marshalling around them.

'Just wait, someone will come along. The best time of year is the empty season. Late January, early Feb,' Phoebe said. 'Then, if you're lucky, it feels like this whole place is yours.'

They followed the path away from the deer, through a clearing in the trees, and beyond to a patch of long grass.

The leash was the kind with a big plastic handle that concealed more cord. Phoebe clicked a button that allowed the dog to roam further. Benson seemed to have forgotten the deer and was content to sniff tree roots. They sat on their coats. Mina unwrapped the sandwiches she'd made that morning—tomato and Swiss cheese. Phoebe got out her phone, frowning at the lack of signal. She held it up to the sky, leaning back so her shoulder nudged Mina's. Mina stroked Phoebe's hair. The strands were slightly coarse, coarser than Benson's, as if Phoebe were a tougher breed. Mina wreathed her fingers in the red strands.

'Do you think I'm a narcissist?' Phoebe asked.

'Obviously not.'

'Theo says I'm a narcissist.'

'You must know the story of Narcissus?'

'We learnt it in primary school,' Phoebe said, and smiled as she described how she'd been given a silver star for her drawing of the boy who fell in love with his own reflection. She'd pencilled him daffodil-gold hair. Mina tried to imagine a tiny Phoebe; each finger, toe, eyelid would have to shrink. How odd that this woman once had to learn how to tie her shoe laces and how to count.

Mina said, 'Well, Ovid describes Narcissus looking at his reflection this way . . .' She shut her eyes, spooling forth those long hours of thesis work. '*Spem sine corpore amat, corpus putat esse, quod umbra est.*' Phoebe looked blank. Mina translated, 'Ovid is saying that Narcissus, looking at his reflection, loves a hope or a shadow. His life ends because he's so caught up in his own reflection. You're his opposite. You're trying to build a life.'

'Nerd,' Phoebe said.

Mina headbutted Phoebe's shoulder and Phoebe gave in to

the fall, tipping back to the ground. It was a little cold to be lying in the browning grass. Phoebe's lips, like the leaves, had reddened in the frost. Her cheeks had turned a darker pink as though the wind had blown two poppy petals there. Mina kissed each one, half expecting them to crumple underlip.

'Why the Greeks and Romans?' Phoebe asked.

'As opposed to?' Mina frowned. People were always asking her this. She did not match their idea of the person who would command the myths. She was guilty of the same thought. When she imagined a classicist, she found herself thinking of a man in a tweed suit with a knitted tie and wire-framed glasses. She did not think of herself.

'I don't know. As opposed to something in English. As opposed to something you don't need a whole other language for.'

The answer she gave to Oscar's friends was something about the joy of translation or the elegance of Roman poetry.

Mina said, 'I've always loved the myths. I had this huge book of Greek and Roman myths. It had an orange sun on the cover and Apollo driving white horses. I used to read them aloud to my grandma, again and again. I don't know how the poor woman put up with me. I was obsessed with Persephone getting taken down to Hades. We'd already learnt about the earth rotating. I knew it wasn't literally true that her kidnapping caused the seasons. But it felt essentially true. It felt like it explained something about what it meant to be alive.'

'Essentially true?'

'Okay. I was like seven, so I probably didn't use those words in my head. I probably just thought they were magic.' But she had felt it. She knew she had. It had felt truer than the tilt of the planet or its long spin around the sun. This world made so much more sense if it was filled with angry, hungry gods. Right now, Persephone would be travelling muddy-footed down to Hades. Her dress would be trailing through moulting leaves and the crushed paper cups that once held hot chocolates or lattes or whatever people were drinking to keep warm.

Phoebe paused as if considering Mina's answer, then leaned forward and kissed the tip of Mina's nose. 'You're cute,' she said. And then, more hesitatingly, 'But, seriously, you don't think blogging's weird?'

'No weirder than anything anybody does.'

'And I have to take photos of myself, you know. I'm part of the product.'

Mina considered. 'Okay, then. Let's not take any photographs today. Let's have a photo-free day. Let's just be us.'

So there were no photos of Mina climbing a tall tree until she was up in the green-brown-gold envelope of leaves. There were no photos of her fists raised in victory as she looked down to Phoebe watching and laughing. Or of them whooping at this simple victory. There were no photos as they kissed against the steady trunk of the same tree, Mina's palms pressed to the bark. There were no photos of the tarnished silver woodlouse that ambled along the bark, which Mina didn't alert Phoebe to because she didn't want the kissing to end.

There were no photos of dusk blurring the trees into the sky. Or of the cloud that rose from the trees that was not a cloud at all but birds, a flock, pulsing and flowing through the air.

'Starlings,' Phoebe said. 'They fly here in the winter.'

'Don't birds go south?'

'England has a milder climate than where they come from. Did you know a flock of starlings is called a murmuration?'

'Murmuration,' Mina said. 'Murmuration. Murmuration.' She pressed her mouth against Phoebe's arm. 'Murmuration. Murmuration. Murmuration,' she kissed into the skin.

'Stop it! That tickles.'

'Starlings. It sounds like they should be from the stars,' Mina said.

As they lay watching the flock, each bird cut a black star against the sky. There were more birds than all the wishes Mina had ever held. Enough birds to wish for Oscar, for Phoebe, for Psyche, for Cupid, for her grandma flitted past. Her arm wrapped around Phoebe, Mina wished on each of them. 'Stay with me tonight. Don't go back to Theo's. Stay with me.'

And Phoebe nodded, her chin bobbing against Mina's forearm.

It was only on the train home, with the warm weight of Benson in her lap, that Mina regretted the day had slipped away undocumented.

Oscar's father stood in front of the hallway mirror straightening his coat sleeves.

'Dad, are you going into town?' Oscar asked. 'Is it safe for you to drive?'

'It's fine.'

'How about I come with you?'

'Oh, stop fussing. You're behaving just like Ami.'

'It's for me. I'm out of multivitamins. You could drop me off at the store.'

'What're they called? I'll grab them. I have a check-up with my primary-care doctor. It might take a while.'

'I can wait,' Oscar said.

The car had reclining heated seats. Oscar had never been a car man but as his legs stretched out he had to admit it felt good. The car was a sofa mounted on a four-wheel drive. Generous driveways and tall pines sped past the window. The ocean shimmied in and out of view.

'There's a bell in town,' his father said. 'You ring it if you see a whale.'

'That's cool.'

'Ami saw one once, but someone got to the bell before her.'

'Dad, I'm glad you're okay.'

'They took my spot.' His father gestured to a car with a big sticker on the front: *MY DAUGHTER MADE THE HONOR ROLL*. 'Look, I'll drop you off by the store.'

Oscar's vitamins were among the other bottles promising health and beauty. He was never sure if they helped, but it must be better to give the brain and body as much as you could. He walked to the place his father had told him to wait, a cluster of benches with a view of the water. A girl in silver Dr. Martens sat sideways on a bench so that her boots were propped up on the seat. Her legs were shapely, two neat arcs of calf. Sunglasses were tucked into the top of the denim dress.

'Have you seen any whales?' he asked. 'I was told they come into the bay.'

She fumbled in her pockets, dug out some earbuds and jammed them in. Oscar felt stupid. What was he doing talking to this girl? She must be only twenty, and she'd come here to sit in peace. He opened his phone and looked again at the picture of Mina that the app used. Next to her image was a red exclamation mark. The app didn't know where she was. But her battery was on 78 per cent and yesterday it had been on 62 per cent so she had charged it. She was alive. He should speak to her. He'd never imagined that he would avoid his wife. He hadn't wanted to be that man. Perhaps she was right: they never should've got married. They could divorce, he supposed. That was what people who never should've got married did.

Divorce. Damn, that was a big word. It was one of those words that attached themselves to you. Oscar Umeda— college-educated, married, divorced.

He'd have to find a lawyer. He thought of his wife's mouth

twisting against Phoebe's. He thought of his father's heart stopping. Was there a place to find reviews for divorce lawyers? Could you trust adverts online? Why was it that some sorts of tiredness, like running, left you feeling clean? Whereas others, like marriage, left you merely exhausted? If his father died and he and Mina split, Oscar would be the only Umeda. But his father wasn't going to die.

A day without Phoebe. It shouldn't be a big deal. Yesterday was still sweet in her mouth. It was almost enough. Almost. But not quite. Because Oscar was everywhere in the apartment. And her phone never rang. And again and again she looked at that little map, at his little unchanging face. She willed him to come home, to write a list, to tell her they'd sort all this out. Did missing Oscar make Phoebe a distraction? Did wanting Phoebe mean she didn't love Oscar? The desires elbowed each other for more room in her skull. Phoebe. Oscar. Oscar. Phoebe. She wished either of them were here. Anything, so she wasn't stuck alone with the monologue in her skull. It was just her and the birds.

Oscar jabbed answer B on the app. Then C, D, D, E.

90%!!!! celebrated the rabbit, and pink confetti fell across the screen. If he'd only had a minute longer it might've been 100. But the app was right: all of life was on a timer. A timer that he had not set. He'd wanted to be introduced to their contacts in imports. But he wasn't ready.

JLPT's listening component demanded: *One is able to listen and comprehend coherent conversations in everyday situations, spoken at near-natural speed, and is generally able to follow their contents as well as grasp the relationships among the people involved.*

Mina would make a joke of that. She would ask, 'Who ever fully understands the relationships among the people involved?' That was the problem with being with someone for so many years. You started saying their lines for them. Being married to an insane person meant insanity slithered into your words.

Next he'd do the one where you had to catch birds flying past carrying the correct kanji in their claws.

A message from Theo—*Finally put the case to bed. Drink?* Theo's text had its usual chipper tone.

Can't. America, Oscar typed. *Work trip.*

Boo! Guys putting together 5-a-side in 2 weeks. Back by then?

Think so, Oscar wrote. He had no idea. But it would be good to feel a ball at his feet and the knock along his muscles that meant he'd hit it just right. Or the feeling of knowing exactly where his teammates would be, of coming together, of everything just working.

The first few weeks of school Oscar had been Billy-no-mates. He was chubby back then. When some kid asked, 'What's wrong with your face?' all he'd done was shrug. Nobody asked what was wrong with Theo's face. Or perhaps they did and he kneed them in the stomach. The second week, Theo's mum sent him a fresh new Arsenal football. Everyone wanted to kick it around. Oscar was just watching from behind a book until Theo beckoned him into the foul-filled game on the lawn. By God-gifted chance Oscar scored two goals between the school-satchel goalposts. After that everything was easier.

Just before GCSEs a boy in their year killed himself. No one knew exactly how, though the halls foamed with rumours. The adults kept saying how shocking it was. He'd been a boy no one talked to, not even the other nerds. Oscar's main memory was of sitting behind him in science, watching the dandruff tumble onto his jumper.

Back then Oscar had thought, There but for the grace of God go I. Maybe it should have been the grace of footie.

Mina suggested that it would be easier for Phoebe to keep some stuff at 4B. That way she wouldn't have to keep rushing across town to change outfits.

Phoebe brought the canvas suitcase from her brother's place and left behind the pair of squat nylon twins. On the Tube, Mina steadied the weight of the bag. Phoebe's arms were busy stopping Benson wandering down-carriage. At the door to the apartment, Mina groped in her tote for the keys. 'One second,' she said, and turned to see Phoebe waiting, the sun catching the buttons of her coat. Mina stopped with her hand on the knob just to look at this human who was about to follow her inside.

Somehow that day had room for everything. Each hour became a palace of details. The clocks had moved like this when she was a child, as if they understood that she needed more space inside each minute because each minute had so much she needed to see. The tea drunk on the orange couch. Phoebe on the bed, her hair spread out in two wings, as if at any moment they might flap and carry away the lovely head. Benson in St James's Park, drawing back on his haunches at the sight of the baggy-beaked pelicans.

Oscar would call it a fish day. Never, not once, did she mention her husband, though she thought of him—his big hands, the way he liked to bite. Phoebe was soft-lipped. If she never said his name, she might be able to pretend that she was an actress in two different movies, one with a male co-star and one with a female. Two stories whose consequences would never overlap.

Oscar sat in the cold outside. It was past midnight. The stars and moon were buried under cloud but car headlights spilled along a distant road. Bugs darted towards the porch lamp in hopeful loops. The weather had turned. He'd put on his father's blue windbreaker. He got more bars of signal out here and he wanted to check in about the decorators. England was eight hours ahead and there the day was already beginning. So far he'd heard nothing from them. It wasn't encouraging. Getting the flats done was the least he could do. His father was supposed to rest, and Oscar didn't want to push him to discuss what stepping down might mean.

The head decorator took a long time to pick up, and when he did, the line was blurry with static. The man made a grunting noise when Oscar identified himself. Oscar asked how the project was going.

'Oh, yeah, meant to give you a call. My boys are held up at the last job.'

'We need this done.'

'It's a busy time of year. Everyone wants new walls by Christmas.'

'So why did you say you could do it?'

'Sorry, what was that? Driving. Reception's all buggered up.'

Oscar looked up at the house, which was grey in the porch light. Above him, Ami and his father would be asleep. It would not be useful to yell.

'When can you start then? Realistically?'

'Next week. You're top of my list.'

A sound came in the far distance, like a child screaming. It was probably an owl. Oscar hung up. He looked again at the picture of Mina in the app. The profile photo was

230

misleading. It made it seem like his wife was wandering London in her wedding dress. It would be simpler if she was that sort of madwoman. He should call her. He should do so many things. He should practise Japanese.

He called his mum. She picked up on the first ring.

'Oh, good. I was just thinking about you.' She sounded brisk. 'Are you free next weekend? You and Mina both. My friend Lydia, you know Lydia, from the poetry group. She gave me the best recipe for vegan cottage pie. Perfect for Mina.'

'Can't Mum. I'm still in America. When I get back, I'll visit.'

The Pacific night gulped down trees and roadways. He listened while his mother listed the ingredients of vegan cottage pie and told him about Lydia's divorce.

She talked until it was far past his time to sleep. He went upstairs, but had no desire for bed. So he took the skipping rope from his bag and returned to the porch. By the low light, he began a simple routine: double jump, one foot, criss-cross, side swing. When skipping you couldn't let your mind wander, if you did you'd trip. He made himself concentrate on the rhythm and the flip of the rope until all else sweated away into the night.

Phoebe woke with a gasping cough. Under her eyes, blue veins stood out. She was beautiful in illness. The veins emphasised her pale cheeks, the way the veins in marble exaggerate its whiteness. She sat up and said, 'I feel disgusting.' And then, a few minutes later, 'I think I have a fever. Do you have a thermometer?'

They didn't. Mina laid her hand on Phoebe's forehead, which did feel warm. But so did Mina's hands. Phoebe coughed, her body hurtling with the force of it.

'Let me try something,' Mina said. 'Don't move. My grandma showed me how to do this.' She leaned forward so that their foreheads were touching and their noses aligned. Forehead to forehead, it could almost be the moment before a kiss. Despite all the kisses that Mina had placed on Phoebe's mouth, as many kisses as leaves covered the street outside, she was tempted to steal another. She forced herself to concentrate on the oblong where their skulls met.

'Yes, you're hot,' she said. 'Definitely. I think you should stay home from work.'

'God, my manager is going to be so pissed off.'

'I'll make you some toast,' Mina said.

'Use the French butter?'

'What?'

'Chef gave me some last night to take home.'

'Why?'

'Because he likes me.' Phoebe smiled like a child who had

232

got away with something. Then she coughed again. The cough was phlegmy. It was the cough of a human woman unlikely to transform into a flower or a deer. But, unlovely as it was, Mina loved it.

The nugget of French butter was wrapped in gold paper. It was a yellow so pale it was almost white. Mina held it to her nose and sniffed it. She always used spread. It was what they'd had growing up because it was cheaper, and then it was what she had later because she was trying to consume mostly plants. On the hot toast, the butter turned transparent. She cut the pieces into triangles and arranged them in a pinwheel on the plate.

She wondered if this was how Oscar felt when he cooked? This pleasant satisfaction of a small and simple task. In their relationship, he had always been the cook, the one with the recipes, the one who got measurements spot on. It was a pattern they'd fallen into: she did the washing and he cooked. Had she felt pleasure folding his shirts and tucking them neatly in the drawers? Or making the little cannonballs of his socks? Perhaps when they'd first moved in together, but it had become a habit of her hands. Was feeding her a habit of his hands? Oscar. Oscar. There was revulsion in his voice when he said, *I can't talk to you.*

Today the decorators would come, and she must let them in. Strange to think that from so far away her husband could send men to the door. What would they make of Phoebe? It didn't matter. They were decorators, not priests or social workers. The thought of them telling Oscar tingled like a scab she knew she must not pick.

The toast was no longer steaming. She hurried to Phoebe. There was no need to be a bad girlfriend and a bad wife.

Phoebe ate in huge bites, getting butter on her chin.

'Is it good?' Mina asked.

'Mmm . . .' Phoebe replied. Crumbs dropped onto the bed,

and Mina picked them up one by one. It was kind of nice, being the healthy one. She felt useful.

'Can you get me a paracetamol?' Phoebe asked.

'Paracetamol?' Mina asked.

'Yeah. Paracetamol.'

'I don't think we have that in the US.'

'Can't explain. Can you just get it. Head hurts.'

A note pinged through on her phone. *Decorators delayed one more week*. She was grateful for the reprieve. She didn't want big-booted men breaking into their small world. Not yet.

The pharmacy sold Mina a packet of small painkillers. It was busy. This was the time of year when sickness blew in with the rain. Every street corner seemed to have someone coughing into their coat or their hand or right into her face.

Oscar was never sick. He just didn't get ill. Mina didn't know why. In the decade they'd been together, she had never, not once, had to bring him a pill. The one time he got food poisoning didn't really count, as he'd dealt with it entirely by himself while she stood outside the bathroom door, asking, 'Can I do anything?' She must stop comparing Phoebe to Oscar. She must.

Back in the kitchen, Mina popped the recommended dose out from the silver foil, poured a glass of water and carried them to the bedroom.

'Nurse is in,' Mina said.

Phoebe sat up and swallowed. Her lips were almost colourless. Then she retreated below the covers. Mina flicked off the lights, ready to leave Phoebe in peace.

'Stay with me,' Phoebe said.

Mina lay down beside her.

'Can I be little spoon?' Phoebe asked. The back of Phoebe's neck was sweat shiny.

Just when Mina thought she was asleep, muffled by the

pillow, Phoebe said, 'Thank you. It's been a while since anyone nursed me.' She took Mina's hand and held tight. Mina lay still until a thousand pins and needles prickled her palm.

Oscar and his father walked in silence. There was driftwood all along the beach, the logs stacked into pyramids. The ashes of old parties blew themselves out across the sand and the wind whistled inside a plastic cup that threw itself towards the sea.

'My doctor says I should be exercising more,' his father said.

'Yeah?'

'I was thinking maybe you could help me get started? One of my friends has one of those step tracker things.'

'You don't need that,' Oscar said. 'You just need to begin.'

'Tomorrow?' his father asked.

'Okay.'

'You know, if you want you can keep it going,' his father said. 'Umeda Trading.'

'My Japanese is still ちょっと.' Oscar gave the word for a wobbly ambiguity, something that is not quite right, a word he had always known applied. But as he said it, he thought about one of the kids who worked for George. A skinny girl with a smart mouth who wore her ponytail slung through her baseball hat. A girl who grew up in Osaka, and who often looked on the verge of laughter. She'd said she was homesick, was thinking of moving back but that she didn't know what she'd do once she got there. All Oscar needed was someone bilingual.

'It's up to you,' his father said. 'But it would be nice to keep the name alive.'

Of course he would do it. Mina would be—he stopped himself because he didn't know what Mina would be. Would she be excited for him? Worried about it? Dead? No. He couldn't deal with that now.

November

After two more days in bed, Phoebe went back to work. Mina pulled the laundry from the washing machine and wondered at how easy it was to tell their clothing apart. Phoebe's spangled dresses gleamed. Mina's black jeans lay among them, like slugs in the flowerbed. She hung the laundry. She gathered the dirty clothes that Phoebe had left by the bed into the now empty laundry basket. She stacked Phoebe's bangles on the windowsill. They were light. Scratches in the goldish veneer revealed an aluminium interior. Mina picked up the thinnest and slid it over her hand, pushing and pushing it until it was as far up her arm as it would go, flesh caving under metal. There was a pleasure in the pressure from something Phoebe owned. Mina thought of the sharply angled wrist.

Why? her brain asked. Why this girl? Mina had seen so many wrists in New York and so many in London. Wrists were everywhere, grazing bus poles, leaning on benches, spurting out from cuffs. Why this wrist? Was it because Phoebe was a woman? But so many of those wrists had been female.

Mina sloshed water into Benson's bowl and tried to put aside the thought. It didn't matter, did it?

Why? her brain asked again. Mina thought that if her brain could be a person, a person who wasn't Mina, it would be a bitch. It would cut its hair blunt, wear fierce glasses, and tell her she was problematic.

Is it because she's English? Mina's brain asked. Do you think it's because she's foreign and exciting?

No, Mina thought. It's not that.

236

The brain crossed its unreal arms.

Because she's young? Or maybe it's just because there's something wrong with your brain.

But you're my brain, Mina thought. How can I love her because of you and doubt it because of you?

You love her? the brain asked.

I don't know. She smells of life.

That stinks of false romance. And what if it stops just like the pills?

Benson lapped at the water, slopping it all over the floor.

The brain reminded her of a seminar she'd taken on Women in Rome. Hadn't Cato said a woman could be killed by her husband if found to be an adulteress?

Oscar just told me to be happy and fucked off, she thought.

But he's your husband, her brain said. *You're greedy. You're selfish and greedy. And fucking undeserving. You're even letting the crazies down. When they say depressed people can't be trusted they'll point at you. When people say women are weak they'll point at you. When they say bisexuals are greedy they'll point at you. You're pathetic.*

I feel like I'm drowning every day, she thought, and when I kiss Phoebe, sometimes, just for a moment, it makes me feel like I've broken past the surface of the water. Is that greed?

Even this is some ridiculous construct you have. A way of making it seem like you're doing more than just talking to yourself.

Benson finished his water and sat on his haunches looking up at her, his fuzzy ears alert.

'Oh, cutie,' Mina said, and pressed her nose into his fur. He smelled of soil after rain, somehow mucky and clean at once. His breath fell across her face. No magical mutt heart-healing took place, but she held him close anyway.

'Let's go on a walk,' she said to the dog.

*

It was late when Phoebe returned. She began talking as soon as she was in the door.

'God, this fucking couple they just wouldn't go home. We had to tell them the bar was closing. And you just know they're fucking around or thinking about fucking around. That's why they don't go home. Because they probably have spouses and kids who are waiting up for Mummy and Daddy.'

Phoebe moved too quickly for Mina to kiss. She stripped off her waitress uniform, dropping it at her feet. 'My head is killing me.' She pulled a cigarette from her bag and lit it. The filter tip clashed with her hair. Oscar would be upset if the apartment smelled of tar and nicotine. Oh, fuck him. Why did she still think of him?

'I don't think you're supposed to smoke if you've just been sick,' Mina said.

'Oh, don't be a puritan. I'll quit in the morning.'

Mina opened the window.

'It's fucking freezing out,' Phoebe said.

'I was just trying to get some air into the place.'

'I'm tired.' Phoebe dropped the cigarette into the mug of coffee that Mina had let go cold. 'I'm going to bed.' Her rapid feet on the old floorboards creaked.

Mina followed her to the bedroom. 'I miss you,' she said.

'I'm right here.' Phoebe pulled on a floppy Ramones T-shirt. Her own or one of her almost-ex-husband's? Mina didn't ask.

'Are you mad at me? I just don't want you to get sick, to get cancer, and die. They say smoking's like roulette. You're fine, you're fine, you're fine, and then one of them gets you.'

'Well isn't that a cheery thought.'

Mina followed Phoebe into the wide bed.

They lay facing each other. Nose tip to nose tip. Mina was thankful for the slatted blinds that never quite closed and the slivers of light that threaded across Phoebe's face.

'I really like you,' Mina said. 'A lot.'

238

'What are you? Fourteen?' Phoebe asked. 'You like-like me? Is that what you're saying?'

'Um.'

'Stop looking so worried. I like-like you too.'

They kissed. Mina nosed her way under the covers and between Phoebe's knees. The sheet slid over her back onto the floor. Phoebe twisted and rocked so that Mina found herself trying to hold the woman down. She needed to get better at keeping their bodies aligned. God, she hoped she'd get to practise this.

After they'd gasped to a level of mutual satisfaction, Phoebe rolled over.

'Do you have to?' Mina kissed the cliff of Phoebe's shoulder blade.

'Have to what?'

'Sleep facing away from me.'

'I can't sleep with someone else's breath in my face.'

How had she been so quickly reduced to a someone? Mina slung her arm experimentally over Phoebe's back. She could feel the warmth of Phoebe pressed against her stomach. It wasn't comfortable. Her bones were smaller than Phoebe's and the spooning was a stretch. After only a minute Phoebe said, 'Would you mind? I just sleep better if no one's holding me.'

So Mina let go and the shadows moved across the ceiling. Did Phoebe want to sleep alone? Was it just that half a bed was better than her brother's sofa? The questions squirmed in Mina's lungs. She rolled over to check her phone. It was the zero'th hour. A new day had begun only a few minutes ago. And begun like this.

Phoebe sighed. 'Go to sleep, Mina.'

'I'm trying to. It's just you feel so far away.'

The binder was as thick as a briefcase. The pages were thick and plastic and stuck to one another as they turned. Each one had a business card. The cards were thick white cream. Some were embossed with the owner's name in roman letters, some in kanji, some sprang for both. The geekiest kid in Oscar's school had had such a binder for his Pokémon. And once, just for laughs, someone had torn them all out and thrown them across the room in rainbow flashes. The business cards were not as bright.

The desk was pushed close to the window and there wasn't really room for two behind it, but Oscar had angled a kitchen chair so that they could sit side by side. He noticed that his father smelled old. Not unclean, just old, a smell he'd noticed before only on buses or subways, his head pushed too close to some clucking granny. Or perhaps he was making that up. His father was sixty-nine, too young to smell like an old man.

'And this is Tanaka-san, he works for the two sisters. The one with the brewery up north. He's good with people and he loves Jack Daniel's. Always bring him a bottle around New Year's, but don't let him drink it with you. He'll never go home. And then his wife will be angry. And if his wife is angry, he'll be in a bad mood.'

Oscar's laptop was perched on the edge of the table and he wrote *Tanaka, Jack D, NY, don't drink with*.

There were pages and pages of the compendium. Later, Oscar would have to put this in a spreadsheet. That was assuming any of it would carry over. There was nothing to say that Tanaka-san would want to drink with him or that Tanaka-san's heart would not blip out.

His father's finger slid down to the next card. The nail was thick and slightly yellow, very ridged. As a boy, he'd tried to memorise this man. But, between birthday visits, his father's features ran like honey so that each year he was surprised by the face that appeared.

'This is Ito-san. He has a granddaughter at Rutgers. She's studying international relations. He's very proud.'

Oscar tried to imagine Ito-san but saw only an image of his own father's face. He tried again so Ito-san looked more like the guy who ran a ramen place up in Harlem. It wasn't much better.

'This is Sato-san. He died last year. You don't need to know anything about him.'

'Dad,' Oscar said.

'Yes?'

'Why didn't you take me over this sooner?'

'I thought there'd be more time.'

One week since moving in and two whole weeks total since the kiss. Mina did not mention the two-week anniversary. It was important not to freak Phoebe out. It had been long enough for Mina to detect the edge of a pattern. When Phoebe spoke in her sleep, the mumbles were too quiet to decipher. When Phoebe looked up at the corner of the ceiling and Mina asked what she was thinking, Phoebe said only, 'Nothing much.' As soon as she'd met him, Mina had known what Oscar was thinking. He basically drew her a spreadsheet of his life plans. But Phoebe . . . Phoebe just smiled at her.

Phoebe sat on the end of the bed while Mina crouched behind her to blow dry the red hair. The strands rippled between Mina's fingers. Phoebe craned back into the heat.

'That's lovely, all tingly,' Phoebe said.

'I told you so,' Mina replied.

Mina cupped her right hand under the bowl of Phoebe's skull, feeling the weight of those secret thoughts. The moon of Phoebe's face was caught in the window glass. Tonight was a waitress night. There would be seven hours to spend alone in the flat. Seven more hours to try to force her research to make sense. Seven hours of staring at Oscar's photo on the phone. Seven hours of trying to believe she hadn't irredeemably fucked everything up.

She flicked off the dryer and kissed the top of the chrysanthemum curls. 'I wish you could just stay with me,' she said.

Phoebe smelled of Mina's shampoo.

'Tell me about one of your women,' Phoebe said. 'The ones that survive.'

'How about Penelope? You know, Odysseus's wife. Her husband doesn't come home from the war and everyone assumes he's dead. So these men come to her hall to eat and drink and demand that she marry one of them. But Penelope says first she must weave her husband's funeral shroud. All day her fingers dance across the loom. Every night she unpicks it, which means she can put off the new marriage by another day. She survives by cunning.'

Mina wove her fingers under Phoebe's hair as she talked, feeling the rhythm of her words.

'Didn't her husband fuck a sorceress?'

'Circe, and actually the goddess Calypso too,' Mina conceded.

'Not that cunning, then, to sit there waiting for some great bullshitter to come home.'

'True.' Mina rested her palm on Phoebe's dryer-warm head. She'd always liked that story for the moonlit unstitching. It was so easy to unpick at night the statements you made in the day. The day-brain might call someone gone, but the night-brain would believe they'd return. And in this story, he does. He returns to hold tight his wife and son. When would Oscar come back?

'Mind if I eat dinner at the restaurant?' Mina asked.

The neck tilted upright and away. Phoebe turned, and two lines cracked between her eyebrows. 'Why?'

'I just want to see your life. I want to know you.'

Phoebe looked uncertain.

'I'll take Benson on a walk first. I'll get him good and sleepy. He won't even notice I'm gone.' Mina dared to press a stream of kisses up Phoebe's neck towards her cheek.

'I suppose. Just, I don't know, can you act like a normal customer?'

243

Mina's face was too close to understand the context of the rising cheekbone, but she hoped it was a smile.

Mina got to the restaurant early. She knew that the hours had not yet begun, but somewhere inside, Phoebe would be laying out knives and forks, adjusting wineglasses, chit-chatting to colleagues Mina had never met. She waited on the park bench. It was cold now, properly cold, and she kept her hands plunged into the pockets of her black raincoat, the only jacket she'd brought to this wet country. Even the pigeons were hiding from the clawing wind. She had to be a normal customer, which meant she couldn't be the first one in. Eventually the first customer arrived, a woman in a suit and neon pink running shoes. Mina followed her.

Inside, the restaurant was warm. Mirrors were screwed to every wall. The wood panelling reflected the mustard-yellow light. She was shown to a corner table. Mina scanned her view for Phoebe. Phoebe leaned towards the running-shoe woman. The folded half-apron wrapped her hips snugly. It was a nonsensical piece of uniform. She was not a chef. But Mina could see the appeal of the apron-string bow. It called out to be untied.

The petite notepad in Phoebe's hand was not so different from the one she took to galleries. She didn't seem to need to look down as she wrote. Her eyes were reserved for the diners' faces. Even from across the room, Mina recognised that graceful attention. It was the sort of attention for which people paid a hundred dollars an hour to their therapists.

'Anything to drink?'

Mina looked up at her own assigned server. An unmemorable boy. But Mina didn't need Phoebe's customer-service smiles: she wanted the real crooked-tooth variety.

There were three vegetarian options. She requested tap water and the endive salad. She hadn't learnt the word endive until her twenties. Her grandmother had never made salads. The vegetables she served must've had specific Chinese names. But when Mina asked, all her grandmother said was 'Green vegetable'. Or 'White vegetable'. Which had seemed adequate at the time. Now Mina had no idea how to replicate those meals.

Phoebe darted to a closer table. An older man sat with his young wife and sons. The woman was dab-dab-dabbing at one boy's mouth. The man was looking straight at Phoebe's breasts. The thin shirt left their slopes visible and vulnerable. He touched Phoebe's arm. Mina stood. Her legs moved quickly towards the pair. But by the time she arrived at the table the woman was asking if it was possible to get the sole meunière without the butter, so Mina just brushed against Phoebe, hip skimming hip. Phoebe looked up. Mina realised that Phoebe's eyelids were bright yellow, as if a sunflower petal had been painted across each one. How had she not noticed earlier? Phoebe flicked her head around, and quick-marched to the kitchen.

It was hard to make the meal last. The endives were so meagre. Mina sliced the salad into sawdust. When all that was left was the oil-wiped plate, she ordered tea and let it go cold. Phoebe bustled and bussed tables. She never looked up or over. No smile rolled off her lips. Mina opened her phone to reread Phoebe's last blog—a Halloween post about Edvard Munch. Mina looked up and Phoebe was out of sight. And although Mina knew that she would come back, Mina had a dread that Phoebe had vanished, crawled into an oven, or sprinted away through a back door.

Ami stood chopping apples into quarters. The knife glistened as it slid through each one.

'I'm thinking of getting Ichiro a sister,' Ami said. 'We've only had him for a year—we wanted to start small. But they're herd animals, really. They're happier together.' She picked a slice up from the board and bit into it. 'Want one?'

'No, thanks,' Oscar said. 'I was thinking, I should probably go back and deal with the flats.'

'You know, you and Mina don't have to go back to New York afterwards. You could stay with us. There's room. Your father would like that.'

'I don't know,' Oscar said. 'Mina's been teaching in New York for a while.'

'Ah . . .' Ami said. 'How is Mina?'

'The usual,' he said. Though that night he'd dreamt of fucking her, not a subtle dream, no hidden messages, just fucking, her body going up and down and her head flung back. On waking up he'd reached out his hand to the space where she wasn't.

'Wait a minute,' Ami said, and washed her hands with the cinnamon-scented soap. 'Just stay right there,' she added and padded out of the kitchen.

When she returned she was holding a package tied with a loop of red ribbon. 'I meant to give this to you on the day,' she said, 'but after the cake, and then . . . Well, it didn't feel like the right time.'

She seemed to expect him to open it so he did. The ribbon unspooled with a quick tug. He ran a thumb under the tape so as not to tear the paper. He opened the narrow box. A scarf.

'Thanks, you didn't have to,' he said.

'It's alpaca and lambswool,' Ami said.

'Not llama then?' he asked, trying to sound amusing.

'No, not llama.'

'That's cool. Thank you.'

They paused. Oscar put on the scarf to show willing. Ami reached up and adjusted it. It felt veterinary, as though he was a creature whose collar needed fixing. He almost expected her to pet him.

Ami gathered up the gold paper and began to fold it into quarters.

'Did you ever leave him?' Oscar asked.

'Him?'

'Dad.' Who else? The dentist?

'Well, I thought about it.' She said this in the same tone she might've used to explain that she'd considered, then rejected a holiday to Canada. 'It was complicated. I broke his favourite bottle of wine on the kitchen counter. It went everywhere.' She made a blowing-up gesture with her hands. 'But I loved him. And at some point you just have to decide to forgive a person.'

Maybe in thirty years he and Mina would tell people that. They'd say it was complicated and no one would quite understand why they were together. But they'd make it work. They'd get a bigger house and animals to over-love. Maybe. Or maybe they'd be living in separate apartments, next to strangers' bodies. Or maybe his wife would have smashed or snapped or cracked or broken herself, and when they called him to pick her up it would not be a barefoot woman he found but a body. Oh, he was so tired.

Standing in Theo's apartment was uncomfortably like tres-passing. Mina laid a finger on one of the guitar's strings and it twanged indignantly. Phoebe's husband, soon to be ex, needed her to post him something she'd taken. So here they were. Phoebe pulled a fuzzy, neon pink, leopard-print coat from the suitcase.

'That's what he wanted?' Mina asked.

'Of course not.' Phoebe slid the coat over her shoulders and twirled. 'Everyone says leopard is basically a neutral. If you're bold enough, you can do whatever you want.'

The thing her husband needed was a pot of lemon-scented beeswax, the wax the yellow of ear gunk. Mina tried to imagine Phoebe throwing all her belongings into suitcases, her palm making a fist around this jar. What would Mina grab hold of if she were leaving? Phoebe shoved the furniture polish into the pocket of the coat. 'I'm going to make a coffee. Want one?'

Mina followed her to the galley kitchen. Phoebe poured two teaspoons of instant coffee into a mug imprinted with the name of Theo's university in a faded font. When Mina kissed Phoebe, the kiss tasted of Nescafé Gold. Phoebe's fur coat brushed Mina's neck.

Phoebe pulled away. 'Hey, let me put my mug down at least.'

Mina took the mug from her and placed it in the sink.

The kiss had barely begun before Phoebe pulled away. 'Shit! Where's Benson?' She strode out of the room. Benson was gnawing a leather seat cushion, head tilted to get a mouthful.

'Bad dog. Bad.' Phoebe shook a finger. Benson played dead, his huge paws hooked in supplication.

It would be best, Phoebe decided, if they allowed him to get his yahs-yahs out in the park. It was a narrow strip, ringed with trees. The fence posts were topped with an arrowhead design. The shafts were thick enough to slay elephants. Phoebe chose a bench under a willow. On the one opposite a woman looked at her phone and smoked.

'God, I could kill for a cigarette,' Phoebe said. 'This coat always had a pack in the left pocket. It reeked. Go on, sniff it.'

Mina did. It smelled of nothing. The only thing she could detect was the faint whiff of a wet city. 'I can't smell anything,' she said.

'Exactly. Nothing. That's what my marriage smelt like. Nothing! You know it was him I gave up for?'

A French bulldog with alert ears and an Argyle sweater waddled towards them, swishing his pale behind. Mina used to tutor a kid who lived on Madison Avenue. The father walked like that. Benson, off-leash, dashed towards the Frenchie. The smaller dog's muzzle pulled back toothily. Benson retreated under the bench.

'Typical,' Phoebe said, and reached through the slats to run a finger over Benson's skull.

The smoking woman jiggled her black patent shoe as she typed. Her whole body was stiff and concentrated, apart from that nervous shoe. Up and down it went. Mina was overcome by the idea that the anxious woman bore almost as much relation to Mina's life as Phoebe did. If Mina died, Phoebe would probably only be sad for an afternoon, maybe a week, a month. Didn't they say mourning lasted half the time you'd known someone?

'What's your ex-husband like?' Mina asked.

'I don't want to talk about him,' Phoebe said.

'That's not fair. You've known Oscar longer than I have. But I can't imagine Brendan.'

'He's the sort of man who'd rather ring me than buy a new pot of furniture polish.'

It seemed a bad moment to ask what made Phoebe willing to fetch it. Mina took Phoebe's free hand. And Phoebe let her.

From above Mina heard the clunk of something heavy being moved. The decorators had decided to start on the upstairs flat. They had nodded at the work she had already done, acknowledging it but refraining from comment. She wondered if this was the famous British reserve or if her DIY left them speechless.

It was almost six. She should offer them more tea and chocolate-chip cookies. That morning Ed had told her he took his tea with three sugars and Tomek took his black. She laid out the store-bought cookies in a flower shape. She balanced the plate in one hand, while holding the two mug handles in the other. She stepped slowly, careful not to spill. The journey was convoluted for such a short distance. She had to walk from 4B to the exterior walkway, to the fourth-floor landing, up the stairs, onto the fifth-floor walkway and into 5B. As she stepped out onto the first of the two walkways, she blinked against the low sun. The trees had all thrown away their leaves, but the air was warm and the breeze mild. Were Novembers in England always gentle? By next year, she couldn't be here any more. She tried not to let the thought bother her.

Mina peered over the edge of the walkway's railing. Four storeys down, pushed against the courtyard's wall, the industrial containers were stuffed with trash. Pigeons perched on the surface, flashing their blues and purples. It felt strange to be so far above the birds.

In 5B, Ed and Tomek were packing up. They'd stripped

away the birds completely and now everything was naked. People talked about naked walls, and Mina had always thought they just meant an absence of stuff. But the stripped walls really did look like flesh—the flesh of a very old English lady, mottled all pink and white, with faint scraps of green and blue. It was like being squeezed between a duchess's thighs.

The two men were of similar height and wore matching heavy boots and dusty jeans. Tomek was the first to look up. She thought of him as the pretty one. He had light blue eyes, like those balloons that say *It's a boy!!*

'We were just heading out.' He shrugged apologetically and scratched the back of his neck.

'But, thanks, a biscuit would be grand.' Ed grabbed a cookie, consuming in two bites. He was the less pretty one. A stud pierced his right earlobe. Did it indicate a love of punk?

'Tomorrow we'll start stripping downstairs,' Ed said. 'That okay?'

'Great,' she said.

'One for the road,' Ed said, as he grabbed another cookie. And then they both headed off.

Soon she, like the birds, would have to be removed from the apartment. But, unlike the birds, she could not be chucked onto a scrapheap. Yet it didn't seem real. In some parallel life, Mina and Oscar would be going to the farmers' market or writing invitation lists for one of his parties. Why had she sent him that text? It had been so easy to type those three words: *I kissed Phoebe.* It was true, of course. But lots of things were true. She could have written, *I miss her too, the person I used to be. The person who thought she was in control of her own brain.* She could have written, *I miss the way my forehead slots just below your shoulder.* She could have written, *It is an emergency, please come home.* But she hadn't. She'd tasted Phoebe's mouth and it had blurred into hers and she had felt herself rock against another person and now that was done and she could not take it back.

She took a sip of the unmilky tea before heading downstairs. As she walked along the balcony, a whirl of leaves rose in the wind. They spiralled as if an unseen spirit were spinning there. Then, without warning, they dropped to the ground.

She needed to see Phoebe. But Phoebe was at work. Perhaps Mina could eat at the restaurant. It hadn't disturbed Phoebe too much the last time. She thought of the overpriced endive salad, and the aphid-green pools of olive oil. Mina needed a job. Perhaps tonight she could talk to Phoebe about whether she'd ever move to New York. Bloggers could blog from anywhere. Phoebe would love New York. But no. Two weeks was too soon to ask someone to move continents. Anyway, Mina should get things sorted first. It would be easiest to begin with the tutoring. Her hands moved flicker-fast across the keyboard.

Dear Ms Davies,

How is Alfie? Is he enjoying junior year? My research here is coming to an end. Let me know if you and Alfie would like me to return. Though if he's comfortable working with Boris, that's no problem.

All my best,

Mina

She read it aloud. Her voice sounded jaunty. She could do this. Of course, immigration to the United States was complicated. But surely it would be easier for Phoebe with her red hair and pale skin than it had been for Mina's Shanghainese grandmother. New York seemed full of the English. They were everywhere, on TV, at her university. She'd introduce Phoebe to people and they'd marvel at her cute accent. Though

Mina wasn't sure which people. The problem with going to college with your husband was that most of your friends were shared property in the same way that the microwave and the pillows were. It didn't matter. She'd have Phoebe. They'd make new friends. Be happy, Mina thought, be happy.

She fed Benson dinner, ran him around the park until his paws dragged, brought him back to 4B, arranged his blanket for him, and refilled the water bowl. Around nine, she prepared to set out for the restaurant. It was a late dinner and her stomach ached, but it meant that she'd finish eating close to the end of Phoebe's shift and they could walk home together.

Benson was curled in his bed in the corner of the apartment. His tail was tucked under his paws. Good. Everything was to plan. And her gift for Phoebe had arrived. Mina re-examined the collar, running her fingers over the silk bow at the front. The lady in Wisconsin called it a BowWow Bow Tie. Mina had chosen XXL to accommodate Benson's fluff. She'd settled on a lavender that would complement Benson's fur. Phoebe would love it. Mina was sure it would play well online.

Oscar's father was wearing thick grey sweatpants, the kind you never saw at the gym any more. His T-shirt had the name of one of the breweries, the one started by two sisters. The kanji flapped as he jogged.

'Come on,' Oscar said. 'You can do it.' He was jogging backwards, the way he'd seen personal trainers do in the park. It was a weird feeling, the world expanding as you tumbled into it.

'Mild exercise,' his father said, between breaths. 'Mild.' His red face lifted to the sky.

'We've only just left the house. We're barely out of the drive.'

His father wasn't even fat. Oscar had been a fat kid. He knew the sear of chub sizzling from muscle. His father didn't even have any weight to carry.

'I was thinking,' Oscar said, 'maybe we can go next year. You can take me to meet Sato and the rest.'

'Sato's dead.'

'I can see you slowing down,' Oscar said.

'No, I'm not.'

They jogged on, applauded by the plock-plock of pine cones falling in the wind.

'I was thinking that the red rice beer would be the best fit for Eileen Johnson.'

Wind caught the fine hair of his father's head, lifting it up.

'How about we try skipping rope.' Oscar had thought they might do it on the beach, but the top of the drive would do.

'Jump rope? Isn't that for little girls?' his father asked.

'Boxers skip. It's cardio. It's good for your heart. Also it's important to have a balanced exercise, you don't only want to be running.'

His father raised an eyebrow. 'Skipping at my time of life.'

Oscar handed him the rope. His father raised it over head, flipping it until it hit the ground where it fell with a slap. But he tried again. And this time got in three jumps before stumbling.

'This is harder than it looks,' his father said.

'You'll get there with practice. You're trying to get too much height.' Oscar demonstrated the small jump required.

His father went again. His sweatpants billowed. They would need better athletic gear. Ami must know where the nearest mall was. The rope went taut with speed. 'One, two, three, four, five, six,' Oscar counted aloud. The rope smacked his father's calves.

'Again,' Oscar said. 'You've got this.'

Again his father lifted the rope. His jumps were uneven and the nylon cord dragged on the ground. But he kept going, stopping occasionally to breathe.

They turned home when a soft rain began to tickle their scalps. 'Guess you can teach an old dog after all,' his father said.

'I'll be teaching you tricks in no time.' Oscar coiled the rope so it fit in the pocket of his basketball shorts.

His father replied, 'You know, you'd make a good dad.'

After the restaurant closed, Mina waited outside to walk Phoebe home. Tonight Phoebe seemed to take longer. Mina walked around and around the benches. It wasn't a big deal. Phoebe would just be splashing water on her face or making polite goodbyes.

When she emerged, Mina caught her by the crook of the elbow for a kiss.

'Not here,' she said. 'It's not professional.'

'I don't think anyone noticed.'

Phoebe was walking quickly. Her scarf was triple-wrapped under her chin and Mina longed for that neck.

'Wait,' Mina tried, 'I got you a little gift.'

'Show me at home.'

Home, Mina thought. Home. It was home.

A few pumpkins still haunted doorsteps and windowsills. Their faces were caved in, expressions more senile than menacing.

'I didn't know you did Halloween here.'

'It's an American thing,' said Phoebe.

'But you did a blog post about it.'

'I post about lots of things.'

'You don't need to be like this. I won't come to the restaurant if you don't want me to.'

Phoebe walked silently, her hands in her pockets. It wasn't

that cold. What had triggered this mood? PMS? No: that was the sort of accusation a man would make.

'Do you believe in ghosts?' Mina tried.

Phoebe raised an eyebrow.

'What? Ghosts aren't an American import.'

'No. I don't know. Maybe.' Phoebe was looking upwards, but when Mina followed her eyes there was nothing to catch onto, just sky, trees and a few window squares. Mina thought about her grandma. Her grandma thought the ancestors were always there, wandering around, judging you, intervening on your behalf. When she lost the keys, she'd talk to her dead husband, who had apparently always known where the keys were. When she found them, she'd thank him. It was in this way that Mina knew many of the likes and dislikes of a man she'd never met. Grandma had been convinced that Grandpa adored Mina. Mina was such a good girl. She got such good grades. Grandpa was so proud. Not *would be*. *Was*. The question was not in doubt. Every Qingming, her grandmother made all his favourite foods: pork dumplings and burgers and Canadian bacon and sugared doughnuts and fresh rice. Mina had been prepared to tell Phoebe all this. But Phoebe did not seem interested.

At home, Benson did a clumsy jig. He included Mina in his joy. Her return too was worthy of celebration.

Mina handed Phoebe the gift. The tape at one end had come unstuck and waved forlornly. Phoebe slid the out the bow tie.

'It's for Benson. I saw them online and I just thought he'd look really cute.'

'Mina. Um. I don't really believe in clothes for dogs.' She turned it over in her hand as if she were being forced to inspect a dead frog.

'It's just a collar. A collar with a bow. Look.' And Mina bent down, patting her knees. It took her a minute to fasten the bow because Benson kept trying to lick her hands as she worked. 'There we go.'

'Okay. He's a bit cute. But can we sleep? I'm exhausted.'

It was very dark and her body was soft and naked in the bed. Under the covers the chill eased away. Phoebe said it so quietly, 'I got my decree absolute today.'

'Decree absolute?'

'The thing that says your divorce is 100 per cent final.'

Then she rolled over, and no matter what Mina asked, Phoebe could not be shifted back around.

His father was taking a nap so Oscar sat alone at the desk with the binder and his laptop. The plan for the afternoon was to put all these names and numbers into a spreadsheet. He'd put in region, speciality and his father's advice. Digitised, it would all be in one place, and safe in the cloud where fire and flood could not reach.

The binder took up most of the desk. With each flip the plastic pages made the sharp smack of a kiss. He thought, with amusement, his card was probably in somebody else's folder. After Oscar had changed his name to Umeda, his father sent him new business cards. They arrived in a long box. It was as heavy as a small dumbbell. The paper was thick. *Umeda Trading*, it said on one side. And then on the other his new name: *Oscar Umeda*.

It implied something sacred was being preserved, in the same way that the butcher Coleridge & Sons made you think of young boys learning to chop pigs at their father's feet, their sons after them chopping the descendants of those pigs. He'd propped one up at the edge of his desk. When Mina got back from teaching, she demanded one to keep in her wallet for no other reason than that she wanted to have this thing of his with her. He'd thought, This is my family.

As he flipped the pages of the business-card binder, carefully transcribing names and telephone numbers, he kept thinking about Mina. Did she still have that card in her wallet? Perhaps he could still care for her without being married to her. He'd pay alimony or an allowance. But he wouldn't be responsible for loving her and holding her. He wouldn't fall asleep next to her wondering if the next day might be the day she chose to vanish.

Maybe it wouldn't be so bad if some day he was the only Umeda. A name wasn't such a heavy thing to carry.

Phoebe was working. It didn't look like work. But Mina had been told that it was necessary that Phoebe be online. Liking a certain number of posts was required. It was imperative that she left a certain number of comments. Blogging was a community you had to give back to. You had to be friendly. To be friendly online, you had to be unfriendly offline. Phoebe hunched over the laptop. She was wearing one of Oscar's shirts. It exposed the delicate scaffolding of her collarbones. Her freckled feet poked out from under crossed legs. She lit another cigarette, sucking hard from the side of her mouth. She'd had two just that morning. The stubs lay in a water glass that balanced uncertainly on the arm of the sofa.

Phoebe glanced up. 'Stop watching me. I can't concentrate.'

'I wasn't. I was thinking.' Mina turned away. She had her own laptop to weigh her down. She'd been contacted by one of the universities she taught at regularly. A member of faculty who was supposed be teaching next term had received a large grant and wanted to head to Sicily. Could Mina cover for him? It was only one university gig but it was a beginning. Hopefully, she'd be able to get her old classes back next year. Ms Davies had also written back.

Yes! We'd love to have you. When can you start?

Each word had zinged gloriously along Mina's spine.

In their bedroom, the painters were at work. The sound of the radio covered the lick of the brushes. The station pumped out the same hit every quarter-hour. The beat bounced Mina's marrow. Phoebe had headphones on, but as the radio repeated itself, she cast an irritated look over her shoulder.

'Shall I make us lunch?' Mina asked.

'I think I'll go to a café. I work better alone.'

'Oh, okay.'

'And I'm meeting a friend for dinner so don't expect me back for a bit.'

'Sure.' Mina tried to keep her voice relaxed and casual.

Phoebe shut her laptop. A shiny vinyl sticker adorned the front. It proclaimed the name of her website in a swooshing calligraphic font. She pushed the headphones down so they collared her neck. She walked to the basket of fresh laundry that Mina had done that morning and pulled out her socks. She tucked her left foot inside, adjusting the jeans to preserve their line. As Phoebe put on the right sock, Mina had a terrible intuition that she'd never see the freckled toes again. She tried and failed to remember their precise dotted distribution. Impossible. A simpler task would be to record the height of anklebone from heel. As high as Mina's thumb?

'I've been thinking. Can you not come to the restaurant when I'm working? It's distracting.'

'In a good way?' Mina tried to sound flirtatious.

Phoebe yanked her Scandinavian backpack from the door-hook. She removed some receipts from the bottom, smoothing them neatly and leaving them aside. Then she began to fill the backpack, starting with the laptop.

'It helps,' Mina said. 'It helps to see you.'

'Helps with what?' Phoebe seemed to be looking for something, her eyes darting all over the room.

'Sometimes I get sad.'

Phoebe grabbed her camera and placed it inside the backpack.

'And when I see you, my insides lift. It pulls me upwards. Oh, I don't know.' Phoebe's expression seemed either pitying or incredulous. Mina kept trying. 'You keep it out.'

'Keep what out?' Phoebe undid her ponytail and shook out her hair.

'This feeling I used to have.' How was she supposed to tell Phoebe about wanting to die? She could say that, statistically speaking, after two attempts she was more likely than not to be her own undoing. But she didn't want to freak Phoebe out. 'You make me happy,' Mina said. 'You're like . . . you're like good weather. You know how everything is easier when the sun's out? You're like that.'

'The sun is a giant ball of burning gas. Too much of it will give you cancer.' Phoebe pulled on a green raincoat that brought out the pink of her lips. 'If divorce has taught me one thing, it's that people don't fix each other.'

And then Phoebe left. It wasn't forever. Not yet. Benson was curled up in the corner. The tips of the bow tie were just visible under his fluff. Phoebe wouldn't vanish without him.

The song vibrated again through the apartment. Mina decided to be happy. They said being happy made you smile, but that smiling also made you happy. Surely dancing would pump joy through the arteries. As the song surged, she began. Her dancing was just a sway of hips and hair. It was a wiggle of fingers and a shake of the elbows. She danced as if showing off, though whether for Oscar or Phoebe or the gynaecologist only the air knew. In the bedroom Ed and Tomek were hard at work, but here Benson watched her with wet eyes. She tried to think only of the song. Everyone was dancing to it that month. It was being played in gyms and restaurants. It was being played in New York. It was being played in cabs and in the short distance between earbuds and ear canal. As she danced, she must be with all those people. All their happiness.

It wasn't until the lights of the Travelodge had almost all blinked off that Mina gave in. The computer, which remembered her old vices, autofilled. *How to make a n* became *How to make a noose*. The voice on the video explained the

Ichabod knot. The voice was even. It repeated itself. It told her how ranchers had used the knot to tie cattle to posts. A different voice on a different video said a traditional noose had thirteen loops, but you wouldn't need that many. That was just superstition. A thirteen-loop rope would be very long. Mina had no length of cord. But her hands danced the second dance of the day, her fingers folding over fingers, miming the steps that would be needed.

She wasn't planning on anything. It was just a comfort to know you could escape.

Tissuey light fell over Phoebe's sleeping face. Her lips hung slightly open. Mina had seen fish lying on ice, their mouths spread. The pink inside the sea bass was the same as the pink inside Phoebe. Though Phoebe would not taste of sea and salt but of sleep-musted life. Mina wished she could lie there and be content in this. Under the lids Phoebe's eyes moved, watching a scene Mina would never see. Sleeping, Phoebe nestled closer. Her breath pushed across Mina's lips.

Mina had once thought she'd write about an obscure passage of Ovid. The story of Iphis and Anaxarete. Once a common boy, Iphis saw the noble Anaxarete. He became obsessed. Legend did not tell if it was due to the sweep of fabric over her rounded behind or her young body slim as an unlit candle. Every day he brought flowers to her door. He begged her nurse to pass on his compliments, but she didn't reciprocate. Legend didn't specify the flowers. Lilies for purity? Poppies for the undoing of purity? Did she step over the wilted petals or did they adhere to the pad of her sandal? She never spoke to him and yet he wanted her. So, one night he stole to her door and hanged himself from the lintel he'd once garlanded. He left a note to the effect that he hoped she enjoyed this offering more than what he'd left before. He told her he loved her but that her heart was unfeeling metal. He did not explain why he loved a girl he called cruel. His body wilted from the rope, like a bloated bloom. The next day, her servants removed the corpse. Iphis was carried through the

264

streets. As she watched the boy, who would finally torment her no more, poor Anaxarete was turned to stone. For some reason, of all the burnt, tortured, transformed girls of legend, it was Anaxarete who had stuck in Mina's mind. Perhaps because it was not a god she had defied but a lone boy and his hungry body. Mina had tried to hold back the roar of despair. She'd tried to think instead of the women who survived.

What would Phoebe make of the legend? And what would have happened if Anaxarete had given in? Would Iphis's desire have burned on? Would he always have been afraid that she'd change her mind and slip away? Or would she slowly have become commonplace? A snorer. A sniffler. A wife like any other.

Mina reached out to touch the faint wrinkle that framed Phoebe's mouth. Phoebe groaned and shuffled deeper under the sheets.

Mina climbed out of bed. She sawed two slices of bread and placed them on the oven rack. Her phone lay charging next to the microwave. She flicked through her emails as the smell of warm sourdough rose. Various New York establishments wanted to tell her about their newest promotions.

An email from Oscar: *I arrive Thurs.*

Oscar coming back. It seemed so unlikely. He'd been gone for almost a month. Phoebe had updated her blog five times.

Mina poured coffee beans into the grinder. The beans had been recommended by Phoebe's blog. The grinder roared under her fist. Oscar was coming back. Oscar would walk into this flat. He hadn't given a flight number or time. In the past he'd always forwarded her his itinerary details so that she wouldn't worry. As if knowing the number of a flight would keep it in the air.

She pulled open the oven, angling out the toast. Phoebe's French butter nestled on the refrigerator shelf. She removed it. The butter had gone hard. Mina scraped it against the toast, which cracked under the force of the knife.

Benson trotted into the kitchen and barked hungrily up at her. She ran the wing of the butter knife over her fingers. Kneeling, she let his tongue slap her skin. His dog-breath was sour, similar to hangover-breath. She'd have to wash her hands. He seemed to enjoy it no more and no less than margarine.

'Do you ever miss them? Your old owners?' she asked.

He tilted his head as if considering her point. She pasted more butter over her fingers. It was good to have this animal love her for a minute. His body was created to love, from his golden ruff to his wine-dark eyes. Imagine being in this world only to love.

She put the two pieces of toast onto a plate, waited for the coffee to filter, then carefully walked to their bedroom. Phoebe had kicked off the covers, revealing swathes of leg and fire-freckle feet.

'Wake up, sleepyhead.'

After Phoebe had eaten, she seemed in a gentler mood. It was a Saturday and the decorators weren't coming. They could spend all morning in a tangle of limbs. She'd have to tell Phoebe that Oscar was coming back. But not yet. Not when she was smiling and licking crumbs of toast from the side of her mouth. Mina couldn't think of the right way to say it. She looked down at her hands and saw the wedding ring wrapping her finger. There had never been a right moment—a definitive moment—to remove the swirl of golden leaves. Or there had been, but she'd missed it. Or maybe she just hadn't wanted to lose this last proof that her husband had loved her, had chosen her, had wanted her to be his. Carefully she took it off, her hands working under the table and out of Phoebe's vision. She slid it into her pocket, where it pressed accusingly against her hip.

'Can we go see that ring?' Mina asked. 'The one in the

V&A? You could do a jewellery post. I bet your readers would like that.' Hadn't Phoebe said the lover's rings were more beautiful than the husband's? Perhaps in the museum she might see there were different types of love.

The jewellery room was pearled, silvered, glittered, gilded. Mina had the impression of a lurid night sky. School groups goggled at the expensive stars.

Phoebe's eyes trailed over the brightness. Mina skimmed the sober descriptions of the hoard. The jewels had been bought, stolen, given from, to and by poets, artists, wives and queens. Mina didn't notice the ring until Phoebe stopped in front of it. It was simple. So simple that it seemed only one more link on the chain from which it hung. *1858* was engraved into the 22-carat gold, the year Janey had married William. The panel below declared in bland serif that Dante Gabriel Rossetti *was in love with Janey* and that much of the jewellery on display was from him. Rossetti had given her gold filigree, citrine, emeralds, rubies, a plaited gold Burmese bangle. The gifts of lover and husband were entombed together—husband left and lover right. As they lay by a riverbank, did Rossetti wrap his teeth around her finger, tugging off the wedding band? Did he transform ring finger to a plain finger, long and white and lovely?

Mina said, 'I once thought I'd get my wedding ring tattooed. Nothing fancy, just a simple black line on my left ring finger.'

'Why didn't you?' Phoebe splayed her own empty hand in front of her.

'Oscar didn't want to. He didn't feel like a tattoo sort of person. Then it felt silly to do it by myself.'

Phoebe's mouth slid into a side-smile. 'Well, there's a metaphor for marriage if I ever heard one. Two people not doing something together.'

Children poured around them in a blue-shirted, clip-board-clutching army.

'Oscar's coming back,' Mina said.

Phoebe said nothing and looked fixedly into the display. To the left of the wedding ring was a box just wider than a pack of cards. It was gold with a glass window. Inside, William Morris's hair was whirled into a ring. She stared at the hair of the dead man whose wife didn't love him. Perhaps that was the reward for being a famous artist and thinker: people remembered how he'd been betrayed.

'Say something,' Mina asked.

'You told me he left.'

'He did.'

'He's coming back, though?' Phoebe drummed a finger on the display case. Mina waited for an alarm but nothing happened.

'The apartment is his father's,' Mina said. How many of these jewels were apologies? How many were promises? 'It's nothing to do with me,' she added. 'He's not coming back for me.' But the words came out wrong, all maudlin and not reassuring.

Oscar would have written differently if he was. He would've asked if she was okay.

The door of one of the beachfront houses opened and a woman emerged. Her Lycra leggings shimmered as her glutes stretched and compressed. Her feet cut delicate triangles into the sand. Oscar felt his jogging pace pick up to match hers.

'Wait,' his father's voice came from behind him. Oscar turned. His father raised a hand in the international symbol for *stop*. His mouth hung open and Oscar could see the slab of his tongue, as thick and pink as a heart.

'Are you okay?'

'Fine.' His father bent over as he panted.

Oscar ran through the symptoms of angina in his head: sweatiness, shortness of breath, pain in the chest, nausea. 'Are you sure?'

'Mmm . . . Water?'

Oscar was carrying the water bottle. He unscrewed the cap and pushed it into his father's grip. His father chugged. The colour in his neck was bright and uneven.

'Need to sit,' his father said, and did so on a log of salt-white driftwood.

Oscar asked again, 'Are you sure?'

His father reached into the pocket of his sweatpants and took out a plastic bottle. He shook out two small orange pills. 'Baby aspirin, supposed to take it twice a day. Good for the blood.'

'Okay,' Oscar said, and sat down next to him. He wondered if he should be calling an ambulance. How to tell good sweat from bad? He shouldn't have been paying so much attention to that curve of ass. The woman ran on, her body shrinking into a slit of shadow. On the log, ants cut busy tracks around their hands.

'Let's do this again,' his father said.

'Sure. Tomorrow? My flight isn't until the afternoon.'

'No. I mean after you handle the apartments, we'd like it if you came to stay.'

'Thanks,' Oscar said, and didn't remind his father that this plan had already been suggested.

'Do you remember when we went to the zoo?' his father asked.

'Yeah,' Oscar said. It had only been the one time. He'd been young, he knew that, but old enough to read the big letters at the entrance, his mouth making the shape of the O. Old enough to know his mother didn't approve of the zoo or of keeping things in cages. But they'd gone anyway, after his birthday lunch, just him and his father. There'd been a tent of birds zigzagging in the air and a snake that didn't move at all but lay like something stuffed. Then there had been the tigers. Or was it one tiger? The memory was of molten fur. The window was cut into a brick wall and Oscar stood nose to the pane. The tiger, unlike the snake, did not hide at the back of the cage but came right up close, pacing back and forth in front of the glass. It was so near that Oscar saw each hair of the pelt. The fur was as individually bladed as sunburnt stalks of grass. He put his hand up against the cool glass and watched the fur move behind his fingers. It was almost like stroking. And his father, who had been silent for most of the visit, other than to ask Oscar if he wanted an ice cream, said, 'Animals in cages go nuts so they pace back and forth.'

Oscar had tried to look into the yellow eyes to see the madness but he saw only yellow and orange.

In the taxi home, his father had asked, 'How about you come stay with me and Ami this summer?'

But Oscar had still been thinking about the tiger's yellow eyes and wondering if it had gone mad immediately or if it was slow, and what madness was. He knew instinctively that this wasn't the madness of the Animaniacs or mad professors. The edges of his mouth felt sticky with ice cream. The day had been too cold, and his nose was clogged. He didn't remember what he'd said, only that he'd thought, No.

That summer he hadn't gone to his father's house but stayed with his mother, listening to the clack of her keys and running his red Hot Wheels racing car along the edges of the floorboards, making clacks of his own.

'Ami wanted to know . . .' His father looked embarrassed. 'Have you thought about a family of your own? Not that we're not your family . . . What I mean is, are you going to make me a granddad?'

'It's complicated with Mina. The doctors say there's something wrong with her ovaries.'

270

'Ah,' his father said. Oscar knew well enough that there were treatments out there, like IVF. For a moment he allowed himself to pretend the only thing wrong with Mina was her reproductive system. Doctors would be consulted until eventually his boy and his girl were born. They'd visit this beach. Their small bodies would run down to the water. They'd hold hands as they stepped into the sea, yelping at the chill. The brother would hold his sister's hand so she wouldn't fall. The girl would look like her mother; she'd laugh the way her mother did, with half-closed eyes. But he supposed if he was ever going to have children he'd have to imagine them with new faces. New un-Mina faces.

Oscar felt the cold seep through his T-shirt. He said to his father, 'Yeah, I'll come back. So you'll have to keep up the running.'

His father laughed and said, 'がんばりましょう' and Oscar laughed to hear the words from his father's mouth and not from the buck teeth of the language app's animated rabbit. *We will do our best.* Yes, he thought, we will.

'**D**on't. You'll smudge me,' Phoebe stepped back to avoid the kiss. Her lipstick was the red of a freshly scraped knee. 'Is this your phone charger?'

'I don't know. I think so. You can use it. I'm fully charged,' Mina said. Phoebe looked at her like she was very stupid. She dropped the charger on the sofa next to Mina, as if it was a microphone and she were some rock star. The prongs pointed forlornly skywards. Mina thought she should tidy before Oscar showed up. Phoebe had rolled her suitcase into the middle of the room. Oscar wouldn't like that. Tomorrow. He would be here tomorrow.

Oscar would be here. Oscar. In her mind she dragged out the syllables of his name. Ohhh-scccarrr. He seemed like someone she'd made up. An imaginary best friend. Even New York seemed made up, a diorama someone had constructed to sell postcards.

'I'm going,' Phoebe said, interrupting Mina's thoughts. Phoebe was wearing earmuffs.

'Are those new?' Mina asked.

'Listen, I'm going.'

'You don't work tonight.'

'What's wrong with you?'

Mina laughed. She'd tried to tell Phoebe everything that was wrong, and Phoebe hadn't wanted to know.

'Mina, it's not working. And this isn't right.'

'I'll explain to Oscar that we're . . .'

'We're not anything. This was . . . I don't know what this

272

was. I'm leaving. And I need to know you're not going to follow me. You're not going to show up at the restaurant or my brother's. Or anywhere else. I have enough drama in my life. It's my fault, really. I thought I deserved something fun. You're cute but I never wanted anything intense.'

Phoebe swept a hand to encompass the breadth of the room. The black earmuffs washed her out. As Mina tried to chase Phoebe's sentences, they skimmed away from her. Phoebe was talking about things being too much. Or Mina being too much. It occurred to Mina that break-ups, like marriages, have scripts. The words were already provided. The memorising started when you were a kid, before you'd even had your first kiss. You watched it on TV.

'Is it your husband?' Mina asked.

Phoebe stopped buttoning her coat. She ran a tongue over those little teeth. She closed her eyes. 'No, Mina. It is not my husband.'

'You know, I don't think I ever saw a picture of him. What's this guy you saw fit to marry like?'

In Mina's head he was ugly. He had over-plump cheeks and a quiff of blond hair, like a cherub. Perhaps that was because Phoebe seemed like the sort of woman who, as a girl, had only had ugly friends. An ugly husband would remind everyone how lovely Phoebe was. No, that wasn't fair. Beautiful girls who only had beautiful friends would be called cliquey. There was no right sort of friend and there was no right husband for Phoebe. Mina imagined someone tall, someone with abs, and eyes as smooth as sea-glass. No. That would not be better.

'This isn't about him,' Phoebe said.

'What is it about?'

'Are you really asking me that?' She waved her arms at the walls or at Mina. It wasn't clear which. The arms were lovely, long and slim, dimpled at the elbows. They were arms you

273

could lose yourself inside. All Mina had wanted was to vanish into this woman's arms.

'Oscar did leave,' Mina said. 'He did. It wasn't . . . I just hadn't . . . But I want you to come back to New York with me. There are museums in New York. There are bloggers in New York.'

Phoebe clicked out the extendable suitcase handle. 'This was supposed to be fun, you know. A fun fling.' Phoebe pulled her tote bag onto her shoulder. 'It wasn't supposed to be more than that.'

'Stay, please.' Mina didn't know what she was asking for. But Phoebe couldn't leave. Every blood vessel in her body rushed along its path.

'Benson, come on. Come to Mummy,' Phoebe called, and the dog trotted over to her without a backward glance. 'Right now, I can't do anything.' Phoebe paused. 'Heavy.'

Mina went to Phoebe and grabbed the slim, familiar arm. 'Please,' she said.

'Mina, stop it.'

The kiss slid off Phoebe's tensed face. Her hair smelled of tobacco.

'Please,' Mina said again.

'I'm sorry, but I've got enough of my own shit to sort out.'

Phoebe shut the door quietly. The automatic latch clicked to lock.

'But I ordered pizza,' Mina said. In the empty apartment, her hands opened and closed. Her chest ached. And she wished she had someone to hold, even if that someone was only Benson. His warm fur, brushing against her eyelids. But he was not her dog.

The pizza arrived in a wide cardboard box. After tipping the delivery guy, she stood in the hall holding it. The grease and heat soaked through the base, stroking her palms. It was almost a comfort.

274

The affair, if that's what it was, wasn't a month old. Yogurt came with a longer expiry date.

A breeze blew through the trees and tickled windows. In the hallway, Oscar double-checked his passport. Photobooth-photograph Oscar Umeda looked back at him from behind plastic. Ami hugged him.

'I wish I could drive you,' she said.

'It's better you stay here with Dad,' Oscar replied.

'Don't talk about me as if I'm not here. I'm not dead yet.' His father's hair was wet from the shower, and under the comb-lines were visible the freckles of an old-man skull.

The lights were off when Oscar arrived. Daylight sliced through the shutters, striping the blank walls. Good, the painting was done. He stepped into the hall. Something gave under his foot, his knee locked, and he grabbed the doorknob for balance. Just a shoe, lying lumpen in the hall. He picked it up and moved it to the side, next to an umbrella he didn't recognise. The space seemed to have swelled since he'd left. Where was his wife?

'Mina?' he called into the shadow. No response. Oscar turned on the lights. One was out. He checked the app but, of course, she'd hidden herself from its signal. It was three o'clock in the afternoon and the lights were out. There was a sour smell in the flat.

The bedroom was dark too. The bed was humped. As he walked closer he saw his wife's face covered by a mess of hair. Her roots had grown out long and dark. She didn't move. His lungs swelled against his ribs. 'Mina?'

The smallest movement, a sliding downwards deeper into the bed. There she was. His horizontal wife. On the plane he'd practised saying, 'I don't think I can help you any more.'

As he looked at the shape of his wife, he felt very tired. He told himself that there is always a moment in a run when you think you can't do it. You start coming up with reasons to stop. But the thing is, if you have the energy to come up with excuses you have the energy to run. All he had to do was tell her.

'Mina, it's three o'clock. No, it's three oh seven.'

'Leave me alone.'

'Get up, Mina. Come on. Get up.'

'Go away.'

He wrenched the duvet off. She was wearing jeans, and one sock. Her fly was undone. The lace of her underwear was revealed in the gap. It was weeks since he'd eased the elastic over her hips. Weeks. He sat down on the edge of the bed and stroked her calf. Mina rolled over. Her face was buried in the pillow. Creases of cotton surrounded her skull in exclamation marks.

He didn't want to drag her physically from the bed. His back was sore from travel. His head ached. He didn't want to have a fight. Anyway, it wasn't like anything could hurt her there. She'd have to get up eventually.

He flicked all the switches. The sitting room was host to a box of pizza, uneaten. The cheese had gone cold and grease-shiny. More grease had seeped through the cardboard. The assembly smelled of unbrushed teeth. It turned his stomach. As his gut writhed, it reminded him of its presence. He hadn't eaten on the plane. The food had been all starches.

He picked up the pizza box, folded it into the trash. He grabbed some kitchen roll and wiped off the smear of grease that glossed the table. If Ami had decided differently, he might've grown up here. He would've rolled his Hot Wheels cars over these floorboards. This would be the wall against which he would've bounced a tennis ball. That would've been the corner he slumped into, Game Boy in hand. He would've had two mothers. People said that you married someone like your mother. If he'd had two mothers, he supposed, he would have been like his father, a man who always wanted more. But he had only wanted one wife. Was that so much to ask for?

In the fridge there was bread—more starch. It would have to do. He turned the oven on to preheat. The orange light glared up at him. A pat of French butter had appeared. Président, slightly salted. Mina had never liked butter. She always chose margarine. She said she didn't like to think of a milking machine squeezing aching udders. Why would she buy this? He slid the bread onto the metal grille.

As the oven clanged shut, Mina appeared, wearing the blanket like a cape.

'You're awake,' he said. 'Do you want some toast?'

She shook her head and stared at her feet. He saw it was a bear day, the hairs sticking up at all angles.

Still staring at her toes, she said, 'I have a new mole. I found it last night. Here.' She bit her lower lip and pointed at the arch of her chin.

'I can't see it.'

'Look closer.'

It was flat and smaller than a poppy seed. She might have drawn it on with a single dot of a ballpoint pen.

'You're sure it's not a spot?'

'It's not a spot. My spots don't look like that. Don't think it's cancerous. I'm just getting older.' She raised her chin in challenge. He ran a thumb over the dot. He shut his eyes. Behind the red-black of his eyelids, he paused, letting the thumb dwell on her skin. It was as soft as it had ever been. His thumb fitted neatly under her lip. It was a warm furrow. Her breath shivered.

The words that came out were not those he intended. 'I love you.'

Mina stepped back, the warmth of her gone. 'But you weren't here. You should've been here to see it.'

'How could I have been here? And what difference would it have made?' His presence didn't stop bananas spotting. It hadn't stopped her trying to kill herself, not once but twice.

'You didn't want to talk to me. You didn't want to see me,' Mina said.

'I did.'

'No, you didn't.'

'I did. Just not immediately.' He didn't know why this distinction felt so important. 'Mina, you tried to die. Guess what? Dying is leaving someone too. If you die, you never respond to texts. You told me you wanted to leave New York. I said okay. You said you wished we weren't married. And then you told me you kissed my best friend's sister. So, forgive me if I didn't know what to say to you.'

'You're still worried about Theo?'

'Mina, I think we should separate.' It was out now.

'Separate?'

'It's not like we have kids to stay together for.'

She bit the lip he had so recently been touching. Mina wasn't crying. She spoke slowly, looking down at her hands. 'When I met you, not that night, sometime just after, I decided I could finally relax. Like all of life had felt like walking through this windowless shopping mall. You know, the kind which is so big it has more than one Starbucks. And I'd see all these things I was supposed to want but didn't. Or things I did want but couldn't afford. And then one day there you were, like a bench. A stable place to rest. A place to just be.'

'A bench. That was what our marriage was to you? A bench.'

'You're missing the point.' She slid to the kitchen floor. God knew if it was clean. 'I was trying to find the life I wanted. I was researching PhD programmes, I was studying for quizzes, I was trying to look cool at parties in dorm rooms that stank of bong water. I was so tired, and you were so stable and good.'

She put her face between her knees. She was right. He was good. He kept his voice careful and kind. He could be a good man about this. He was so bloody tired.

'I'll be in 5B if you need anything. Tell me when you want

279

me to book your plane ticket to the States. Can you think of anyone you want to stay with? I'll sort out everything with the people sub-leasing our place.'

He couldn't sell the flats while she was living there, ordering pizza, weeping. He had to ease her out. He flicked through memories of their friends. Who would be amenable to Mina?

Mina stood on the exposed walkway. She looked down. Beside the bins yet more trash bags lay in great black pillows. Pigeons moved their grey backs over the grey ground. A lance of light speared the wall on the other side of the courtyard, burnished the bricks copper. The smell of cooking flew upwards. She imagined falling down that gap, ending her life in this strange city. She imagined the heads that would lean over railings to look at the mess of a woman, who had smattered like pigeon shit over the ground. She put her palms on the railing. The cold turned her fingers red. She wrapped her hand around the rail tightly, and her knuckles blanched white. She shifted her weight from her feet to her hands. Slowly, her toes lifted off the ground. The heat of effort burned in her upper arms. It would be easy to jump from this balcony. Would the pigeons peck her eyeballs? There would be blood, she assumed. Or would it all be internal, an inward collapse? But she didn't want to die in public. Even animals went off alone to die. A car honked. She did not climb over. She did not jump.

Her arms slackened. Her feet hit the floor with no sound. Sometimes Mina wished she smoked. Smoking gave a person the excuse to stand alone in the cold for a precise amount of time. When the ash approached the fingertips, the cigarette told them it was time to go inside.

The elevator chimed. She turned, embarrassed, ready to see Oscar and his glare of disapproval. A wire trolley slid through the open door onto the balcony. The figure that followed the trolley was bent in concentration. A red beret was pulled down over her ears. The neighbour. Mina hurried to hold the door.

'Oh, hi,' Mina said.

The woman grabbed the rail so that one hand balanced on the trolley, the other on the balcony. Her bright Perspex rings caught the light. The old woman was smiling, and her teeth were as brown as old books. 'Oh, my dear, don't fuss.'

Mina wasn't aware of fussing, but after the accusation she wondered if she should. The cold didn't seem to bother her neighbour. Should she be encouraging her to go inside?

'Liking it here?' the neighbour asked.

'Oh, yes. London is lovely.'

'Too bloody cold but it always has been. This building has cold bones, if you ask me. I'm moving to Corfu.'

'But you said you'd lived here for decades.'

'Exactly.' The neighbour began to explain how she'd bought the flat for nothing. Bought it from the government and now it was worth a mint. A mint and a half! She was getting out. She would lie in the sun for the rest of the days God gave her. Mina nodded and smiled, imagining red bikinis and beautiful young people swimming in the golden light, like fish kept for this woman's special entertainment.

The fresh paint was a bluer white than he remembered choosing. Perhaps it was a trick of the weather and the month that thundered down around him. He might have lived here, among all those birds. It wasn't useful to sit around wondering about the past. He was acting like Mina. He texted Theo.

Might as well get that out of the way. They arranged to meet up at the pub they used to go to before a night out. The streets were crowded. Images of Christmas trees were painted, pasted, and printed on glass. Christmas shopping already?

By the time Oscar got there, Theo was already sitting on

a bar stool. He had two pints of Camden Hells. Oscar asked how the game was going and Theo pointed to the TV, making a face of theatrical anguish. He asked how Mina was doing in the offhand sort of way that another man might've asked about traffic. Relief cut through Oscar. Phoebe had not told Theo. There was one less disaster to contain.

He bought the next round. Somewhere into the third, he was listening to Theo complain about how the dog had chewed up his Gibson.

'Do you still play?' Oscar asked. Back when they'd lived in dorms, he'd often seen the guitar lying across the bed, like a beautiful woman.

'Not as often as I'd like.' Theo stretched under the table, his loafers gleaming lazily in the sticky light. 'Not with that infernal dog back.'

'Back? Phoebe's been away?'

'To give her credit, she tries to stay out of my hair. Well, you know, she was crashing with Mina for a bit. And then she vanished for, like, two weeks. New boyfriend, I assume, but they must've had a falling out.'

Someone scored a goal and a cheer rose around them, as loud as waves crashing against a rocky shore.

She had taken a shower in an attempt to feel clean. Thwock, thwock, thwock, came the noise from the bathroom. She must not have rotated the nozzle all the way shut. Mina shivered. She patted the pillow that belonged to Oscar or Phoebe. They'd both let her sleep closest to the door. They'd both known she needed that. Now she felt the emptiness at her back. If Phoebe were here, they'd be sleeping back to back, their spines aligned. If Oscar were here, his long arm would be draped over her. Greedy, she thought. She'd been greedy. But was it greedy to cram food into your mouth when hunger shredded your stomach? Was it greedy to eat so much you were sick all over yourself? Dogs ate like that. Seagulls. Fish. They ate and ate with a hunger that didn't stop.

'I am a dog. A fish,' she said to the room. She thought of running upstairs to say it to him. She thought of asking for his love back, as if it were a muffin tray she had once borrowed and needed again. Pathetic. She did not deserve Oscar or Phoebe. But even as she thought that, she thought, Deserve? You did not deserve? Do you think you're on some TV interview? Do you think you can fool anyone by sounding so pathetic? So irresponsible? You don't deserve? It's as if you think just by claiming guilt you'll make yourself unguilty.

Mina closed her eyes, as if by doing that she might shut out her mind. But the thought came anyway. It's as if you think you're on stage. It's as if you think, by lying there in the foetal position, someone is going to feel sorry for you.

She opened her eyes again. The lights were off and she could just see the outlines of the room. The furniture had blurred into slabs of shadow. What would it be like to be your own shadow? To follow yourself around, making human gestures but never making any decisions? To grow and shrink but to have no control? Would it feel that different from being a person?

Phoebus Apollo granted the Sibyl as many years of life as grains in a pile of sand. But she forgot to ask for eternal youth so she was doomed to age and age. Her body scraped away until she became so small she was just a voice in a jar. When asked what she wished for, all she said was *I want to die*. Mina sounded out the Greek: ἀποθανεῖν θέλω. The words stumbled in her mouth. She said it again, more confident now of the flow.

Mina imagined her death and the pan out to sky and rain. Or sky and sun. Sky. And herself gone. Just gone. Not even knowing she was gone. The pan out would belong to someone else's eyes. Phoebe getting off the Tube at Angel, or Oscar looking out of the window, pausing as he boxed away her things.

They were both going to think it was about them. Perhaps she should leave a note—*It's not your fault. My brain is broken.*

Would her denial seem like an insult? They'd think she was being passive aggressive. But could she be responsible for their assumptions? It might be a good thing. Maybe their lives would feel more purposeful afterwards, like *I'm so wonderful, someone died for me.*

A Swedish study had found that women whose siblings committed suicide were 1.5 times more likely to commit suicide themselves. But Mina had no sisters. Her dad would be upset. He'd worked so hard for their small family. But how much worse to throw herself on him because she couldn't cope with something so simple as life? She'd save him from her living failure.

There was the problem of how. There was always the problem of how. The statistics were easy enough to get. Guns were the best. Guns were by far the best. But she didn't have a gun. She didn't have a gun here and she didn't have one in America either. She just hadn't been able to imagine herself driving out to Virginia, flashing ID, and returning with portable death. She'd easily imagined Dido forcing steel through her own skin and the funeral pyre's smoke smudging the sky. She'd imagined abandoned Ariadne's body dancing on the end of its rope. But Mina couldn't imagine swiping a credit card a few states over. So it had been pills that first time. Pills were easy to picture, so she'd gone with them. Idiot. Idiot. And then the bridge, where she had done nothing at all, just looked into the same river tourists snapped selfies in front of. Idiot. Idiot. Idiot.

The decorators had splashed paint on 5B's floor. If only he'd noticed earlier, he could've bought sandpaper.

His phone began to buzz, and singing up from the screen was the +1 that indicated the number was American. Trust Americans to have made themselves the number-one country in the world.

'Hi?' he said.

'It's your dad. Well, no, this isn't your dad, this is Ami. Hi. Sorry.'

'What's wrong with Dad?'

'He's okay now.' Ami was talking quickly, and the line buzzed loudly as if a wasp were trapped in the wires.

'Now?'

'We're in the hospital.'

'What?'

'A few hours after you left, he doubled over. It was bad. He couldn't stand. They think it might be an infarction.'

'An infarction? That's a heart attack.'

'Yes. He told me not to call you. He didn't want you to worry, but I thought if it was my father . . .'

'So what's going on? Should I come back?'

'He's getting fitted for a stent.'

'A stent?' He must have read about it, but right now a stent sounded like a gardening tool, something his mother would use to tie roses to a trellis. 'I should've stayed.'

'I'll keep you updated, but they're saying it should all be routine.'

'I can turn around, go to the airport.'

'It'd all be over by the time you got here. Get some rest, Oscar. Look, sorry, I have to go. I'll let you know as soon as it's done.'

The small of his back ached. He punched it with the ball of his fist. He thought of his father in a hospital bed. He realised the bed he was picturing was Mina's post-suicide-atempt hospital cot. And then he thought of Mina in bed downstairs, the slick of drool dried to her face.

Exercising, he could always tell the difference between good and bad pain. Growth and damage were distinct in a way he couldn't describe but his tendons understood.

Oscar stripped off his coat, then his shirt, his shoes, socks, trousers, until he was down to his boxers and the draught tugged on his chest hairs. The pigeons watched from the window. Their heads were hunched into their puffy grey shoulders. Their orange eyes stared. He began his shoulder rolls. Then hamstring stretches. Then press-ups. Then squats. Then star jumps.

Mina had found what she was looking for. Oscar's dressing-gown cord was too short for the fairy-tale thirteen loops. She made a simple noose of only three. It took a few tries. It was hard to remember when to loop under and when to over. The first time, it looked wrong and she had to begin again. The second, she made the head loop too small. The third was okay. She ran a hand around the inside of the noose. It was fluffy. She slipped it over her neck and it hung, innocent as a scarf.

There were no rafters and no beams. The door hooks were tiny brass beaks that looked unready for her weight. The only choice was the bathroom and the shower rail. She considered herself in the sink's mirror. Normal woman, in the middle of her life. Her skin faintly imprinted by the years. Dark eyes, the pit of the pupil just visible in the iris. Chin a little softer, a little more rounded than she would have liked it. Some tattoos, but everyone had tattoos these days. On the whole, nothing special. Noose around her neck.

She moved aside the swishing curtain. She climbed onto the edge of the bath. It was wet. The shower rail had a good diameter. It seemed made of the same stuff they used for subway handrails. Had anyone ever hanged herself on the subway?

There was no point in tying herself to the rail if it would

286

just break. It would be better to test it. She tugged hard on the rail. It didn't seemed to move. Both hands wrapped tightly around the bar, she let her feet slide off the edge of the bath. She felt the weight leap straight to her fingers. The shower rail gave a metallic sigh. Her elbows hurt. She swung for a moment more, like a kid on the monkey bars, then placed her feet back on the bath's edge. The rail had held her weight. This place would do.

Mina looked down at her bare feet. Her nails needed cutting. A callus had formed on the left big toe. Her baby toes had never fully straightened out. They looked so strange. Giant jelly beans. She lifted her right foot up in the air experimentally. She curled her toes around the bath's cliff-edge. Her mother had died in a bath like this, unceremoniously and alone. Like mother like daughter, she thought.

'So, I guess this is goodbye,' Mina said to the bathroom. The bathroom ignored her. She laughed for no reason. It wasn't that she thought this was funny. But everything around her was so ordinary, so boring, and yet here it was, the place she was going to die. A farce to spend so long going back and forth only to end up here.

She thought of the way a neck breaks. The way, without oxygen, the brain wilts and withers.

She strung the cord over the shower rail and stood on tiptoe. Her lump of a brain had stopped generating death wishes. It should be singing now. It should be cackling and dancing, pleased that it had finally won. Instead, she felt blank. If she got down now, no one would know. She would not be signed into anyone's custody. But at the same time, wasn't this the only logical course of action? She'd been complaining about wanting to die all this time. If she'd lost Oscar and the ferrous flicker of Phoebe, if she no longer loved the city she grew up in and had failed to find a new home, what else was there to do?

She made a simple knot. Oscar would be upset. But he'd get over her. People did. People moved on. She knotted it again.

In the silence of the bathroom, she heard—thump, thump, thump. She turned, the cotton straining against her neck. No water was coming from the faucet or the shower. Perhaps it was the radiator then.

She wrapped her hands around the shower rail, feeling its width and its strength. Her toothbrush reclined on the sink. A pool of toothpaste had calcified around the head. Phoebe's hairbrush lay flung in a corner. Red hair was clumped in the bristles. Mina wondered what other people looked at before they died. She doubted many had a sea view. What did a beautiful view matter if just moments after the memories were etched in, they were erased?

Thump, thump, thump. It was distracting. She needed to concentrate. The sound was relentless. It was like someone smacking the floor again and again. Pipes? It was coming from above her head. Thump, thump, thump. Was Oscar hanging pictures up there? Building a fort? Should she have written him a note?

Get on with it, said her brain. Oh, she thought. You're back. She checked the knot with her fingertips. The key to a painless death was to break the neck. Otherwise the suffocation would be slow, her brain losing air, her face turning scarlet, then purple, then white. She should jump with force. She bent her knees and felt the knot shove against her throat.

Thump, thump, thump. Was it so much to ask, to die in the quiet? She didn't need waves or Wagner, just the peace of a bathroom at night. She had lived three decades and she was going to die chafed by the crash and wallop above her. She wanted some peace and a long quiet. She wanted not to think about pipes, hammers, thumping. She closed her eyes.

Thump. Thump. Thump.

Why wouldn't it just shut up?

Thump. Thump. Thump.

Was it getting louder? What was it? Were these really her last living thoughts? There was nobody to record them, but she'd thought they'd be better. She'd thought she would die thinking of the antimatter black of death. Or that she'd die thinking of the clowning eyebrow wiggle her grandmother had made when Mina told her about the mean kids at school. But she was going to die wondering whether the plumbing was malfunctioning. Every day, she had tried to force herself not to think about death. And now, when she was trying to die, life rushed in to distract her.

She thought, Get on with it. Get on with it. This is exactly why you need to just jump. Just jump and all of this will be over. There won't be a You to have these thoughts. They'll be gone. None of this will matter.

Thump. Thump. Thump.

What if it was Oscar? What could he be doing that would make that noise? Did he hate her so much that he was just punching and punching the floorboards, pretending they were her face?

She couldn't die distracted. The bathroom would be here later. She could still jump. She could leave this earth in peace. She would just go, find out what the fuck was going on upstairs and come back down.

She spread her legs to stabilise herself. With one hand she held the bar above her head. With the other, she found the tail of the knot. The knot undid. But as the cord flopped down, her foot slipped, and her body slammed into the tiled wall.

'Fuck.'

She stood in front of the mirror with the dressing-gown cord hanging from her throat. The noose was as tough to undo as it was to do up—harder, perhaps. She had not practised the motions needed to escape. She wormed a finger under the fattest loop. An uncomfortable choking sensation caught her breath and she winced. The cord came free.

With the noose gone, her neck looked just the same as it always did. There was not even a rope burn to record those few minutes. She ran a hand over the side of her neck, feeling no difference. Lying on the tiled floor, the cord looked like any other bit of laundry. The thudding continued above her head.

She stepped out of the bathroom. In the hallway, she shoved her feet into the sneakers that she'd thought she'd never see again. She felt oddly weightless. Her key turned 5B's lock. The thumping was louder as she opened the door. Oscar's suitcase loitered in a corner. She didn't bother taking off her shoes. The sound was coming from the main room, and she followed it, her steps matching the beat.

The table had been pushed against the wall. In the centre of the room, Oscar was jumping rope. The rope flipped over Oscar's head and under his feet, skimming the floor, becoming an O encircling her husband. His feet bounced again and again. Thump. Thump. Thump. The jumps were slow, almost clumsy. 'Oscar?'

He kept jumping. His arms were sleeved in sweat. His eyes were shut. And they stayed shut. Oscar's face had gone an odd purple colour. He was flushed from hairline to neck, apart from two startling dots of white on his cheeks. He shone with so much sweat that she couldn't see the individual droplets.

This, she thought, was what he'd look like if he were drowning. As his head bobbed over the waves, he would gasp like that. His arms would flap up and down. Up and down beat his arms. How long could he have been jumping? She knew her husband enjoyed testing his body. She had stood at the end of the New York Marathon applauding. But this felt different.

'Oscar?'

He did not stop. He gulped air. He sniffed. It occurred to her that her husband might be crying. It wasn't certain. It might just be sweat and snot and air. It might have been a trick of the bulb that hung from the ceiling with not even a puff of paper to cover it. The light-bulb swayed on its wire.

Thump. Thump. Thump.

Quietly she began, 'Fortune teller please tell me what my husband's name will be:

A?

B?'

He dropped the rope with a final thud.

She stepped towards him and touched his chest. Sweat slid against her palm. His body was hot. For the first time in months, Mina was sure what to do. Her body understood. Her bones and her skin and her stomach and her liver all understood.

She lifted his sticky arms up and around herself. Oscar said something, but it came out as a gust of air. His sweat slicked the side of her face. She let it run into her mouth and down her neck. Salt. The heat of him was uncomfortable, but she leaned into that too-warm body.

'I know,' she said. 'I know. Breathe. Breathe.'

He did. His chest ballooned against her.

'You're okay,' Mina said. 'You're okay.' She was sure they were the right words, the only words that mattered. 'Close your eyes,' she said. And he did. Jaw hanging open, he chugged air. Mina pushed herself up onto her tiptoes. She kissed his left eyelid. She kissed the right. She felt his eye move under the skin. What did he see back there? Just blood and heat? Or something else?

'You're okay,' she said. 'I'm here. You're okay.'

As his breath slowed, Oscar let himself be held. His wife's body was familiar. Her head tucked under his chin. Each

291

small expansion of her ribs pressed against his own. It was good to breathe beside her breath.

Once a bat had flown into his dorm. It knocked itself against walls and ceiling until finally it had scrabbled onto Oscar's duvet, just between his knees. He'd captured it in his palms. Its toothpick claws had left scratches, but as he'd walked to the window he'd been aware only of the heartbeat. The beat had filled his fingers, going faster than he'd thought possible. Theo had opened the window and Oscar had stuck his hands out into the night. Before letting go, he'd waited, holding the beat: a whole life in his hands.

Mina moved to step back, but Oscar's arms stayed tight across her shoulders. She leaned into her husband's damp shirt and let his hands move through her hair.

'Wait,' Oscar said. He gulped another breath.

'You're okay,' she said.

Eventually, they sat on the floorboards, their backs pressed against the pale walls. Mina's face was sticky with his sweat. His arm and hers stayed touching. Their shared shadow stretched across the floor.

'Did I tell you about the time I held a bat?' he asked.

'Tell me again,' she said.

Author's Note

If you are fighting with your own sadnesses or love someone who is, this note is for you.

The seed of this book emerged from the struggles of people very dear to me and from my own challenges. Not everyone who is sad is sick but I have been sick and I have loved those who were sick. However, the characters within this book are fictional beings. Their views are their own and should not be taken as advice.

This novel is not intended as a celebration of or an attack on the psychiatric-pharmacological process. How you decide to handle your illness will come from talking to professionals you trust, those who love you, and your own sense. For some the journey to health is fast, and for others it is long and slow and full of setbacks. Sometimes a particular medication or a particular therapy will work wonders for one individual and not succeed for another. Whether you have a long or short road to health is a mixture of luck, circumstance, and biology. In writing this book, I hoped simply to write the story of two people attempting to walk that path together.

But I would like to say this:

Every day you try again is an act of bravery. Although this is worthy of pride, you may not feel able to be proud of yourself. So I would like to wish you congratulations on being here today.

Thank You

This book was only possible because of the generosity of many.

Thank you to everyone who read and supported *Harmless Like You*. You gave me the courage to keep writing. Thank you to the bookshops which stocked *Harmless Like You* and gave it a way to meet readers.

Special thanks and appreciation must go to my agent Lucy Luck who fights all my battles and to Francine Toon for being such a wise editor and friend. Indeed, thank you to everyone at Sceptre and Conville and Walsh for taking me into your fold. Especially—Louise Court, Natalie Chen, Susan Spratt, Helen Flood, Megan Schaffer, Rebecca Folland, Hazel Orme and to the translation team at C&W.

To Sophia Brown and Jessica J. Lee for their excellent proofreading.

The epigraphs of this book are taken from the work of B.J. Marples' "The Winter Starling Roosts of Great Britain, 1932-1933", from the Journal of Animal Ecology and from a loose adaption of the OED online definition of augury.

Forever indebted to Paul and Francine for their knowledge of classics. While writing this book, I consulted many sources but in particular: Charles Martin's translation of the *Metamorphoses*, Harold Isbell's translation of the *Heroides*, Tom Payne's translation of *The Art of Love*, Mary Beard's *Women and Power*, Seamus Heaney's *Aeneid VI*, Mary Lefkowitz, and Maureen Fant's *Women's Life in Greece & Rome*.

Thank you to Hedgebrook without which many of the scenes of this book would not have been written. Thank you to Gladstone's Library where I sat under stained glass and sliced away wobbly sentences. Thank you to Asian American Writers' Workshop and to Kundiman—two organizations whose work and power I am forever awed by.

Thank you to Henry Sutton and Stephen Benson at UEA, who guided me throughout this project. Thank you to Karen Tei Yamashita who read the first pages and told me to believe in this voice.

Thank you to Paul who sat with me as I read aloud the first shaky drafts of this book. Thank you to Alice who is a well of kindness and intelligence and without whom there would be no title. Thank you Ilana without whom this would be a different book. Thank you Aby who sat with me for so many days and told me to follow my nose. Thank you Tony for everything before and after writing this book.

Thank you to the friends with whom I talked through the kinks of this book—Eric, Emily, Kathleen, Lee, Lindsay, Lizzie, T Kira, both Saras, and Sharlene! Thank you to all my friends who asked, 'How are you doing?' and listened to the rambling answer.

Thank you to my father, my mother, my brother. Thank you to Gloria and Peta for everything you do. Thank you to my grandmother for her snark and love.